The GEM THIEF

OTHER BOOKS AND AUDIO BOOKS

BY SIAN ANN BESSEY

Forgotten Notes

Cover of Darkness

Family Is Forever

Kids on a Mission: Escape from Germany

Kids on a Mission: Uprising in Samoa

Kids on a Mission: Ambushed in Africa

Teddy Bear, Blankie, and a Prayer

Deception

Within the Dark Hills

You Came for Me

The Insider

One Last Spring

To Win a Lady's Heart

For Castle and Crown

The GEM THIEF

SOME THINGS AREN'T ALWAYS AS THEY SEEM.

SIAN ANN BESSEY

Covenant Communications, Inc.

Cover image: Abi Symons © Arcangel Images. *Oia Town in Santorini, Greece-By Night* © Portishead1. Courtesy of istockphoto.com.

Published by Covenant Communications, Inc.
American Fork, Utah

Printed in the United States of America
First Printing: November 2018

24 23 22 21 20 19 18   10 9 8 7 6 5 4 3 2 1

ISBN: 978-1-52440-773-5

For Kent, Anna, and Elizabeth

My memories of the Mediterranean are all the more treasured because I share them with you.

ACKNOWLEDGMENTS

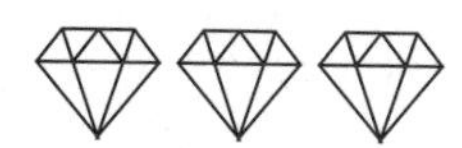

THE RESEARCH FOR THIS BOOK took me into the fascinating world of gemology and jewelry design. I owe a huge thanks to Rick Merrill, jeweler and owner of Main Street Diamonds in Rexburg, Idaho, for sharing his time and expertise with me. His insights were invaluable, and he has given me a new appreciation for the natural beauty and exquisite workmanship to be found in this field.

Thanks also to my son-in-law, Tyler Sommer, who guided me through EMT and hospital protocols; to my friend, Traci Hunter Abramson, who fielded several law enforcement questions; and to my sister, Emily Manwaring, who gave me constructive feedback on my first draft and is a constant source of support.

I appreciate all those behind the scenes at Covenant who work to make my books the best they can be. Many of them are unsung heroes, but I must make mention of my incredible editor, Samantha Millburn, my publicist, Stephanie Lacy, and the cover designer for this book, Hannah Bischoff.

Finally, this novel would likely never have happened without the support of my husband, Kent. Not only does he encourage me in my writing, he gifted me the background material for this book by taking me on a cruise of the Mediterranean. It was an incredible experience, and one that I hope I may share, in part, with each of you through the story of *The Gem Thief.*

CHAPTER 1

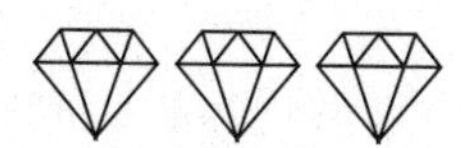

THE MOMENT GRACIE MILLER STEPPED out of Rosie's Cafe carrying a cup of hot chocolate, an ominous rumble sounded from the glowering skies above. The first drop of rain hit her shoulder before the thunder had completely faded, and within seconds, rain was falling in sheets. All around her, pedestrians scrambled for cover.

A few yards to her right, a scruffy teenager with a shaved head, multiple piercings, and a vicious glare barreled down Madison Avenue's sidewalk on his skateboard. "Watch it!" he yelled.

Clutching the strap of her shoulder bag with one hand and her steaming drink with the other, Gracie leaped out of his way. The boy whizzed past, his arm swinging wildly and clipping the base of Gracie's cup before he careened off the sidewalk into the midst of the snarled morning rush-hour traffic.

"Hey!" Gracie cried as half the hot chocolate slopped out of the cup, burning her fingers and splattering her clothes.

Drivers honked their displeasure as the skateboarder weaved through the cars, leaving Gracie standing on the sidewalk, fuming about rude teenagers and the cost of getting hot chocolate stains out of her dry-clean-only silk blouse.

Not far away, a traffic light turned green, and suddenly cars were surging forward, their tires hissing in the water already collecting on the road. A yellow taxicab shot past, churning up liquid from the gutter and spraying Gracie's skirt, legs, and shoes with dirty rainwater.

She stumbled back from the curb. "You've got to be kidding me!"

At the nearby crosswalk, a strident beeping accompanied a flashing light, and a herd of impatient New Yorkers surged across the road. Tamping down her frustration, Gracie dropped her soggy cup into the nearby garbage can, hitched the strap of her sodden bag higher on her shoulder, and dashed through the rain to join them.

By the time she reached the front doors of Samuel Hamley Fine Jewelry, her shoes squelched with every footstep and her brown hair hung around her face in wet, stringy ropes. Wiping the raindrops off her face with her equally wet hand, she reached for the large brass door handle. The door swooshed open on smooth, silent hinges before she had a chance to open it herself, and Samuel Hamley's silver-haired doorman, Walter, greeted her with upraised eyebrows and the hint of a smile.

"Well now, Miss Gracie," he said, traces of his Southern roots evident in his inflection. "It appears that this ol' summer thunderstorm may have gotten the better of you."

Gracie rolled her eyes. "The rain wasn't even the worst of it. If Mrs. Katsaros hadn't called to say she was coming in this morning, I'd have turned right around, gone home, and crawled back into bed."

Walter chuckled. He stepped behind the mahogany table just inside the door, pulled a small white towel out of a drawer, and handed it to Gracie. She accepted it gratefully. She had a sneaking suspicion Walter used a cloth just like this to polish the storefront's glass doors and brass door handles, but she wasn't going to turn down a towel, no matter its reason for being in the drawer.

"Thank you, Walter."

The older man gave a pleased nod. "Anytime, Miss Gracie."

Gracie wrapped the towel around the lower portion of her dripping hair and squeezed out some of the moisture. A small puddle had already formed on the tile beneath her feet, and she eyed with concern the plush beige carpet that marked the beginning of the showroom.

"Don't you be worryin' too much 'bout the carpet, Miss Gracie," Walter said, following her look. "Yours won't be the only pair of wet shoes that comes in this mornin'."

Logically, Gracie knew Walter was right. But leaving dirty, wet footprints across the pristine floor covering of the high-class jewelry store went against everything in her nature. Even now, nine months after being hired as a designer for one of the most prestigious jewelry companies in New York City, she hadn't lost the sense of wonder she'd felt when she'd first walked through these doors.

The thick, luxurious carpet was almost the same color as the walls. Marble pillars broke up the spacious showroom into smaller areas, each furnished with two or three glass cases and a couple of elegant Queen Anne chairs. A shimmering chandelier hung in the center of the room, and strategically placed can lights spotlighted the glittering jewelry within the glass cases.

Two well-dressed sales ladies hovered unobtrusively in the shadows, and Gracie knew their supervisor, Max, was not far away, should either of them need assistance with a customer interested in a big-ticket item. Not that Samuel Hamley ever sold anything that wasn't expensive, but sometimes the number of zeros on the price tags took Gracie's breath away, and she couldn't imagine telling a customer the asking price without stuttering over the words. She was far better suited sitting at her desk on the second floor, designing settings for the incredible jewels the buyers for Samuel Hamley provided, than trying to sell the finished product to a prospective customer.

"I'd better head upstairs before Mrs. Katsaros gets here," Gracie said, handing Walter the damp towel. The wealthy patron had called yesterday to say a ring Gracie had designed needed adjusting.

"Too late for that," Walter said, taking the towel and putting it behind the table. "She beat you by five minutes."

Gracie froze. "She's already here?"

"Yep. Her driver dropped her off at the door the moment I unlocked it." He brushed away Gracie's obvious horror. "It was Mr.

Hamley she asked for. She always wants a quick word with him before doin' any other business. I'm bettin' you've got a couple mo' minutes before anyone even misses you."

Gracie was already halfway across the room, her worries about spoiling the carpet forgotten. When she reached the elegant staircase that led from the back of the showroom to the offices on the second floor, she took the steps two at a time. Her wet shoes squeaked against the polished wood, and by the time she reached the top, she was out of breath.

Immediately in front of her, floor-to-ceiling windows ran the length of a long room separated into smaller working areas by short dividing walls, artfully placed potted trees, and an occasional sofa. Half a dozen people were already at their desks; a couple more were gathered around a large table in the center of the room, poring over photographs of Samuel Hamley's upcoming fall line. Gracie spared her desk in the far corner of the room a brief, longing look before turning to her right, where Kelly Wright sat guarding the entrance to Henry Hamley's office.

"I was getting ready to send out a search party," Kelly said as Gracie approached.

Gracie grimaced. "Has Mr. Hamley asked for me already?"

"No," Kelly said. She glanced at the clock on the wall. "But he's getting close to his max on time alone with Mrs. Katsaros, so you'd better prepare yourself. Any second now, it'll be your turn to pretend to be interested in whatever it is rich women talk about."

Gracie stifled a smile. In many respects, Kelly was Gracie's complete opposite. Her unorthodox, forthright personality was the antithesis of Gracie's quiet, conservative manner. Standing at a diminutive five feet two inches, Kelly embraced the opportunity to wear leopard-print, six-inch heels; whereas, at five feet eight inches, Gracie preferred flats. Kelly's blonde hair was short and spikey; Gracie's long brown hair fell softly below her shoulders. Both women were in their midtwenties and had worked at Samuel Hamley less than a year, but while Kelly happily juggled all the demands of Samuel Hamley's current owner, company employees, and their customers,

Gracie preferred the solitude of her small corner of the large office space, where she could work on her designs without interruption.

No one could deny that Kelly monitored her boss's schedule with the precision of a Samuel Hamley watch, but beneath her vibrant eyeshadow and New York attitude, she was one of the most genuine, kind people Gracie had met since she'd moved to the big city. And right now, Gracie needed an ally.

"Can you stall him for three more minutes?" Gracie asked.

Kelly peered at her over the top of her bedazzled reading glasses, obviously seeing her properly for the first time. "Uh, did you lose a fight with a giant espresso machine?"

"It was a single-cup-of-hot-chocolate-and-gutter-water combo," Gracie said.

Kelly sniggered. "Remind me not to try it."

"You won't need reminding," Gracie said, reaching for the large box of tissues on Kelly's desk. "Can I use some of these?"

Before Kelly could respond, the intercom on her desk crackled to life.

"Send Gracie Miller in."

It was Mr. Hamley. And he did not sound happy. Kelly glanced at Gracie and pushed the button to reply.

"She'll be there in two min—"

"Right away, Kelly."

Gracie yanked some tissues out of the box and gave the largest brown stain on her pale-blue blouse an all-but-futile blot.

"Go!" Kelly hissed. "He's much more likely to be mad at you for keeping him waiting than for the color of your shirt."

"Right," Gracie said. "Maybe he'll think I came to work dressed as an impressionistic painting."

Kelly raised her eyebrows. "Hey, that's not a bad idea."

Gracie groaned, tossed the wet tissues into the garbage, walked up to Mr. Hamley's door, and gave a single knock.

"Enter."

Tucking her wet hair behind her ears, Gracie raised her chin, turned the handle, and walked in.

She'd only ever been inside Henry Hamley's office twice before—when she'd interviewed for her current position and when she'd been given the assignment to design a ring that would best display Mrs. Katsaros's four-carat pink diamond. This time was no less nerve-wracking. The well-appointed office oozed intimidation almost as well as the company's CEO.

Mr. Hamley was sitting at his oversized mahogany desk. Behind him, the large picture window displayed a multimillion-dollar view of the Empire State Building, and on the wall to his left hung a large, framed oil painting of his father, the founder of the company, Samuel Hamley. Subtle track lighting spotlighted the cut-glass vase, ornate clock, and photograph of a very young Henry Hamley standing beside an older Audrey Hepburn at one of her many award ceremonies. It didn't take reading the brass inscription to guess that the diamond choker the famous actress wore was a Samuel Hamley original.

The only bright spots of color in the room came from the arrangement of fresh flowers on the corner table that Kelly delivered every week and the yellow dress Mr. Hamley's current visitor, Mrs. Katsaros, wore. Mr. Hamley himself was wearing his standard pin-stripe gray suit and navy-blue tie. When Gracie walked in, he lowered the jeweler's loupe he was holding and turned his attention from the ring on his desk to her. Immediately, the frown on his face deepened.

"You are aware of the company's dress code, Miss Miller?"

"Yes, Mr. Hamley. I apologize for my appearance. I'm afraid I left for work unprepared for the thunderstorm."

Mrs. Katsaros, who was sitting in one of the two wingback chairs across from Mr. Hamley, chimed in. "My dear child, you're soaking wet. You'll catch your death of cold in those clothes." She looked over at Mr. Hamley. "You must send the girl home to change, Henry."

Henry Hamley gave the woman a long-suffering look before pointedly ignoring her. "Miss Miller, I wish you to take a look at Mrs. Katsaros's ring." He held out his gold-rimmed loupe.

Gracie nodded, hoping the plush carpet would mask the sound of her squelching shoes as she moved over to the desk. "Mrs. Katsaros called to tell me it might need to be resized," she said.

Mr. Hamley remained silent but handed her the loupe and pointed to the stunning jewelry sitting on a small square of black satin on the desk. Unable to quell the thrill she felt in seeing the ring again, Gracie carefully picked it up and placed it on the palm of her hand.

She sensed the difference immediately. Whether it was the slight variance in the ring's weight, the gleam of the band, or the stone itself, she couldn't tell, but the moment she held it, she knew it was not the ring she'd crafted so lovingly. Raising her eyes to Mr. Hamley's, she wondered what he was thinking. Was this a test of her skills? Of her integrity? His expression was blank and told her nothing, so she held the ring between her thumb and first finger, put the loupe up to her eye, and studied the asscher-cut diamond carefully.

Mrs. Katsaros's $250,000 pink diamond was flawless, something that might, under normal circumstances, make a positive identification difficult. But the diamond cutter had removed the natural stone's only blemish by cutting extra facets to the standard asscher-cut, so not only had his decision added luster and value to the stone, but it had also made it all the more unique.

Shifting slightly so she could view the ring under one of the tracking lights, Gracie studied it from all angles. The basket head mount made it difficult to examine the jewel from every side, but she saw enough to validate her original guess. She moved her study to the metal. A few scratches were evident on the shank, and Gracie caught the hint of a yellow undertone to the silver-colored band.

Slowly and deliberately, she placed the ring back on the satin cloth. "That's not Mrs. Katsaros's ring," she said.

"Of course it is." Mrs. Katsaros sat forward in her chair. "You were the one who designed it for me."

Gracie glanced from Mrs. Katsaros's indignant expression to Mr. Hamley's grave face, and a sick feeling settled deep in her stomach. Did Mrs. Katsaros truly not know? "I'm not sure if I should be flattered or upset that someone has made such a good copy of my work," she said. "Your Samuel Hamley ring was a flawless pink diamond in a platinum setting, Mrs. Katsaros. That one is a moissanite-and-white-gold replica."

The older woman blanched. "Is she right, Henry?"

"Yes," Mr. Hamley said. "I suspected as much when you handed it to me, but I wanted Miss Miller's opinion before saying anything."

"But how's that possible? You saw me take that ring off my finger yourself. If I'm not wearing it, it's in my safe at home."

"I think you'd better call Quinn," Mr. Hamley said.

Mrs. Katsaros fumbled through her purse until she found her cell phone, then pushed a few buttons. "Quinn, where are you?" She listened to the reply. "I . . . I have a bit of an emergency. Can you meet me at Samuel Hamley?" She nodded a couple of times. "Yes. But I'd rather you talk directly with Henry. Come straight to his office." She disconnected the call and stared bleakly at the beautiful ring on the desk. "He's only two blocks away. He said he'll be here shortly."

"Take a seat, Miss Miller," Mr. Hamley said, pointing to the second wingback chair. "There's no point in you standing while we wait for Mr. West."

Gracie eyed the hunter-green upholstery uneasily. Mr. Hamley had obviously not thought through what her wet clothes would do to the expensive fabric. "Perhaps a desk chair would be better," she said.

"The chair will dry as well as you do," he said, brushing off her concern impatiently.

Gracie lowered herself gingerly onto the chair and stayed perched on the edge while Mr. Hamley pushed the button on his intercom.

"Bring in some coffee, Kelly," he said. "Four cups."

"Right away, Mr. Hamley."

Gracie glanced at Mrs. Katsaros. Her hands were clasped tightly on her lap, and she was watching the ornate clock as though willing its hands to move faster. Gracie guessed that the fretting woman and Mr. Hamley were similar in age—early sixties perhaps—but where Mr. Hamley was almost completely bald and wore a virtually perpetual frown, Mrs. Katsaros had a crown of pure white hair and was almost always smiling. Except now. Now she looked absolutely miserable.

Feeling as though her pronouncement somehow made her responsible for the older lady's unhappiness, Gracie reached out and touched her hand. "I'm very sorry, Mrs. Katsaros."

Her words seemed completely inadequate, but she honestly didn't know what else to say. "I'm sure you'll find your ring" would be a lie. "I'm sure your insurance will cover the cost of it," sounded empty and callous. Despite her personal investment in Mrs. Katsaros's ring, the shock and dismay Gracie felt over the loss of such an incomparable piece of jewelry had to be nothing compared to what its owner was feeling.

To Gracie's surprise, Mrs. Katsaros took her hand and squeezed it. "Don't worry, my dear." She had a slight shake in her voice that lessened as she spoke. "Quinn will know what to do."

Gracie didn't know who Quinn was, but she hoped for Mrs. Katsaros's sake that he had some stellar connections in the underground world of jewel thieves or the complex world of law enforcement. If not, he would likely require access to a powerful magic wand.

A knock sounded on the door, and Mrs. Katsaros looked up hopefully, but it was Kelly who entered carrying a round tray loaded with four mugs of steaming coffee and a small bowl containing sachets of sugar and mini cups of creamer. Gracie didn't like coffee, but she was starting to feel chilled, and simply holding a hot mug in her cold hands was enough of a draw for her to accept it when Kelly offered.

"No spilling," Kelly said softly, her lips twitching as she fought to keep a straight face. "I'd hate for you to spoil your current look."

Gracie rolled her eyes. "Any chance you've got a blanket out there?" she whispered. "Not that I'm trying to cover up this masterpiece or anything. It's just that if the air-conditioning keeps kicking on, I'm going to go from filthy wet to frozen stiff before this meeting's over."

Kelly gave her a conspiratorial nod, then she turned to hand Mrs. Katsaros the sugar. When she was sure they all had what they needed, Kelly left the office. She'd been gone only a few seconds when the intercom crackled to life again.

"Mr. West to see you, Mr. Hamley," she said.

CHAPTER 2

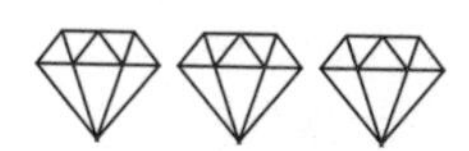

Quinn West listened as Henry Hamley called him in on the intercom. He glanced at his watch. He had forty-five minutes before his weekly board meeting began. He could only hope that his Aunt Dorcas's crisis didn't stall him that long. Making excuses to his senior partner for being late or—even worse—for not showing up at all was not something he enjoyed doing. Especially if the best reason he could give for his absence was his aunt's need for help in making an expensive purchase at Samuel Hamley. He tightened his hold on the folded, wet umbrella in his hand. This morning's unexpected detour needed to be fast.

"You can go in now, Mr. West." The secretary with spiky hair and sparkling glasses gestured toward Henry's office.

"Thanks," he said, walking briskly to the door and offering a token knock before opening it.

Henry rose to meet him as he entered. Quinn had spoken with the man on several occasions, but their conversations had always been brief and focused on his aunt's most recent jewelry purchase.

"Good of you to come, Quinn," Henry said, extending his hand.

Quinn shook it. "Of course."

His aunt had also risen to her feet. She reached for him and kissed him on both cheeks—a habit she'd picked up from her late Greek husband, Alessandro Katsaros.

"It's my ring, Quinn," she said, taking a step back from him.

To his alarm, her chin wobbled as though she were fighting tears. He glanced at the distinctive piece of jewelry on Henry's desk. "What about your ring?" he asked.

"It's not mine."

"Aunt Dorcas, your check cleared the bank months ago. The ring is most definitely yours."

"What your aunt means," Henry said, "is that the ring she wore to the store this morning is a fake."

"A fake?" Quinn stared at him, stunned to silence. This had to be a mistake. Or someone's sick joke. But one look at his aunt's face told him they were serious. "Explain this to me," he said.

His mother's sister shook her head. "I can't explain it. That's the worst part. There's been no break-in at the condo. It hasn't gone missing. To the best of my knowledge, it's been in my keeping ever since the day I walked out of this store with it on my finger."

There was a movement at his right, and for the first time, Quinn realized someone else was in the room.

"This is Gracie Miller," Henry said. "She's the ring's designer. I had her come in this morning to take a look at it."

A young woman with a smudged face, straggly, wet hair, and stained, wrinkled clothing stood and offered him her hand. For a split second, Quinn paused, wondering if her hand was as dirty as the rest of her. She must have sensed his hesitation because she immediately withdrew her arm.

"Someone has gone to a lot of work to replicate your aunt's ring," Gracie said. There was a slight chill to the vivid blue eyes that met his, and Quinn guessed she'd taken his foolish reluctance to shake her hand as a snub. "The differences might only be caught by a gemologist or a fine jeweler, but I can assure you the ring on Mr. Hamley's desk is a pink moissanite set in white gold."

"How much is a ring like that worth?" Quinn asked.

Gracie shifted her feet uncomfortably. "I would guess somewhere around $3,500."

At least $246,000 less than the original. Quinn worked to keep his shock from showing, but Dorcas gave a strangled sob and reached for her chair. To his surprise, Gracie stepped over and gave his aunt's shoulder a comforting squeeze.

"We'll have to bring in the police," he said.

Henry gave a resigned nod. "I agree."

Quinn began mentally revising his schedule to allow for an interview with local law enforcement. There was no way he'd let Dorcas face questioning alone. His board meeting was history. He clenched his jaw, already foreseeing the nightmare ahead. At some point, he was going to have to tell his partner what was going on because quite apart from a personal concern for his aunt's welfare, they both had a vested interest in the outcome of an investigation of the ring. Theirs was the company that insured all of Dorcas's property.

"We're not going to the police," Dorcas said.

Quinn faced his aunt, his stress mounting at the stubborn set of her mouth.

"Even if they're not able to recover the original ring, Anderson and Gough will want a full investigation done before they even consider a claim," he said.

"No police," Dorcas repeated. "You remember what happened when Alessandro reported his stolen car? Police traipsing in and out of our house for weeks, reporters parked outside the front doors day and night, twisted lies about us in the newspaper." She eyed him fiercely. "I will not go through that again—even if it means losing the ring and the money it cost."

Quinn remembered how difficult that experience had been for his aunt. Alessandro had started life as the son of a dock worker in Piraeus, but through hard work, ingenuity, and a little luck, he'd worked his way up to become the owner of the largest, most lucrative cruise line in Europe.

It was the type of rags to riches story the media loved, and they'd followed Alessandro through the milestones in his adult life, from the launching of his largest ship to his public appearances at various charitable functions, from his move to New York after the death of his first wife from cancer to his marriage to an American spinster whose background was as unremarkable as his was extraordinary.

If anything unusual happened in Alessandro Katsaros's life, the media had wanted to know about it. The loss of the Greek billionaire's top-of-the-line Porsche from a parking garage in Manhattan had made the front page of all the gossip rags and had remained a hot topic of celebrity news for weeks. Even though he'd been away at college at the time, Quinn remembered the fuss and knew how much Dorcas had hated the intrusion into their private lives.

"That was six years ago," he said, hoping he could reason with her. "Alessandro's been gone for three years. I really don't think you'll get the same kind of hounding you did when he was alive."

"Then you don't know the paparazzi," she said. "The ring was purchased with Katsaros money." She paused. Despite her obvious desire to take a firm stand, her chin was quivering again. "If they catch wind that it's missing, those wolves will be out for blood."

"We can ask the police to keep the investigation under wraps."

She gave him a withering look. "If you believe that's going to happen, you don't know the NYPD either. Too many people would be involved. All it would take is one officer showing up outside my building in a patrol car or a report left on someone's desk a few minutes too long or the mention of the Katsaros name over a drink—"

A knock interrupted them. At Henry's gruff response, the door opened and his secretary appeared.

"Sorry to disturb you," she said. "I thought Gracie might need this." She took a step into the room and handed a multicolored blanket to Gracie. In a soft voice meant only for Gracie, she added, "Walter's grandson left it here last time he visited. It was the best I could do."

Gracie's eyes lit up with gratitude, and Quinn was struck again by how very blue they were. "Thank you, Kelly," she said, reaching for the blanket with trembling hands. "It's perfect."

With shock, Quinn realized she was shaking with cold. Why was she here in dirty, wet clothes?

"No problem," Kelly said, slipping back out the door as quickly as she'd entered.

"Are you okay?" Quinn asked.

Gracie had unfolded the blanket and was wrapping herself in a collage of superheroes. "I'm fine," she said stiffly before turning back to his aunt. "What about using a private detective?" She was obviously anxious to return everyone's attention to his aunt's problem.

Dorcas shook her head. "I don't know any private detectives, and I won't share what's happened with anyone I don't already trust."

Quinn accepted the cup of coffee Henry offered him and took a sip. It was black, sugarless, and tepid, but he barely noticed. His thoughts were following the direction Gracie had set. Did he know anyone who had both law enforcement experience and an existing friendship with Dorcas?

"Steve Nyborg," he said, placing the cup back on Henry's desk as his taste buds registered the drink's foul flavor.

"Your old college friend?" Dorcas said, her brow furrowing. "What does he have to do with anything?"

"He's been working for the FBI for the last few years. His office is in Philly, but I bet he'd come into the city if I asked." Quinn gave his aunt a knowing look. "Especially if I told him you'd bake one of your apple pies for him."

For the first time since Quinn had entered Henry's office, Dorcas managed a small smile. "He did have a fondness for those, didn't he?"

"That's putting it mildly," he said.

Quinn and Steve had been roommates at Columbia University, and since Steve's father was in the military and had been stationed overseas, Quinn had invited him to stay at Dorcas's condo with him whenever the holidays had rolled around. On the first Thanksgiving he'd spent with them, Steve had tasted Dorcas's homemade apple pie and he hadn't left the table until he'd finished the entire dish. From that time on, he had requested Dorcas's apple pie for birthdays and Christmases, along with the next three Thanksgivings.

After he and Quinn had graduated, Steve had been recruited by the FBI and Quinn had gone on to graduate school for an MBA.

Their busy schedules and the miles that separated them made it harder to keep in regular contact, but their friendship was solid, and Quinn had no doubt Steve would do whatever he could to help.

He studied his aunt, trying to gauge her response to his suggestion. She plucked at a small piece of lint on the arm of the dark-green chair before looking up at him.

"I think I may have enough time to make an apple pie in the next day or two," she said.

With relief, Quinn pulled his phone from his pocket. "I'll call him right now."

"Good," Dorcas said, coming to her feet. "Then I'll go home." She reached for the ring on the desk and slid it onto her finger. "Thank you for your help, Henry."

The older man rose and nodded awkwardly, but before he could say anything, Dorcas turned to Gracie.

"Where do you live, my dear?"

Startled, Gracie rattled off an address in Upper Manhattan.

"Perfect," Dorcas said. "That's not more than a couple of minutes out of my way. I'll have my driver drop you off. It's long past time you changed into something warmer."

Gracie gave Henry a hesitant look, and Quinn hid a smile as Henry mumbled something about seeing Gracie back at the office after lunch. The older man obviously knew better than to go against Dorcas Katsaros. Quinn's anxiety lightened fractionally. His aunt would rebound from this loss. Her strong personality was already reemerging.

CHAPTER 3

Gracie stood between Mrs. Katsaros and Walter at the front door of Samuel Hamley Sunshine broke through the thunderstorm's residual clouds as a black Cadillac purred up to the curb. A young man dressed in a suit jumped out of the driver's side and hurried around the car to open the back door.

Gracie turned to Walter. "I'll wash your grandson's blanket and bring it back to you."

"No problem, Miss Gracie," Walter said with his signature broad smile. "I reckon Isaiah's been without it long enough; a few mo' days won't be making any difference." He pointed at Mrs. Katsaros, who was already climbing into the car. "You'd best get on if you're hopin' to get a ride home."

"Thanks, Walter," Gracie said, hurrying across the sidewalk to where the young man was still holding the car door.

"Don't worry about the seats," Mrs. Katsaros called from inside the vehicle. "They're leather, and they'll wipe off. Just slide in and make yourself comfortable."

Gracie got in, and the driver closed the door behind her.

"Would you give Brent your address?" Mrs. Katsaros said once the young man had taken his place behind the wheel.

Gracie obediently recited her address to the driver. He nodded, and as the car pulled away from the jewelry store, it felt as though she'd entered a different world. The car was unlike anything she'd seen before. Along with the leather upholstery, tinted windows, and polished wood trim, there was a sunroof, miniature TV screens for each seat, and a small icebox full of drinks. There were more gadgets than she knew what to do with, and when Mrs. Katsaros requested that the heat be turned up, the driver simply pushed an icon on a touch screen beside him, and immediately, warm air flowed around Gracie's damp feet.

"This is incredible," Gracie said.

Mrs. Katsaros chuckled. "You've not ridden in a chauffer-driven car before."

"Is it completely obvious?"

"More like completely refreshing," Mrs. Katsaros said. "The thrill in your eyes brings back memories of how I felt on my first ride."

"When was that?" Gracie asked, suddenly curious about the woman beside her.

"About ten years ago."

"Really?" Gracie made no attempt to hide her surprise.

"You didn't know I was relatively new to this life of luxury?" Mrs. Katsaros said, her eyes twinkling. "I must have mastered the art of appearing high-class better than I thought."

Gracie laughed. "You've got it down."

The older woman looked thoughtful. "I wonder what my old friends in Cheney, New Hampshire, would think of that."

"Is that where you're from?"

She nodded. "My sister, Libby, and I were born and bred there. We'd both put down roots in the small town, and I don't think either of us had any plans to ever leave." She gave a small sigh. "Funny, isn't it? How life throws you curveballs you don't even see coming?"

"What brought you to New York?" Gracie asked.

"The love of a good man," Mrs. Katsaros said. She leaned back in her seat, a small smile playing across her lips. "Not the answer most people expect from an old lady, but true nonetheless."

"Will you tell me your story?" Gracie asked. She sensed a depth to Mrs. Katsaros that she'd not recognized before and guessed that the woman had experienced her share of heartaches, along with the happiness that love may have brought.

The older woman glanced out the window. Despite the congested roads, they were making good time. "It won't be long before we reach your apartment, so I'll give you the condensed version."

Gracie nodded encouragingly.

"Back in the days before everyone booked their own flights and hotels online, I ran a travel agency in Cheney. When internet bookings became popular, my business took a hit. Except when it came to cruises. For some reason, people still wanted to work with an agent to book a cruise. So I made that my specialty.

"Over the years, I scheduled hundreds of cruises for other people, but it wasn't until after Quinn left for college that I went on one myself. I chose to cruise the Mediterranean with the Greek company GCL. The ship stopped at places I'd wanted to see all my life, but the highlight of the trip was not any of the ports of call; it was meeting the owner of the Greek Cruise Line, Alessandro Katsaros."

She smiled. "I sat at his table for dinner the first night of the cruise, and despite our different circumstances, we found that we had a lot in common. Our passion for travel and the recent loss of a loved one to cancer were the most obvious. But we quickly discovered other shared interests and recognized loneliness in each other.

"I made a habit of booking that same cruise every six months for two years. Alessandro made a habit of being on board each time. And then, when he decided the time had come to relocate to New York, he drove up to New Hampshire to find me."

A slight blush touched her lined cheeks. "We were married three months later."

The driver was pulling up outside Gracie's apartment building, and Gracie knew their time together was over. Impulsively, she leaned over and gave Mrs. Katsaros a quick hug. "One day, when we have a little longer, will you tell me the full version?"

Mrs. Katsaros laughed and patted her hand. "Only if you call me Dorcas," she said. "My friends don't call me Mrs. Katsaros."

"I'd like that," Gracie said, warmed by her kindness. "Especially if you call me Gracie."

Brent opened the back door, and Gracie slipped out.

Turning around, she lowered her head so she could see the white-haired lady inside. "Thank you so much for the ride."

"You're welcome, Gracie. I enjoyed having your company."

Brent closed the door between them and hurried back to his side of the car. Gracie stepped onto the sidewalk and raised her hand in farewell. The tinted window lowered a few inches, and Dorcas waved back. The moissanite ring on her finger sparkled, and Gracie's heart sank. For a few short moments, she'd forgotten the devastating discovery of the morning.

The Cadillac pulled away from the sidewalk, and Gracie turned to climb the stone steps outside the remodeled townhouse. She punched the code into the lock on the front door and let herself in. The dark, narrow hall led to the door of the first floor apartment. Gracie ignored it and headed for the steep staircase, climbing up until she reached her small, one-bedroom apartment on the third floor.

The moment she was inside, Gracie took off her wet shoes, crossed the narrow room that served as both living room and kitchen, and entered her bedroom. A quick glance at the clock beside her bed told her that if she was fast, she might have enough time to eat a sandwich for lunch before heading back to work. Opening the closet door, she pulled the nearest dress from its hanger and grabbed some clean underwear from her dresser drawer, then headed straight for the shower.

The warm water washed away the stickiness and soothed away the chill, but it did nothing to calm Gracie's thoughts. One minute, she was reliving the skater's collision with her cup of hot chocolate, and the next minute, she was picturing Dorcas's devastated expression when Mr. Hamley had confirmed that her ring was a fake. Gracie's emotions ran the gamut between outrage and sorrow, and somewhere—squeezed in between all the other muddled feelings—there was a good measure of embarrassment and irritation that Quinn West had refused her hand.

Admittedly, her appearance hadn't helped. But even if she had looked like a drowned sewer rat this morning, it was no excuse for his rudeness. Gracie scrubbed the shampoo through her hair a little more vigorously than usual. Dorcas Katsaros may not have embraced the attitude of superiority so common among Samuel Hamley's rich and famous clients, but it appeared that her nephew had made it his own.

Anxious to move on from the memories of her awkward interaction with Quinn West, Gracie turned off the water, stepped out of the shower, and steered her thoughts toward the mystery of Dorcas's ring. How had the rings been switched? And when?

Gracie had designed the shank specifically to set off the stunning pink diamond. It was intended to be a one-of-a-kind piece of jewelry, and so the mold had been destroyed as soon as the ring was cast, and her original sketches, along with all the ring's specs, were now locked in the vault at Samuel Hamley.

Her hand froze midway through brushing her hair. Had someone accessed those papers? Who, other than Mr. Hamley, could open the vault?

Gracie put on her dress and hurried back to the bedroom. Pulling her phone from her bag, she dialed Samuel Hamley's number. When the automated response clicked on, she pushed *2 and waited for Kelly to answer.

"Samuel Hamley Fine Jewelry. Kelly speaking."

"Kelly, this is Gracie."

Kelly's professional tone instantly warmed. "Hey there, how was that fancy Cadillac ride?"

"Incredible," Gracie said, unable to keep from smiling.

Kelly laughed. "As incredible as Mr. Quinn West?" She lowered her voice. "Tell me that very fine man left Mr. Hamley's office with your phone number."

"Uh, do you happen to remember what I looked like when he came in? He wasn't interested."

"Lame sauce." Kelly sounded genuinely disappointed. "I really thought he was a long-brown-haired-girl kinda guy." Gracie heard the rustle of papers. "He's not into spiky short hair. That's for sure. He didn't give me a second look."

Gracie held back a sigh. "Don't worry about it. He probably has a glamorous girlfriend anyway." She moved on to her bigger concern. "I actually called to see if you can tell me who has access to the vault over there?"

"I have one of the combinations. The same one as Pete. Max and Mr. Hamley have the other."

"It has a dual control lock?" Gracie asked. It made sense to share the two codes between Pete, who was manager of the design team, and Max, who was manager of sales. Along with the company's documents, the Samuel Hamley's vault housed a fortune in precious stones.

"Yep. The combinations have to be put in at the same time for the door to unlock. It's a security thing. No one person can open it alone." Kelly paused. "What's up? Why the sudden interest in the vault?"

"I need to look over some of my old sketches," Gracie said. "And I wasn't sure how to access them."

"Mrs. Katsaros's ring?" Kelly guessed.

"Yeah." There was no point in hiding it from Kelly. She was smart enough to put the emergency meeting in Mr. Hamley's office together with Gracie's sudden interest in her earlier designs.

"I'll be here all day," Kelly said. "I'm guessing Max will be too. We'll snag him if Mr. Hamley's not available. Just let me know when you want to get in."

"Thanks, Kelly." Gracie wasn't sure why she felt such relief at her friend's willingness to help. Perhaps she simply needed reassurance that no one at Samuel Hamley was responsible for what had happened to Dorcas. Making sure the original blueprints had not been compromised was a good place to start.

CHAPTER 4

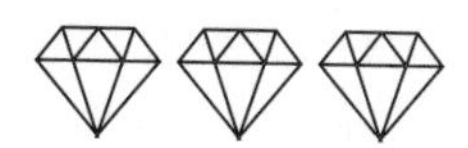

ALMOST SEVEN HOURS LATER, GRACIE followed one of her favorite tree-lined paths through Central Park, the echo of her pounding feet barely registering as she pushed herself to take the incline a little faster. She'd hoped that an early evening run would help dispel her lingering misgivings over what had happened to Dorcas Katsaros, but her thoughts were still troubled by the events of the day.

As soon as Gracie had arrived back at Samuel Hamley, Kelly had grabbed Max and they'd given Gracie access to the vault. Kelly had quickly found the portfolio filed under Gracie's name and had stood at her side as she'd sifted through all the designs she'd worked on since she'd arrived at the New York office. Every single sketch, blueprint, and photograph was there—including the ones for Dorcas's ring. Kelly and Max were understandably grateful that she'd found what she'd been searching for. Unfortunately, Gracie didn't experience the same kind of relief.

She hadn't told Kelly or Max exactly why she'd wanted to revisit her ring design, and because they didn't know about Dorcas's loss, they didn't realize what finding all the papers really meant. But Gracie did. If a perfect counterfeit of her work had been made with the originals still safely locked up at Samuel Hamley, the thief had created a mold for the new ring some other way. Which meant it could happen again. Until Dorcas learned how her ring had been stolen, there didn't seem to be any clear way forward. Gracie could only hope that the person Quinn knew in law enforcement was capable of generating more ideas about how the theft had occurred.

Tamping down her frustration, Gracie exited the park and crossed the street. Keeping her pace even, she headed toward her apartment, waiting until she turned the corner less than half a block from her destination before beginning her cooldown. As she slowed her steps, she noticed a man she'd never seen before standing on the top step in front of her building. Tall and thin, with sandy hair and dark-rimmed glasses, he wore a button-down gray shirt and navy pants. He looked at his watch, then scanned the vicinity as though searching for something or someone.

No longer concentrating on where she placed her feet, Gracie tripped on the uneven sidewalk. She caught herself before she fell, but her stumble attracted the man's attention. His eyes met hers, and she instinctively turned away.

"Gracie Miller?"

Her heart stuttered. How did this stranger know her name? She took an unsteady step backward. One glance up the street told her a delivery truck was approaching too quickly for her to make her escape across the road.

"Wait, Gracie." In an instant, he was down the stairs and within a few feet of her. "My name's Steve Nyborg." He pulled a wallet out of his back pocket and withdrew a card. "I'm a friend of Quinn West and Dorcas Katsaros."

The guy from the FBI. Gracie made the connection before reading the card he handed her that confirmed who he was and where he worked.

"You didn't waste any time," she said.

He grinned. "I'd drive a long way for one of Dorcas's apple pies."

Gracie felt herself relax. It seemed unlikely that the sandy-haired man in front of her could fake that level of enthusiasm for Dorcas's special dessert unless he'd tasted it himself.

"You've talked to her, then?"

The grin disappeared. "Yeah. That's why I'm here. I've come to ask for your help."

"My help?"

"Dorcas said you spotted the forgery right away," he said.

"It's not always that easy, but I'd be out of a job if I couldn't recognize a real diamond."

He inclined his head. "Fair enough. But the truth is, most of us can't, and I need to know if anything else in Dorcas's collection has been switched out without her knowing." He gave Gracie a measured look. "I was hoping you'd be willing to take a look at the rest of her jewelry because, apparently, you're the only person she trusts to do it."

Gracie stared at him. Why had it never occurred to her that Dorcas might have other pieces of jewelry—wholly unconnected to Gracie—that could have been stolen? "Of course," she said. "I'd be happy to."

"Great." He pointed to a dark-blue Chevy on the other side of the road. "I'm parked right over there."

"You want me to go right now?" Not only was she wearing a pair of ratty old sweat pants and her brother's hand-me-down *Sting* T-shirt, but she probably didn't smell that great either. "Can you give me time to take a shower and change?"

Steve checked his watch again. "I wish I could, but I have another commitment in Philly later tonight, and I'm going to be cutting it close as it is." He frowned. "I know it's asking a lot, but I really need to know the scale of this theft before I can do anything else, and I won't be able to get back out here again until next week."

The decision was not hard. Now that Steve had opened the possibility that Dorcas was the target of more than a one-ring-heist, Gracie wanted validation that her remaining jewelry was the real deal as much as he did.

"I'll come," she said. "But I'll need a loupe."

"A loupe?"

"It's a magnifying glass jewelers use." She pointed to the building behind him. "I have one in my apartment."

"Okay." He hesitated. "Can you be . . . ?"

"Fast?" she said.

She sensed his relief. "Yeah."

Gracie started for the front door. "Give me three minutes," she said, already punching in the lock code. She turned around. "I'd say two, but there're a lot of stairs."

His grin was back. "Thanks."

Gracie ran up both flights, her legs protesting with every step. As soon as she entered her apartment, she hurried to the bedroom, located her shoulder bag, and rooted through it until she found the small leather case containing the hand-held magnifying glass. Clasping the case tightly, she tossed her bag onto the bed and headed for the door.

Steve was waiting for her on the sidewalk outside her building. "Got it?" he asked.

She opened her hand to show him the black leather case.

"Great. Let's go." He jogged toward the parked car, and within seconds, he had it running with the passenger-side door open.

Dorcas's condo was less than a mile from Gracie's apartment, but the tall, sleek skyscraper standing directly across from Central Park looked nothing like the old, worn brownstone houses on the street where Gracie lived. Steve pulled up in front of the glistening main doors, and a smartly dressed valet stepped out to meet them. To Gracie's surprise, Steve immediately jumped out of the car and tossed his keys to the valet.

"Mrs. Katsaros is expecting us," he said, "but we won't be long."

"Very good, sir," the valet replied, walking around to the driver's side of the vehicle while Steve opened Gracie's door.

"Where's he taking your car?" Gracie asked as she got out.

"Some secret underground parking place that only people wearing that dorky uniform are allowed to enter," he said.

"I see." Gracie bit back a smile.

"Yeah. I tried finding a parking spot on my own the first few times I visited Dorcas. The first time, it took me so long I was half an hour late for dinner; the second time, I arrived back to find a hefty ticket tucked under my windshield wiper. After that, I decided it's better to just cough up the tip for the valet and save myself the hassle."

Steve nodded to the doorman. The man reciprocated with his own nod of recognition and opened the door to the sumptuous lobby. Gracie followed Steve past enormous potted plants, a gurgling water fountain, and elegant artwork until they reached a wall of gold elevators, where Steve pushed the button marked with an up arrow. The elevator door opened, and they stepped inside. Seconds later, they were soaring upward until a ping announced their arrival on the top floor.

The elevator doors opened into a miniature lobby, complete with two armchairs, a table bearing a beautiful display of fresh flowers, and a large oil painting of New York harbor. The only other exit appeared to be through a wide dark-wood door on the opposite side of the small room. Steve led her to the door and gave a brisk knock. Moments later, it opened to reveal Dorcas wearing a flour-covered striped apron over pink lounge pants and a pink polka-dotted blouse.

"Steve," she said with a smile. "And it looks like you found Gracie."

"I did." Steve took Gracie's elbow and guided her forward. "Your directions were excellent."

"Hello again, Dorcas," Gracie said.

The older woman reached for Gracie, kissing her lightly on each cheek just as she'd done when she'd greeted Quinn in Mr. Hamley's office. "I'm so glad you're here, my dear," she said. "We need your expertise."

Gracie smiled. "I'm happy to do whatever I can to help."

"Come along, then," Dorcas said.

Gracie followed Dorcas and Steve into the most beautiful living room she'd ever seen. To her left, the polished wood floor extended all the way to a wall made entirely of huge panes of glass, with built-in french doors that opened onto a furnished balcony with stunning views of Central Park. A sleek, black grand piano took up one corner of the room, and immediately in front of her, a large cream-colored sectional sofa curved in a semicircle around a parquet coffee table, with two matching armchairs on the other side. An assortment of lamps were tastefully scattered around the room, and a stunning painting of the Acropolis at sunset hung above an oversized gas fireplace on the far wall.

The only hints that she wasn't simply looking at an illustration in an interior design magazine were a pair of fluffy purple slippers lying beside the closest chair, a couple of framed photos on the mantelpiece, and a newspaper open to the half-completed crossword puzzle sitting on the coffee table.

"It smells awesome in here." Steve sniffed the air appreciatively, and Dorcas chuckled, pulling her apron off as she led them into the kitchen.

"It just came out," she said, pointing to a pie cooling on a wire rack on the granite-topped bar.

Steve stepped closer.

"Oh, no you don't, young man," Dorcas said, humor temporarily replacing the anxiety in her eyes. "It's still too hot. Wait until we've finished looking at my jewelry. It should be just the right temperature for the ice-cream by then."

Steve gave an exaggerated sigh. "Fine. But I've waited an awful long time for this."

"Then a few more minutes won't kill you," she said, quickly cutting through the well-appointed kitchen and turning to the right, where she opened the door to what must have originally been Alessandro's office.

A large desk and leather chair were positioned on one side of the room. Bookshelves lined with books, trophies, plaques, and trinkets covered the back wall, a large picture window that looked out across the city skyline filled another, and an Impressionist painting hanging slightly askew dominated the third. Dorcas stepped closer to the painting and lifted it off the wall to expose a safe behind.

Gracie stood next to Steve behind the desk as Dorcas inputted a code on the safe's keypad. She turned the metal lever, and the bolt slid back with a solid click. Seconds later, Dorcas had opened the heavy door and was lifting out eight velvet-covered boxes of varying sizes that she then carried to the desk.

"Here they are," she said. "I have a few pieces of costume jewelry in my bedroom, but these boxes contain everything of value."

Dorcas opened the first box to reveal two rows of sparkling earrings. From pearl clusters to cascading diamonds, from round-cut amethysts to oval-cut rubies, each pair was a work of art.

"Check every one, Gracie," Dorcas said, sliding the box toward her.

Gracie drew her loupe out of its case and reached for a set of pear-cut emeralds. Turning the first one toward the light, she examined it from every angle. Then she repeated the procedure with its mate.

"These are nearly flawless emeralds set in platinum," she said, lowering her loupe.

Dorcas's shoulders sagged with relief. "Thank goodness. What about the amethysts?"

One by one, Gracie inspected the earrings. Every stone passed muster until she came to the very last pair. The matching rubies looked to be close to three carats each and were surrounded by a ring of tiny diamonds. Gracie scoured the stones for any signs of natural imperfection. There were none. She held them up to the sunlight, but the red rays that should have been almost instantly visible were not there.

With a sinking heart, she faced Dorcas. "I think these are synthetic rubies," she said. "I haven't checked the diamonds, but my guess would be that if the rubies are man-made, the surrounding diamonds are too."

Dorcas slowly lowered herself into the armchair in the corner. "It was probably too much to hope for, but for a little while, I really thought we were in the clear."

Battling her own disappointment, Gracie went to put the earrings back in the box, but Steve reached out his hand for them. "Let's keep the forgeries separate," he said. "It will make it easier to figure out what they have in common."

With a nod, Gracie handed them to him, and he set them on a clean piece of paper in the center of the desk.

"Try the next box," Dorcas said, weariness stealing into her voice. "My rings should be inside."

Twenty-five minutes later, Gracie had gone through all the boxes but one. Lying starkly on the piece of paper that Steve had set on the desk were the synthetic ruby earrings, a five-and-a-half-carat synthetic amethyst pendant, a synthetic emerald and moissanite ring, and the pink moissanite ring.

Gracie reached for the last box, and Dorcas rose from the chair, moving to stand across the desk from her. Seeing the raw emotion in Dorcas's eyes, Gracie hesitated. "May I?" she asked.

Dorcas nodded, and Gracie opened the box to reveal an absolutely stunning sapphire necklace. The radiant-cut stone was at least seven carats and was suspended from a delicate platinum rope chain.

"Alessandro gave it to me on the eve of our wedding," Dorcas said quietly. "He said the blue was to remind me of the Mediterranean where we met."

Carefully, Gracie picked up the necklace, running the chain through her fingers until the sapphire lay in the palm of her hand. Raising her hand to her mouth, she breathed heavily on the stone, then watched and counted as the condensation evaporated. With her heart pounding uncomfortably in her chest, she put the loupe to her eye and held the stone up to the light. A few thin lines, like gossamer spiderwebs, intersected half a dozen microscopic bubbles in the center of the sapphire. Slowly, Gracie lowered the stone.

"Have you ever heard of a lead-glass-filled sapphire or a composite sapphire?" she asked.

Dorcas shook her head.

"They're actual sapphires," Gracie explained, "but they're very poor quality. Lead glass is poured into them so their flaws become transparent, and to the naked eye, they appear good enough to be used in jewelry. When they're viewed under a jeweler's loupe, however, it's possible to see the bubbles the glass creates as it cools and the thin lines where the glass has filled in the cracks in the original stone."

"And you can see those things in the sapphire you're now holding," Dorcas guessed.

Gracie's hand shook as she considered what the thieves had taken from the woman before her. "Yes."

Behind her, she heard Steve's muttered expletive, but her focus was on the tears welling up in Dorcas's eyes.

"I'm so sorry, Dorcas."

The older woman pulled a tissue out of a box on the corner of the desk and dabbed at her eyes. "Well," she said. "Now we know." She took a deep breath and cleared her throat. When she spoke again, her voice was firm. "So, Steve, what are we going to do about it?"

CHAPTER 5

Quinn resisted the urge to loosen his tie and undo the top button of his white dress shirt. The Guggenheim's air-conditioning was barely taking the edge off the rising temperature in the crowded room, and he wanted nothing more than to be out of his black suit and tie, riding his road bike through Central Park, far away from this room full of people trying too hard to impress each other.

A few feet away, Mallory Stapleton stood surrounded by men. One of them said something, and Mallory laughed, a sure sign that she was as much in her element here as Quinn was out of his. For about the hundredth time, he wondered what had possessed him to agree to attend the opening night of the Guggenheim's newest exhibit with her. The fact that the painting hanging on the wall next to him looked like something he'd created in kindergarten proved how little he knew about art, and there was certainly no lack of males willing to escort Mallory wherever she desired. Why she'd insisted that he be her date this evening was a mystery; he had to be the most boring guy in the entire museum—and that was saying something.

A waiter walked by, a tray full of drinks balanced on one hand. He paused next to Quinn, but Quinn raised his half-full glass of orange juice and shook his head. Assured that Quinn wanted nothing stronger, the waiter moved on. Quinn watched him effortlessly weave in between the small clusters of New York's wealthiest businessmen and -women, the headlining politicians, and a handful of celebrities. The sound of enthusiastic voices and laughter filled the room; it appeared that the gala was a success.

He glanced at his watch, wondering if Steve had arrived at Dorcas's condo yet. When his friend had finally returned his call and learned what had happened to Dorcas, he'd promised to drive to New York as soon as he'd finished some pressing paperwork. Quinn had wanted to be at the condo when Steve arrived, but when he'd called Mallory to bow out of attending the gala, she'd told him she'd been looking forward to going with him for weeks, had bought a new dress for the occasion, and had thought she meant more to him than some old college friend. A combination of guilt and the inability to tell Mallory the real reason for Steve's visit had compelled Quinn to pick up Mallory in time for the walk down the red carpet.

Now, two hours later, he was ready to leave. Placing his glass on a table, he walked over to the nearby group and inserted himself into the circle next to Mallory.

"Hey, stranger," she said. "Where have you been all this time?"

"I've been around," Quinn said.

She threaded her arm through his. "I missed you."

He was quite sure she hadn't but refrained from saying so. "I hate to cut your evening short, Mal," he said, "but I need to go check on Dorcas."

"Is she sick?"

"She's had a pretty rough day," he hedged. "I promised I'd stop by before she heads to bed. And you know how early that can be."

The flash of annoyance in Mallory's green eyes eliminated any twinge of conscience Quinn felt over cutting her socializing short, and he found himself wondering what she would do. Each of the men in her current entourage had undoubtedly arrived with one of the women who was clustered around a canvas that looked as though it had been run over with a bicycle after the tires had been dipped in red paint. That meant that none of them were in a position to step in as her date.

Mallory tightened her grip on Quinn's arm and flashed a bright smile at her companions. "It looks like we're heading out."

"It was good to meet you, Mallory," one of the men said, raising his glass in her direction.

"You too, Brady," she said. She handed her half-empty champagne flute to the guy at her other side. "Take care of that for me, would you, Tim?" Then pivoting on her extremely high stiletto heel, she nudged Quinn toward the exit.

Quinn stifled a smile. It seemed that this time, protocol trumped personal preference. With a nod to the watching men, he put his free hand in his pocket and walked Mallory out.

The drive back to Mallory's condo was short and unusually quiet. She spent the entire ride texting on her phone. Quinn kept his eyes on the road. Apart from the fact that Mallory's new little black dress was so low-cut it made him uncomfortable, he was happy to skip out on seeing the peeved look on her face over their early departure. When they pulled up to the building, the valet appeared immediately. Quinn handed him the keys and walked around to open Mallory's door.

"I'm sorry we left before you were ready, Mal. It's been a pretty brutal day, and it's not over yet."

She got out of the car, and he closed the door behind her. She stood for a moment, looking up at the lights shining from the penthouse suite high above them. "Dorcas isn't even your mother," she grumbled.

He took her arm, glad that she didn't pull away. "She may as well be. You know that. She cared for me and my mom when there was no one else. Now it's my turn."

She sniffed. "Fine. But you owe me another night on the town."

Somehow, Quinn managed not to groan. Every outing with Mallory for the past eight months was supposed to have been his last. When he'd first met her at the gym in Dorcas's building, he'd been a new graduate student just starting his first job in the city.

He'd been flattered that the cute girl who lived five floors down from his aunt was interested in him, and he'd been more than happy when she'd agreed to be his date to many of the functions he was expected to attend as a representative of Anderson and Gough.

Unfortunately, it hadn't taken him long to realize they had almost nothing in common. He'd been ready to move on months ago, but to his frustration, Mallory didn't seem to see things the same way. When his invitations had dwindled to none, she'd started issuing her own, and thanks to his maddening sense of obligation, he'd accepted far too many of them.

The elevator reached her floor, and they stepped out together. They approached her door, and she withdrew the key from her sparkling black clutch.

"Thanks for going with me," she said.

"You're welcome."

She leaned into him and pressed her lips to his. He pulled back, but she didn't seem to notice.

"I'll see you later," she said confidently.

Silently, he got back into the elevator and pushed the button for the top floor. He had to let it go tonight. There were too many other things weighing on him to add dealing with Mallory and her self-absorption to the load. But like it or not, his next conversation with her was going to be ugly; there was no nice way out of this mess.

Two minutes later, Quinn knocked on Dorcas's door. He didn't have to wait long for his aunt to open it.

"Quinn!" She greeted him warmly with a hug and a kiss on each cheek. "I was hoping you'd make it." She ushered him inside. "Come along. There's apple pie and ice cream."

He followed the delicious aroma and the sound of voices to the kitchen, where Steve was sitting in front of an enormous bowl of dessert across the bar from a girl with a lopsided ponytail. Steve looked up as Quinn entered.

"Well, it's better late than never," Steve said with a welcoming smile. He got to his feet and clasped Quinn's hand firmly. "It's been too long."

"It has." Quinn smiled. "When did you get here?"

Steve shrugged. "I made it into the city just after rush hour, got some more details from Dorcas, then picked up Gracie." He glanced at the clock on the stove. "We've been here about an hour."

"Gracie?"

The girl on the bar stool turned around to face him. "Hello again, Mr. West."

With her back to him and dressed in a T-shirt, sweat pants, and running shoes, it was forgivable that he'd mistaken the jewelry designer for a teenager, but he'd already made one social blunder with the young woman, and he wasn't about to repeat himself. "Quinn," he said, covering his surprise at seeing her in his aunt's condo by extending his hand to her. "Call me Quinn."

Her blue eyes widened, then she shook his hand and smiled. "Quinn," she repeated.

"Where have you been in that penguin outfit?" Steve's teasing voice pulled his attention back to his old friend.

"Says the guy who can't match his socks."

"Matching socks is overrated."

Quinn snorted. "You're totally colorblind but won't admit it."

"Like you won't admit where you've been," Steve said, wiggling his eyebrows.

"The Guggenheim," he said, finally undoing the top button of his shirt and pulling his bow tie free.

"You saw the new exhibit?" Gracie asked.

"Some of it," he said. "Most of the canvases looked like they were covered in tire tracks and food spills."

She laughed, and he paused halfway through taking off his jacket, suddenly feeling awkward. "Sorry. You probably appreciate that kind of art much more than I do."

Gracie shook her head, mirth still shining in her eyes. "I know where you're coming from. I enjoy art, but I prefer paintings like the one your aunt has over the fireplace."

"I knew you had good taste," Dorcas said, putting the ice cream back in the freezer and joining them at the island in the center of the kitchen. "I've always loved that painting. It came from Alessandro's home in Athens."

She handed Quinn a bowl of apple pie and ice cream. It was almost as big as Steve's.

"This looks amazing," Quinn said.

With a smirk, Steve tossed him a napkin. "Here. Even if you don't need it for the dessert, you can use it to wipe the lipstick off your mouth." Quinn glared at him, and Steve laughed unrepentantly. "Who's the lucky girl?"

"It's not like that." Quinn stabbed the fork into his piece of pie.

"Uh-huh."

"I'm serious." A quick glance at Dorcas told him she was all ears. Gracie, on the other hand, was incredibly focused on her pie and ice cream.

"I bet you are." Steve folded his arms and raised his eyebrows. "How serious is serious?"

No wonder the FBI recruited the guy. If he interrogated suspects half as relentlessly as this, none of them stood a chance.

"Mallory Stapleton invited me to go with her."

"The hot chick who lives downstairs?"

Quinn winced. He wasn't going there. Not here. Not now. "Okay, enough about my evening," he said firmly. "We're moving on to what you've decided to do about Dorcas's ring."

"I'm afraid it's not just about the ring anymore." Dorcas had taken her seat again. "Steve wanted to know if that was the only thing that was stolen, so we asked Gracie to come over and check the rest of my jewelry." She paused, her voice becoming quiet. "She found four more forgeries in the safe."

Quinn pushed his bowl to one side, his appetite suddenly gone. "What else has been stolen?"

Steve handed him his phone. He'd taken photographs of the items, individually and as a group.

Quinn's frustration mounted as he flipped through the images. "The sapphire necklace?" He had a pretty good idea of how much sentimental value Dorcas attached to that particular piece.

Dorcas nodded.

He turned to Gracie. "How sure are you about this?"

"As sure as I can be without access to stronger magnification or lab results," she said. "You'd want to look into having a second opinion or more conclusive tests before filing any kind of insurance claim, but I can tell you for sure that Dorcas's ring is not the only piece of jewelry that's been switched out."

Quinn ran his fingers through his hair. "Steve?"

"We've definitely got more questions than answers right now," Steve said. He flipped open a notepad that had been hidden behind his bowl. "First off, how is this happening without Dorcas's knowledge? The obvious answer is that someone is taking something from the safe and replacing it with a fake. Since there's no sign of break-in, the safe would have to be opened by someone with the combination or by a safecracker. Dorcas claims you're the only other person who knows the combination, which makes you suspect number one."

Quinn stared at his friend, and Steve chuckled. "Don't worry. Even if I didn't personally know what a respectable citizen you are, the fact that your insurance company stands to lose as much as Dorcas pretty well puts you in the clear." He tapped the tip of his pencil against the notepad. "According to Dorcas, the only other person who has free access to the house is her maid." He glanced at his notes. "Leticia Lopez."

"It can't possibly be Lettie," Dorcas said. "She's been working for me ever since I moved to New York."

"Which may be when this all started," Quinn pointed out. "We don't know how long you've been wearing the forgeries."

Dorcas bit her lip, and Steve looked thoughtful. "The vague time line does complicate things."

"Dorcas, you told me Alessandro gave you the sapphire necklace the day before you were married." Gracie entered the conversation for the first time. "I know you bought the pink diamond ring about nine months ago. What about the others?"

Quinn slid Steve's phone over to his aunt, and she studied the picture of all five pieces. "Apart from the sapphire necklace, they were all purchased fairly recently," she said. She looked up from the photo. "Within the last three years."

Steve raised his eyebrows and glanced at Quinn. "Isn't that about how long Alessandro's been gone?"

Quinn nodded. "Yes."

Steve scribbled down some notes. "Can you get me the dates you purchased each one, Dorcas?"

"I think the receipts are locked in the file cabinet," she said. "I'll make you copies of them."

"Thanks. Are they all from Samuel Hamley?"

"Actually, no. I've bought a few things there over the years, but the pink diamond ring is the only one from Hamley's that Gracie identified as fake." She paused to think. "Alessandro purchased the sapphire many years ago and had it made into a necklace for me in Athens. I bought the other three pieces at the Venetian Jewelry Show."

Gracie gasped. "You've been to the Venetian Jewelry Show?"

Dorcas smiled at Gracie's awe-filled expression. "I have."

"Uh, humor the jewelry-ignorant guy in the room, would you?" Steve said. "What's the Venetian Jewelry Show?"

"It's one of the most prestigious jewelry shows in the world," Gracie said. "Top-ranked dealers in precious metals and gems attend, and it's become *the* place for European jewelers to unveil their new designs."

Steve raised his eyebrows. "Security would need to be pretty tight for something like that." He turned to Dorcas. "I'm guessing a regular tourist can't just get off a gondola and wander in, right?"

She shook her head. "Admission is by invitation only."

"And when did you start receiving invitations?"

"Alessandro was a regular attendee long before I met him. It's probably where he purchased the sapphire he used for my necklace." Sadness filled her voice. "When Alessandro saw how much I treasured the necklace, he insisted that I go with him each year to pick out something new. Since the jewelry show is held on the first weekend in July and coincides with the start date of our summer cruise, it became a regular part of our trip to the Mediterranean. We'd go see Alessandro's favorite jewelers at the show on Saturday, then board the ship on Sunday.

"After Alessandro died, the invitations continued to come, and I . . . I couldn't bear to give up the tradition that had brought us both so much pleasure. So I went back alone."

"And you made a purchase, then went on the cruise by yourself afterward?" Steve asked.

Dorcas nodded. "Yes. Going back that first year without my husband was one of the hardest things I've ever done."

Quinn experience a pang of guilt. He remembered Dorcas agonizing over whether or not she should go. She'd even asked him to go with her. But he'd been at Anderson and Gough for only five weeks, and he'd felt the need to prove himself worth their generous paycheck before taking two weeks off work. Had he messed up his priorities?

"The crew welcomed me back like family," Dorcas continued. "And they seemed so genuinely glad to see me that it helped dull the pain of being there without Alessandro. And then there are Alessandro's children. They still live in Europe, and going on the cruise gives me a reason to visit them."

Steve studied Dorcas thoughtfully. "So you're saying that three of the five forgeries were purchased at the Venetian Jewelry Show—one each year since Alessandro's passing. After attending the show, you always take the same cruise with the same crew and visit the same ports of call, including one that enables you to visit Alessandro's family members."

"Yes," Dorcas said. "I've done that cruise so many times I often stay on board rather than take the excursions. But I always get off at Piraeus and go into Athens by taxi to visit Nikos for a few hours. Then, at Santorini, Theo sends a car for me, and I spend the day at his house in Oia."

"Are Nikos and Theo Alessandro's sons?"

Dorcas chuckled. "Theo is, but Nikos is as old as Alessandro. They were best friends growing up in Pireaus, and now Nikos is one of Athens's finest goldsmiths." She shrugged. "I think he was the one who first persuaded Alessandro to invest in jewelry. He was also the jeweler who created the setting for my sapphire necklace. Alessandro always wanted to show him his purchases at the Venetian Jewelry Show."

"And you now do the same," Steve guessed.

Quinn had a pretty good idea where Steve's questioning was leading. His aunt's love of keeping up traditions made her behavior easy to predict; the fact that she traveled alone and was relatively inexperienced in the world of fine jewelry made her an obvious and easy target.

With a glance at his friend's grim expression, Quinn posed the next question. "If this Nikos guy is such a good jeweler, why isn't he at the show in Venice?"

"Oh, he used to go," Dorcas said. "That's where I first met him. But he claims he's getting too old for it now. His son, Damien, takes care of the Nikos Antoniou Gold exhibits at all the shows in Europe. I think Nikos still does a lot of the designing, but Damien has already taken over the business end of things."

Steve scribbled a few more things in his notebook, then he glanced at his watch and grimaced. "I'm afraid I've got to get going." He stood, pushing the stool back under the island. "We've made a decent start, Dorcas. When I get back to Philly, I'll put out some feelers." He put up his hand in anticipation of any argument. "Any inquiries will be vague and wholly unconnected to you. It would simply be interesting to know if the Italian police or Interpol have had any reports of jewelry thefts from people attending the Venetian Jewelry Show or taking Mediterranean cruises."

Dorcas's eyes widened. "Do you really think . . . ?"

"Right now, I want to consider all possibilities," Steve said. "Which means I need to give you a homework assignment. I still need copies of your receipts, and I plan on doing a background check on your maid, but if the jewelry isn't being switched out from your home safe, I need a list of any time or place that you remember taking off any of the stolen jewelry—either to show someone else or to place in another safe because you weren't home."

Dorcas suddenly looked anxious. "I may not remember them all."

"Just do your best," Steve said, reaching over to give her a brief hug. "I'm really sorry you have to go through this, but don't you worry; with my brains and Quinn's—well, whatever it is Quinn has to offer—we'll figure this out."

Dorcas managed a weak smile. "You're just buttering me up so I'll give you the rest of the pie to take home."

"Is it working?"

"Maybe," she said, opening a nearby drawer and pulling out a roll of tin foil.

Steve gave Quinn a triumphant grin before surreptitiously glancing at his watch again.

"I'll call a cab," Gracie said. She pulled a cell phone from the pocket of her sweats. "It'll make you even later if you have to drop me off."

Steve frowned. "I'm really sorry. I have to meet someone with information on a case I've been working on. He has an early-morning flight, and he's only going to be in Philly for a few more hours."

"You don't have to call a cab, Gracie," Quinn said, coming to his feet. "I can take you home." She swung to face him, and he tried to brush off the astonishment in her eyes with a shrug. "It's no problem. I'm heading out now too."

She glanced at Steve, but his attention was on Dorcas and the pie pan. "All right," she said hesitantly. "Thanks."

Quinn reached for his suit coat. Steve leaving with all the leftover pie was a fitting end to this terrible day, and yet, Quinn's heart lightened. For some inexplicable reason, having Gracie agree to let him drive her home felt like some kind of victory.

CHAPTER 6

Gracie hadn't thought anything could be more humiliating than facing Mr. Hamley and a wealthy client while dripping wet and covered in hot chocolate and gutter-water stains. But walking through the luxurious lobby of Dorcas's high-rise building beside tux-clad Quinn West with her hair in a disheveled ponytail and dressed in worn-out exercise clothes was shaping up to be a close second.

By the time they reached the glass revolving doors, Quinn had greeted four well-dressed residents by name and Gracie had received at least double that many curious stares.

"Hey, Quinn!" A portly man called out to them from the elevator. "It's been awhile."

Quinn raised his hand in acknowledgment. "Good to see you, Don," he said, ushering Gracie into the revolving door. "Sorry to rush you," he said, lowering his voice so only Gracie heard him as the glass door panel slid forward. "I lived with Dorcas for a few months when I first moved to the city, so I got to know some of her neighbors. I like Don, but once he starts talking, there's no stopping him." He gave her an apologetic look. "I figured we'd both rather not get held up right now."

Gracie wrinkled her nose. "I think I might be a bit underdressed for formal introductions."

Quinn chuckled. "Are you kidding? Don may be a millionaire, but he's never worn anything as cool as a vintage Sting T-shirt."

"Vintage," Gracie said, trying not to smile. "Who knew? My brother will be sick when he realizes what he parted with."

The door rotated a little further, and with a whoosh, the moist outside air greeted them. Gracie exited onto the sidewalk with Quinn right behind her. The doorman signaled the valet, and the young man took off at a run.

"Jeff will have your car here momentarily, Mr. West," the doorman said.

"Thanks, Bill."

Quinn stepped aside as a cab pulled into the drop-off zone in front of the building. Gracie moved to stand beside him and watched silently as a woman got out of the taxi, her short black dress revealing a pair of shapely tanned legs almost as eye-catching as her perfectly styled blonde hair and flawless facial features.

"Well, look who's here." With feline grace, the woman walked toward Quinn. "I didn't expect to see you again this evening."

"Hi, Mal," Quinn said. "You must've decided to go out again."

"Vince Lindon called. There was a party at his place and . . ." She raised her bare shoulders. "Well, the night was still young."

"Great. I'm glad you got to go."

She slid her arm through Quinn's. "It was boring. Vince's parties always turn into a political rant." She turned her green eyes on Gracie. "And who's this?"

Gracie's impression of a cat on the prowl intensified, and she was reminded of how much she preferred the loyal dogs over the calculating mousers at her family's farm in Washington. Looking cat-woman in the eyes, she forced a smile. "I'm Gracie Miller."

"Gracie's a friend of Dorcas," Quinn said. "Gracie, this is Mallory Stapleton. She lives a few floors down from Dorcas."

The hot chick who lives downstairs. Steve's words echoed through Gracie's mind, and she worked to keep disappointment from showing on her face. This evening's interaction with Quinn had almost persuaded her to revise her initial impression of him. But in one area, at least, it seemed that her first guess had been right after all: his taste in women ran toward rich, blonde models.

The sound of a car pulling up drew their attention, and Quinn deftly slid his arm out from under Mallory's. "This is mine," he said, pointing Gracie toward the silver Audi.

Mallory's eyes narrowed. "Are you driving her home?"

Quinn stiffened. Gracie was glad to see that he recognized his girlfriend's rudeness, but she wasn't going to just stand there while he gave someone so unpleasant a placating explanation. She might look like a nobody right now, but she wasn't going to be labeled one. A quick glance over her shoulder told her Mallory's taxi was still parked in front of Quinn's car. The driver looked up from resetting his meter, and Gracie raised her hand. She took two steps toward the empty cab, and the driver immediately got out and opened the back door.

"Thanks for walking me out, Quinn," Gracie said. "I won't keep you any longer." Then without giving him a chance to respond, she hurried into the cab and the driver shut the door behind her.

Quinn leaned back in his desk chair, closed his eyes, and pinched the bridge of his nose with his thumb and forefinger. It was only 10:25 a.m., and already his head ached and the columns of numbers on the computer screen in front of him were starting to wiggle out of alignment. The past twenty-four hours qualified as nightmare material. His rough day had morphed into an even worse night, and even now, he wasn't sure which emotion had kept him awake the longest—concern over Dorcas's stolen jewelry, fury over Mallory's behavior, or his inexplicable regret over Gracie's hasty departure.

In his mind's eye, he relived watching Gracie climb into the cab, her untidy ponytail looking all the more crooked when she turned away from him. He'd caught the smug expression on Mallory's face seconds before it disappeared behind her familiar pout and he'd known that if he allowed himself to give vent to his feelings right then, he would undoubtedly live to regret it. Drawing on every ounce of self-control he could muster, he'd clenched his jaw, turned on his heel, snatched his keys from the hand of the innocent valet, and peeled out of the drop-off zone at a speed that would have straightened Dorcas's curly hair.

There had been several things Quinn had hoped to ask Gracie on the drive to her apartment. Her knowledge of the jewelry business—particularly the area of design—made her an invaluable resource in trying to figure out how Dorcas's forgeries were being made. Did she have any idea how it could be done? Had Steve asked her already?

Quinn rose from his chair and paced across his office, a whirl of unanswered questions tumbling through his head. He paused beside the window that looked down on the bustling streets of New York's financial district. Working in America's commercial center had been his goal for as long as he could remember. To do so as the junior CEO of a well-respected insurance company was a dream come true. And yet, as he gazed down on the sidewalks spilling over with ambitious businessmen and women desperately trying to keep pace with the ever-changing world of economics, he couldn't help but wonder if there was more to life than this. Something important that he was missing.

He reached for the carafe on his desk, poured some water into a glass, and studied the photo on the shelf behind his chair. He'd been twelve years old when that picture was taken. He sat on a bleacher at the baseball park in Cheney, New Hampshire, tousle-headed and triumphant after his team had won the district championship. On one side of him stood his mother, and on the other side was his Aunt Dorcas. They'd been his cheering section at every game.

Taking a drink, Quinn thought back on his early years. He could faintly remember his father, but the memories weren't happy ones. His parents had been high school sweethearts and had married right after graduation. But thanks to a quick temper and no solid qualifications, his father hadn't been able to hold down a job for longer than a few months at a time and had eventually turned to alcohol to drown his feelings of failure. The alcohol had led to abuse, primarily of his wife, and by the time Quinn was six, his parents had divorced and he and his mother had moved in with his mother's unmarried sister, Dorcas.

He'd been ten when he'd learned that his father had been killed in a car accident driving drunk. Thankfully, no one else had been involved, and although Quinn had felt no emotional attachment to the man, his father's death had solidified two personal goals in his young mind: he would do whatever it took to reach the top of his chosen career, and he would never allow alcohol to become part of his life.

His professional goals had driven him to excel in college and acquire a coveted internship at Anderson and Gough. The internship had led to a permanent job after graduation, and six months ago, when old William Gough retired, Quinn had been made junior partner in the firm. His determination to abstain from alcohol had kept him sober during his college days and had given him direction during the torturous sixteen months that his mother had fought and lost her battle with cancer. The agony of watching his mother suffer while being helpless to ease her pain felt as real now as it was then. And Dorcas had been there through it all, consistently supportive, even though she had to have been hurting as much as he had.

His grip on his glass of water tightened as he thought back to his aunt's crushed expression when he'd walked into Henry Hamley's office the day before. It was quite possibly the first time he'd ever seen her innate buoyancy crumble.

Gracie had put her arm around his aunt's shoulders, he remembered. Quinn took a deep breath. He'd been incapable of lifting the burden Dorcas must have felt when his mother had lain dying or when her husband of only seven years had suddenly passed away of a heart attack, but there had to be something he could do this time to ease her loss.

Placing his glass back on the desk, he pulled his cell phone from his pocket and scrolled through his contacts until he found Steve Nyborg. He pushed the call button and waited. Steve answered on the third ring.

"I was pretty sure I'd hear from you today," Steve said. "But seeing as I only made it into the office an hour ago, I don't have much for you yet. So far, the maid, Leticia Lopez, is looking squeaky clean, but I'm still waiting on her bank records.

"I've got a call in to Interpol, the Italian Carabinieri, and the Greek Hellenic Police, but I haven't heard back from any of them yet." Steve paused. "My gut tells me the thefts have a European connection, but I don't know how much help the authorities over there are going to be. Even if the thief has targeted other people, the knock-offs are so well done, most people would never guess they're wearing fakes. Unfortunately, the chances are good that nothing's been reported."

"What about the jeweler in Athens?" Quinn pressed.

There was the sound of shuffling papers. "Nikos Antoniou," Steve said. "I have someone doing some preliminary digging for me, but since I can't tell him why I want to know more about this guy, I have to go carefully."

"I'll see what I can find out about him and his business connections," Quinn offered. "And while I'm at it, I'll check on what Theo and Calista have been up to recently. Last I heard, Theo was running the cruise line from Santorini, and Calista was working for one of the French fashion houses, jetting back and forth from London to Paris to Madrid."

"Is Calista Alessandro's daughter?" Steve asked.

"Yeah. He just has the two kids. I met them both at the wedding and again at Alessandro's funeral. Calista was in New York for Fashion Week about a year ago. Dorcas invited me to dinner while she was here, so I got to see her then too. She acts like she's pretty high up in the fashion industry, but I don't know if she got there through hard work or good connections. She doesn't live in Greece anymore, but I think she tried to be at Theo's when Alessandro and Dorcas stopped there on their cruises. I don't know if she still does now that her dad's gone; I'll have to ask Dorcas."

"That would be great," Steve said. "Anything we can find out about Dorcas's routine onboard ship and onshore would be helpful.

I'm going to see if I can get my hands on a current and past-years crew listing. Dorcas seemed to think many of the crew members have remained the same over the years." Steve's voice became grim. "I'd like to know if there's any extra incentive for doing that."

Quinn stared unseeingly at the concrete jungle outside his office window. With so many people and possible scenarios in the mix, the likelihood of discovering what had happened to his aunt's jewelry seemed slim at best. And Dorcas's insistence upon privacy made their search for the thieves even more difficult. It was as though they'd been handed pencil flashlights when they needed halogen lamps.

"What do you think the odds are that we can . . . ?"

"Hey," Steve interrupted him. "If there's one thing I've learned in this business, it's that the odds are never fixed. Right now, we're just setting ourselves up so that when they shift our way, we're ready."

Despite his concerns, Quinn couldn't help smiling. "That sounds an awful lot like those pep talks you used to give our intramural basketball team when we were down by fifty points at halftime."

"You mean the ones I gave before we turned the game around and won?"

"Yeah, right." Quinn rolled his eyes. "Just keep me in the loop, okay? I'll do whatever it takes."

"You got it," Steve said. "Send me whatever you find on Alessandro's kids and Nikos's business. I'll call Dorcas in a bit and see if she's come up with anywhere else that she remembers taking off or showing someone her jewelry. If she has, we'll check those out too. In the meantime, see if you can't get her safe combo changed by the end of the day."

"Will do."

"I'll be in touch," Steve said. Then he was gone.

Quinn lowered his phone to the desk and turned to his computer. Opening a new window, he entered *Nikos Antoniou Gold*, then he leaned back in his chair and watched as the hits came in.

CHAPTER 7

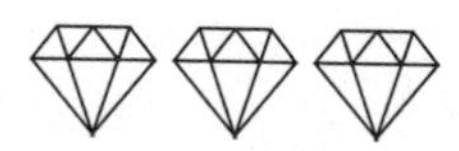

GRACIE STUDIED THE SKETCH ON the desk in front of her. She'd been working on the filigree detail for the Gaelic-style brooch all afternoon, but she still wasn't satisfied with it. Her focus was off, and no matter how hard she tried, the traditional design she'd been going for kept transforming into something that bore an uncanny resemblance to Dorcas's ring.

She gave a sigh of frustration. It had been two days since she'd identified the forgeries at Dorcas's condo, and she had no idea if Steve had made any progress in identifying the jewel thief. It was quite possible that neither he nor Quinn would think to let her know the outcome of their quiet investigation, but she hoped Dorcas might give her some kind of update the next time she came into the store. Unfortunately, Gracie had no way of knowing how soon that would be, and simply guessing at what might be happening was just about killing her.

She stared at her sketch again, concentrating on the center of the brooch where a five-carat emerald would be placed. She needed to create a perfect setting for such a stunning stone.

At her elbow, her telephone rang. Distracted, Gracie picked it up. "Gracie here," she said.

"Hi, Gracie, this is Kelly. I have a Steve Nyborg on the line. He asked to speak to you. Can you take a call right now?"

Steve. Did he have news? She leaned back in her chair, swiveling away from the litter of sketches and diagrams covering the desk. "Yeah," she said. "Thanks, Kelly. Put him through."

"Sure thing."

Two seconds later, she heard a click. "Hello, this is Gracie," she said.

"Hey, Gracie, this is Steve. Do you have a minute to answer a couple of questions?"

An FBI agent wanted to ask her a couple of questions. She tightened her grip on the phone. "Uh, sure." She paused. "Should I be worried?"

Steve laughed, and some of the tension left her fingers. "I don't think so," he said.

"Good to know," she said. "What did you want to ask me?"

"How would you go about making a forgery of the ring you designed for Dorcas?"

Gracie was silent for a second. "Up until two days ago, I'd never given something like that any thought," she said.

"But you have now."

"A little," she admitted.

"And . . . ?"

Gracie took a deep breath. She was going out on a limb here, but she had a feeling they were dealing with a professional, someone who would know the available technology. "If I had access to the right CAD program, all I'd need are photos of the ring taken from three different angles. From those pictures, the computer could generate a 3-D image in wax. The wax replica could then be used to form a mold, which, in turn, would be invested and cast to create a new ring."

"What about the stone?" Steve asked.

"As long as it was a standard cut, it wouldn't be hard to find a synthetic replacement."

"And how fast could it be done?"

This was the tricky part. Gracie knew she was only guessing, but she was pretty sure she would be close. "If I were on a tight time line and had the right equipment, I'm pretty sure I could have a replica made in about thirty hours."

Steve's breath whistled through his teeth. "Now we're getting somewhere!"

What was Steve working on, and how much was he willing to tell her? "Do you have a lead you're following?" she asked.

"Not a lead, exactly. But things certainly seem to be pointing one direction."

"Toward Europe?"

Steve laughed again. "I need to make a couple more phone calls before I answer that. If Quinn or I need to get ahold of you, is there another number I can use?"

"You can call my cell directly," Gracie said, reciting her phone number to him.

As eager as she was to receive updates, especially if they included good news about Dorcas's missing jewelry, she couldn't help wondering if Quinn would talk to her again. Taking the taxi and leaving him standing outside Dorcas's building with his girlfriend was meant to spare him the awkwardness of explaining why he was driving another girl home at night. But when she'd glanced back as the taxi pulled away from the curb, Quinn had appeared more angry than relieved.

"Awesome. Thanks." Steve's voice drew her back from what were becoming irritatingly frequent thoughts of Quinn. "I appreciate your help."

"No problem," Gracie said. "I really hope you can find out what happened and get Dorcas's jewelry back."

"That's the goal," he said.

💎💎💎

Quinn scrolled through his planner and frowned at the many entries filling his calendar. The National Association of Insurance Companies Convention was to begin the day after tomorrow in San

Antonio, and no matter how much he wished it were different, he couldn't see a way out of attending. Almost two thousand insurance representatives from all over the country would be gathering at the conference, and since his senior partner, John Anderson, was going to be in Florida at his granddaughter's wedding over those dates, Quinn had agreed to represent their company.

His secretary had already scheduled meetings for him with reps from their affiliates in San Francisco, LA, Chicago, and Houston. Those consultations began before the convention and lasted through the week. Returning to New York early was not an option either. Six months ago, the convention chairman had reached out to Quinn, asking that he be the keynote speaker at the closing banquet. It was a huge honor and one that neither he nor his company could afford to turn down.

With a sigh of resignation, he placed his phone on the bedside table and dragged his suitcase out from under the bed. Regardless of his desire to help with Steve's investigation and his concern over Dorcas's upcoming travel plans, he was going to Texas, and it was time to stop putting off his packing.

Fifteen minutes later, his phone rang. He glanced at the clock, noting that it was already after 11:00 p.m. Putting down the shirt he'd been folding, he checked the caller ID and reached for his phone. "What's up, Steve?"

"Hey, sorry for calling so late," Steve said. "I just saw what time it is, but seeing as I haven't left the office yet, I figure it's only fair if I disturb the guy who clocks out at five."

Quinn grunted. "Next time we're together, remind me to show you my schedule. You might be surprised."

"Maybe," Steve conceded. "But as the one who's been working the phones since 6:00 a.m. today, I'm going to give you the latest update real fast, then I'm going home to get some sleep."

"Okay," Quinn said. "What've you got?"

"The last of the background checks on the list of people Dorcas gave us just came in." Quinn heard the shuffling of papers. "I have one guy who lost his money on the stock market and is trying to make it back into the big leagues by setting up a sketchy-looking pyramid scheme and another couple who spend too many weekends in Vegas trying to recoup what they lost the week before. Otherwise, I have no obvious red flags. The biggest worry is Amber Winters. She's a columnist for *High Society*, that magazine that features what celebrities wear to those fancy functions that none of us peons can afford to go to. She did a piece—with photos—on Dorcas's sapphire pendant after Dorcas wore it to the Tonys." He gave a frustrated sigh. "Bottom line, those photos could be anywhere."

"And that's a problem because . . . ?" Quinn said.

"Because according to Gracie, a skilled jeweler with the right equipment could make a forgery with as few as three photos taken from different angles."

"You've spoken with Gracie?" Quinn wasn't willing to analyze why that information bothered him.

"Yeah. I called her at work earlier today. And based on what she told me about how fast fake jewelry can be produced and the fact that none of our domestic leads have panned out, I have a theory I want to run by you."

"Go for it," Quinn said.

"I'm still working on how the sapphire pendant and the pink diamond ring fit into this," Steve said, "but for now, let's concentrate on the other three forgeries.

"We know they were purchased at the Venetian Jewelry Show in consecutive years. I think it's fairly safe to assume that gemology expertise and security at a place like that is high enough that no one's going to try pawning off fake stones as the real thing. Once Dorcas gets home, other than the times she's wearing her jewelry or taking it with her on random visits to the friends on her list, the jewels are kept in her safe. If you and the maid—who are supposedly the only ones who could access the safe without sign of break-in—are off the suspect list, that leaves the week that Dorcas is on the cruise as the most likely time that a switch is made."

"Wait a minute," Quinn said. "No one—including Dorcas—knows ahead of time what she's going to purchase at the show. You're telling me you think someone's watching to see what she buys and then is producing a virtually identical fake and trading it out—all within a week?"

"Yep."

Quinn dropped onto the bed. "Can it be done that fast?"

"According to Gracie, if we're dealing with a skilled jeweler who has access to the right equipment, he can make the copycat piece in under two days. Which leads to the next question: when is the tradeoff occurring?"

"On the ship or at the jeweler's shop in Athens," Quinn guessed.

"Those would be my top picks too," Steve said. "But proving it is going to be tough unless we catch the thieves in the act."

Quinn was on his feet again. "No way, Steve. We're not sending Dorcas in on some kind of sting operation."

"Calm down." Steve's tone was measured. "I'm not suggesting that she does this by herself. She'll have someone with her the whole time."

"And you think she's going to go for that?"

"She will if the people are you and Gracie," Steve said.

"I hope you're joking."

"Nope," Steve said. "All Dorcas has to do is follow her routine to the letter. Gracie's there to distinguish the real stones from the fake ones, and you're there to buy a super expensive ring for your new fiancée."

"That's not funny."

"It's not supposed to be," Steve said. "Hear me out, okay? None of the law enforcement entities I've contacted in Europe have any reports of stolen jewelry associated with the show in Venice or the cruise ships in the Med. I know we talked before about the fact that the forgeries are good enough that most people won't notice the difference, but the more I started thinking about who buys this stuff, the more I realized that it's people who know precious stones well enough to view them as an investment. They know how to pick out a diamond from a cubic zirconia or a moissanite." He paused. "I'd be willing to bet that Alessandro would have spotted the fakes himself. But Dorcas can't. She's too new at it. And if that's the case, then it's possible that ever since her husband's death, someone has been specifically targeting Dorcas."

"But—"

"We have to find out if Dorcas is the only victim," Steve said, not letting Quinn get a word in, "and the easiest way to do that is to have someone else buy something at the show and follow her same itinerary. If you go to Venice posing as Gracie's fiancé, you can pick out an engagement ring at the same time Dorcas buys her jewelry. When they're not being worn, both pieces can be kept in the same safe on board ship. Every morning and evening, Gracie can check the jewelry. If Dorcas's piece is traded out but the engagement ring isn't, this investigation instantly shifts from exposing thieves to uncovering who has it in for your aunt and why."

Quinn's mind was reeling. "Can I say something now?" he asked.

"Shoot," Steve said.

"There are so many reasons this plan is a bad idea, I'm having a hard time figuring out where to start," Quinn said. "First off, how do you propose we fund the purchase of tens of thousands of dollars' worth of jewelry, knowing full well that they could disappear without a trace? Second, neither Gracie nor I have any law enforcement experience or authority. What exactly are we supposed to do if the real jewels go missing? Dorcas won't want the whole thing broadcast to the ship's crew or the Hellenic police any more than she wants us going to the NYPD."

"Dorcas is willing to pay for the jewelry," Steve said. "I told her I could call in some favors and have one of the tech guys here provide us with a transmitter small enough that it can be placed on whatever she buys, but even without it, she's willing to take the risk for a chance at getting the sapphire necklace back."

Quinn froze. "Wait. You've talked to Dorcas already?"

"Just a little while ago. She's in."

Quinn gazed heavenward and counted to ten.

"Listen, Quinn," Steve said, and this time there was a slight edge to his voice. "I really think this will work. And so does Dorcas. She can get two guests into the jewelry show on her invitation. If there's any trouble on the ship, she knows the captain on a first-name basis, and I'm a single phone call away. The moment you contact me, even if it's only over a suspicion, I'll drop what I'm doing to get you the help you need."

"And did it occur to either of you that Gracie or I might not be able to leave our jobs on such short notice, or that Gracie might refuse to act as my fiancée? For all we know, she has a real fiancé out there somewhere."

"There's no hidden fiancé," Steve said confidently. "I checked. She had a boyfriend when she lived in Washington, but they broke up when she came to New York, and there hasn't been anyone since."

"Well, I hate to be the bearer of bad news," Quinn said, the memory of Gracie's abrupt departure outside his aunt's building still smarting, "but I don't think she likes me very much."

"She likes Dorcas," Steve said. "And I think she's genuinely willing to do what she can to help your aunt recover her missing jewelry. Besides, most girls would agree to a temporary engagement to Jabba the Hutt if it meant going on an all-expense-paid Mediterranean cruise." His teasing tone was back. "You're not much better looking than old Jabba, but it might be enough."

Quinn ran his hand over his face and gazed at his half-packed suitcase.

"I have to be in San Antonio tomorrow evening," he said. "There's no way to get out of it, and I won't be back here until after Dorcas leaves for Italy."

"Gracie can travel with her," Steve said. "You could join them in Venice the next day." Quinn remained silent, and Steve obviously knew better than to keep up the pressure. "Think it over," he said. "I'm coming into the city tomorrow. I'll catch you at your office before you leave for Texas, and we'll revisit this then."

"I'm in meetings till noon," Quinn warned him.

"Then I'll meet you for lunch," Steve said.

Steve's tenacity was legendary, and Quinn knew that to keep arguing was futile. "How about Marcello's on the corner of Wall

Street and Hanover?" he said, opting for the Italian restaurant closest to his office.

"Great," Steve said. "I'll see you tomorrow."

Quinn lowered the phone, and ignoring the pile of socks stacked beside his suitcase, he headed for the kitchen. Steve had successfully ensured that he'd get little to no sleep tonight, so packing was no longer the priority it had been. He suddenly had all sorts of extra time.

CHAPTER 8

When Quinn reached Marcello's at 12:05 p.m. the next day, the small restaurant was already busy. The enticing aroma of garlic, onion, and freshly baked bread wafted through the open doors, spilling onto the sidewalk where half a dozen round tables had been positioned to accommodate the many customers. Red-checkered tablecloths fluttered in the breeze, anchored down by tall wine bottles, glasses, and dishes full of pasta, salad, and pizza.

Quinn followed one of the black-clad servers into the restaurant and looked around. The light was dimmer inside. In the far corner, the open flames of an enormous brick oven heated the room, and half a dozen cooks were working feverishly to keep up with the demand for fresh pizza. To Quinn's left, a long bar ran the length of the restaurant, and although every bar stool was occupied, a quick glance told him Steve was not among those customers.

"Can I help you, sir?" A dark-haired, dark-eyed girl stood a few feet from the door, menus in hand.

"I'm meeting a friend here for lunch," Quinn said. "Tall, sandy hair."

She pointed to a table next to the window. "He told me to expect you," she said with a smile.

"Thanks." Quinn wove between the tightly packed tables until he reached the one where Steve was sitting.

"Glad you could make it," Steve said.

Quinn dropped onto the seat. "Yeah. It's been a crazy morning."

A young man appeared at the table with a pitcher of root beer and a couple of glasses. "Your pizza will be ready in just a few minutes," he told Steve.

"Thanks," Steve said. He waited until the server stepped to the next table before turning to Quinn. "I went ahead and ordered for you. I figured your love of pizza and root beer probably hasn't changed much in five years."

The corners of Quinn's mouth quirked upward. "Just so long as you eat anything that comes to the table with anchovies on it."

"If they put anchovies on a meat lovers pizza, we're eating somewhere else," Steve said. He gave Quinn a long look. "Have you thought any more about our discussion last night?"

"Yes."

"And?"

Quinn met his friend's gaze. "I'll go through with your harebrained scheme on three conditions."

Steve gave him a guarded look. "Name them."

"First, Gracie has to be a willing participant, without any arm-twisting on your part or Dorcas's. She has to be told straight up that if anyone takes the bait, she could find herself caught up in something nasty."

Steve nodded. "Fair enough."

"Second," Quinn said, "I don't want any transmitters placed on the jewelry."

Steve's eyebrows shot up. "Why?"

"The first thing a jewel thief is going to do when he gets his hands on Dorcas's new purchase is study it under one of those jeweler's loupes. I don't care how microscopic your tech guys think the transmitter is, the thief's going to spot it. And then it's game over. He'll know someone's on to him, and if he's a common crook, he'll cover his tracks to the point that we can't find him or recover the jewelry.

Worse, if the guy's really singling out Dorcas, he could blindside us and go after her in a whole new way."

Steve looked thoughtful. "How about a miniature security camera covering the safe in Dorcas's cabin? If anything's stolen while she's onboard, the video feed would give us something to go on."

"That might work, as long as it's hidden well enough that room service doesn't find it."

"That's doable," Steve said with a decisive nod. "What's your third condition?"

"That you have someone in law enforcement over there ready to step in at a moment's notice."

Steve grinned. "I have a few vacation days owed me, and I'm seriously considering taking a last-minute trip to Greece. How about I promise you a midlevel FBI agent onshore who can pull in local support if needed?"

Quinn felt some of the tension leave his shoulders. Ever since Steve's phone call, he'd been waging an internal battle between his reluctance to have Dorcas risk her personal safety and money and his promise to do all he could to recover his aunt's stolen jewelry. It was reassuring to know that there would be other people he could call on should things go badly.

"Then it looks like all you've got left is to talk to Gracie and see how she feels about it."

The server appeared at their table and placed an extra-large pizza in front of them. "Anything else I can get for you?" the young man asked.

"No. This looks great," Steve said.

The server gave a pleased nod. "Then I'll leave you to it."

Steve picked up a large slice of pizza, folded it in half, and took a big bite. He chewed silently for a few seconds. "As far as Gracie goes, I'm thinking attending the Venetian Jewelry Show is a better selling point than spending the week engaged to you." He smothered a smile. "But for your sake, I will mention that minor detail to her."

"Yeah," Quinn said, reaching for some pizza and hoping it would settle the unaccustomed churning in his stomach. "You'd better."

Gracie spotted Steve as soon as she stepped out of Samuel Hamley. He was leaning against the nearest lamppost, watching the pedestrians ebb and flow in front of the jewelry shop's large glass doors. She watched as his gaze brushed past her, faltered, and returned. Then he straightened and took a step toward her.

"Well, you clean up nicely," he said with a smile.

Gracie gave her pale-pink blouse and navy skirt a self-conscious glance. "Thanks. I think."

Steve laughed. "Can I buy you a coffee?"

She looked at him curiously. What was he doing here? He could have called her at work or on her cell phone if he had more questions. "How about hot chocolate?" she said.

"Hot chocolate it is." He pointed to a nearby coffee shop. "Let's try there."

She fell into step beside him. "What brings you to New York?" she asked.

"I had some things to check on," he said. "And people I needed to talk to."

"Including me?"

He gave her a half smile. "Including you." She eyed him inquiringly, but he shook his head. "It can wait till we're sitting down."

He opened the door of the coffee shop, and she stepped inside, wrinkling her nose at the pungent smell.

"What would you like?" he asked. "I'll go place the order, and you can choose a table."

"Just a regular hot chocolate would be great," she said. "No whipped cream."

"Sounds good." He started toward the counter.

Gracie watched him go, then turned to find somewhere to sit. There was a vacant table against the window, so she headed that direction, pulled out one of the chairs, and sat down to wait.

There were two people ahead of Steve in line, and by the time the workers behind the counter handed Steve his order, Gracie's imagination had conjured up countless reasons for his unexpected presence outside Samuel Hamley—none of them good. With her stomach in knots, she took the cup he offered her and waited only until he took his seat before asking the dreaded question. "Do you have bad news?" she asked.

"No," he said. "I'm here to ask for your help again."

Gracie released the breath she hadn't realized she'd been holding. "Of course," she said. "What do you need?"

Steve gave her an enigmatic smile. "I have a rather unusual proposition for you."

Gracie looked at him, startled. "For me?"

"Yes," he said. He paused as though choosing his words carefully. "How would you feel about traveling with Dorcas to Italy and helping us flush out the jewelry thieves?"

Gracie wrapped her fingers around her warm cup, the drink inside forgotten. "Are you kidding me?"

"Nope," he said. "But before you answer that question, you need to know exactly what you'd be getting yourself into."

Gracie listened in stunned silence as Steve explained his belief that the jewelry thieves were exchanging the real jewels for forgeries sometime between Dorcas's purchase at the Venetian Jewelry Show and her return home from her cruise. He outlined his plan to test the thieves' motives by adding a second expensive piece of jewelry supposedly purchased by Quinn. And then he explained her roles as gem expert and fiancée-of-convenience. "I know it's a lot to ask," Steve said, "but we can't pull this off without someone who knows the industry, and with Dorcas's unwillingness to go public with this investigation, I don't have many players to work with."

"I . . . I see," Gracie managed. To attend the Venetian Jewelry Show was something she'd dreamed of for years, and to have an all-expense paid Mediterranean cruise thrown into the mix was almost more than she could comprehend.

"Is it something you're willing to consider?" Steve asked.

She released her grip on the cup. "I'd be crazy not to, wouldn't I?"

Steve gave her a sheepish grin. "That's what I was hoping you'd say, but since we're going into this hoping that something will go down, you need to understand that there are risks involved. We're assuming that the thieves will make the trade when no one's around, but the bottom line is, we have no idea what they're willing to do to get the goods."

At his caution, Gracie experienced her first frisson of fear. This was not simply a vacation trip.

"How does Quinn feel about the plan?" she asked, suddenly wishing she could speak with him herself. Despite their awkward beginning, she thought he might understand her hesitancy better than the FBI agent in front of her. Especially since he was the one who would have to role-play alongside her for a full week.

"He's willing to go through with it," Steve said.

"And his girlfriend?" Gracie asked. "I can't imagine she's going to be too excited about Quinn getting himself engaged to someone else in Europe—no matter how short the engagement is."

He shrugged. "It never came up, so it can't be that big a deal."

Gracie gave him a doubtful look. Mallory "Catwoman" Stapleton didn't seem like the kind of woman who'd be okay with this scenario at all.

"He's on his way to San Antonio right now," Steve added. "He has business meetings and a conference through next week. In fact, he won't get back until the day after Dorcas leaves for Venice. So if you're willing to make this trip, you'd fly out with Dorcas and he'd join you there the next day."

Gracie pulled her phone out of her purse and pulled up the calendar. "What are the dates?"

He fished a piece of paper out of his inside jacket pocket, opened it, and slid it across the table to her. On the top was a printed itinerary for a direct flight out of JFK and into Marco Polo airport. Beneath that was the itinerary for an eight-day cruise starting in Venice and stopping at various ports in Italy, Greece, and Croatia. Scribbled at the bottom of the paper were three phone numbers prefaced by the letters D, S, and Q.

"That's Dorcas's schedule. She'd book you a seat on the same flight, a room at the hotel in Venice, and a cabin on the cruise. Pretty sure she'd be willing to place a call to Henry Hamley if you encounter any trouble getting the time off work too." He gave her a wry smile. "Money and connections can move mountains."

Gracie took a deep breath. To willfully put herself in harm's way, to act like she was engaged to a man she barely knew—it was crazy. But how many times had she been told the same thing about moving to New York City alone? And she'd done it anyway.

She gazed unseeingly out the window. When she'd shared her decision to take the job at Samuel Hamley with the people she loved, her brother had thought she was nuts. Her sister had been worried for her safety. Her father had been sad over the distance it would place between them. Her boyfriend, Derek, had been furious. So furious, in fact, that even though she'd offered to call him every day and fly home regularly, he'd walked away from their eighteen-month-long relationship and gone right into a new relationship with one of her former roommates.

Only her mother had understood her need to go. She was the one who'd watched Gracie draw, color, and design crowns and tiaras, necklaces, and rings from the time she'd been old enough to hold a pencil. She'd taken Gracie by the hands and told her to follow her dreams and make every day count.

It had taken every ounce of courage Gracie possessed to move to the Big City, but although she'd experienced moments of homesickness since then, she knew she'd made the right decision. Working at Samuel Hamley had given her unique opportunities to grow and develop as a jewelry designer, and along the way, she'd proved her mettle.

What Steve was suggesting was not so different. It would take her completely out of her comfort zone, but it was also the trip of a lifetime. This was her chance to attend the Venetian Jewelry Show and see the Mediterranean. Things she would likely never be able to do again. How could she turn it down without regretting it forever?

"If you want some time to think about it, you can call me this evening," Steve said, pointing to the phone number next to the letter S.

Gracie shook her head. "I don't need extra time." She picked up the paper. "I'll do it."

Steve's relief was palpable. "Thank you, Gracie. Dorcas will be thrilled."

Gracie waited for the feeling of dread to settle in the pit of her stomach. But it didn't come. Instead, like the fluttering of a swarm of butterflies, excitement took flight. She offered him an uncertain smile. "I'll do my best not to let her down."

He smiled. "I know you will." He slid his chair back and stood, obviously ready to go. "I'll let her know so she can make the bookings for you."

"Okay." She got to her feet.

"And you have her phone number if you need to check on anything," he said, pointing to the paper still clutched in her hand.

"Will you tell Quinn too?" she asked, nervousness sending the butterflies into a synchronized whirl.

"Yeah. He won't get the message until he lands in Texas, but I'll make sure he knows."

Gracie nodded. She could do this. Surely her role as one of the extras in her high school production of *Hello, Dolly!* had to count for something. She could act happily engaged for ten days if it meant that Dorcas recovered her jewelry and if her own lifelong dream of visiting Venice was fulfilled.

CHAPTER 9

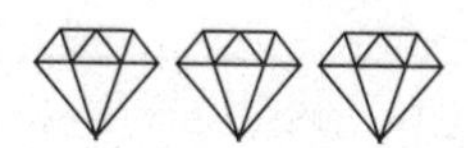

GRACIE STEPPED BACK AND SURVEYED her small kitchen. Everything was covered in a fine layer of powdered sugar. There were globs of frosting all over the counter, smears of food coloring on her fingers, and almost every bowl, knife, and spoon she owned was dirty. It was a total disaster, but as she studied the pan of sugar cookies sitting in the middle of the chaos, she couldn't help but smile. Walter would love them.

It was the doorman's birthday tomorrow. Gracie wasn't sure how many people at Samuel Hamley were aware of it, but he'd let it slip earlier this week after she'd asked him if he was going to the Yankees's next home game against the Houston Astros. She'd known he was a die-hard baseball fan, but when he'd told her he was going to the game to celebrate his birthday, she'd decided it was the perfect opportunity to practice her baking skills and do something for the man who'd been so kind to her.

Taking a large paper plate from a nearby cupboard, Gracie transferred the cookies onto it, alternating the ones she'd decorated to look like baseballs with the ones showing Yankees's logo. She'd opted not to do any with the Astros's emblem, but as she wrapped the plate of cookies in cellophane, her thoughts inevitably turned to the only person she knew in Texas at the moment. Depending on what time his flight had landed, it was now about twenty-four hours since Quinn had learned that Steve had spoken to her and that she'd accepted the assignment. She hadn't expected him to call her right away, but she wished she knew what he was thinking. Was he as uncomfortable with their upcoming charade as she was, or was it no big deal to him?

Her meeting with Steve felt like a distant memory, even though it had been only yesterday. She'd spent last night learning all she could about the ports of call listed on the cruise itinerary while trying not to think about the ramifications of faking an engagement. First thing this morning she'd approached her manager, Pete, about taking ten days off work. Initially, he'd frowned and muttered about fall deadlines, but his attitude had softened when she'd promised to finish her designs for the Gaelic collection before she left, and then when he learned that it would be her first vacation time since she'd been hired, he'd given his reluctant approval.

Relief that she wouldn't need Dorcas to make a phone call to Henry Hamley had quickly turned to mild panic when she realized how much she needed to finish within a week. So she'd remained at the office long after everyone else had gone home today, staying until the brooch design was complete. She would probably need to do the same for the necklace, bracelet, and ring that were to make up the set.

Gracie put the plate of cookies next to her purse so she wouldn't forget them in the morning, then started gathering the dirty dishes. She had just finished rinsing and loading them into the dishwasher when her phone rang.

Leaning across the counter, she glanced at the caller ID, and her heart lurched. She'd added Dorcas, Steve, and Quinn to her list of contacts last night. Dorcas had called this morning to express her delight that Gracie was traveling with her and to let her know all the bookings had been made, but this was the first time Quinn's name had appeared on her screen.

Drying off her hands, she reached for the phone. "Hello."

"Gracie?" There was a fraction of a pause. "This is Quinn."

"Hi, Quinn." She crossed the room and slowly lowered herself into the armchair. "How are things in Texas?"

"Hot, muggy, and too busy," he said.

"Ah, just like New York."

He gave a soft chuckle. "I guess it does kind of sound that way, doesn't it?" He paused. "I heard from Steve."

Gracie's palms were sweating. She wiped them on her pants. "He met me after work yesterday and told me what he'd like us to do."

"And you're okay with it?" Gracie hesitated, and immediately Quinn spoke again. "I'm sorry. It's not that I'm questioning your decision. I just know how persuasive Steve can be, and I want to be sure you're comfortable with the situation."

"I'm okay," she said. "Thanks for asking."

"Well then." He cleared his throat awkwardly. "I was thinking that it might be easier for us to pull off Steve's crazy scheme if we knew a little more about each other."

"I agree."

"It would be a lot easier if I were there, but . . ."

"We can make this work," she interrupted him, hearing the frustration in his voice. "How about we take turns asking each other a question? And if we run out of time before we run out of questions, we can do it again on another night?"

"That sounds great."

"Why don't you go first," she said.

"Uh, all right." He paused. "Will you tell me about your family and where you grew up?"

"I grew up on a farm in Washington State, not far from Tacoma. Apples are our biggest crop, but we plant some wheat and potatoes too. My dad is still farming, but sometime down the road, he'll likely hand things over to my brother, Jeff. Jeff and his wife, Molly, built a house right down the street from my parents'. He's been farming with my dad ever since he was big enough to sit on a tractor.

"Along with my brother, Jeff, I have an older sister. Lucy's married too. Her husband's a dentist, and they live in Tacoma."

"So everyone's close to home except you," Quinn said.

"Yeah." She paused, wondering how much she should share during their first real conversation. "At first, that was really hard, especially when the whole family gathered for birthdays or holidays without me. I attended the Washington School of Jewelry Design in Seattle, so even when I was away at school, I could drive home for special occasions. When I moved to New York, it felt like I was living another world away."

"Does it still feel like that?"

"It's a lot better than it was at first," she said. "Although there are still some days when I'd trade hot, muggy, and too busy for cool, rainy, and quiet."

"I bet," he said. "That sounds pretty good to me right now too."

Quinn sounded as though he honestly felt that way, and Gracie found herself relaxing.

"Is it my turn to ask a question?" she said.

"Pretty sure I went over my quota already, so you'd better ask two."

"Okay. Do you have any brothers or sisters?"

"No. It's just me. My parents divorced when I was young, and neither of them remarried."

Gracie sensed the regret behind his response and immediately reevaluated the direction she'd been going. There were so many things she wanted to know about Quinn. His unique bond with Dorcas was intriguing, and his relationship with Mallory was discouraging, but instinct told her to shy away from asking anything too personal yet.

"What's your favorite late-night snack?" she asked.

"Caramel popcorn," he said. "What's yours?"

"Is that your next question?"

"Yes. Wait. No."

Gracie laughed. "Muddy Buddies," she said. "And since you're still figuring out how this works, you can ask me another one."

"Okay." He thought for a moment. "If you had a free afternoon, how would you spend it?"

"Hmm. I'd probably go to the park and sit on a bench and sketch. How about you? What would you do with a free afternoon?"

"Bike," he said without hesitation. "Or run or swim."

"Now I feel lazy."

He chuckled. "I've been competing in triathlons since high school. But if it's any consolation, I can barely draw a stick figure."

"Are you just saying that to make me feel better?"

"Nope. It's the truth. And I'm pretty sure that question means I get another turn."

She laughed. "Go ahead."

"All right," he said. "What are your top three movies?"

"Uh, *Pride and Prejudice* (as long as it's the one with Colin Firth), *While You Were Sleeping*, and *Tangled*."

"You're a romantic."

"Maybe," Gracie said. "But have you ever considered what great 'how to' movies they are? They've got the answers every woman needs on how to avoid interacting with socially awkward men, how to drop and roll to escape an oncoming train, and how to wield a frying pan as a weapon. Those movies are full of all sorts of life skills."

Quinn laughed. "I'll never watch them the same way again."

Gracie's laughter joined his. "Right?"

There was a slight pause, and when Quinn spoke again, the humor was gone from his voice. "Thanks, Gracie. This phone call has turned out to be the bright spot in my day. But it's getting late in New York, so I should let you go. Can I call you again tomorrow?"

"Yes," she said, smiling into the phone. "I'd like that."

💎💎💎

One week later, Quinn let himself into his hotel room, loosened his tie, and dropped onto the bed. He closed his eyes. Finally, it was over. He'd made it through all the meetings, the presentations, the wining and dining, and his keynote address. His professional expertise and social skills had been stretched to the breaking point, but from his perspective, at least, he could return to New York confident that Anderson and Gough had been well represented.

He opened one eye and glanced at the clock. For the last seven days, he'd returned to his hotel room at about this time and had immediately called Gracie. Over the course of the week, their conversations had developed from the short question-and-answer session of the first day to a two-hour-long discussion yesterday that had covered everything from the virtues of Thai food over Indian food to updates on Gracie's day at work and his final meeting with Paul Strickland of Barclays International. He'd looked forward to talking to her each evening, but tonight he was on his own. Unless their flight had been delayed, Gracie and Dorcas were already en route to Venice.

He reached into his pocket and pulled out his phone. It had been on silent since the closing banquet began, and it looked like he'd missed two phone calls and five texts. After checking to be sure the phone calls weren't anything he needed to respond to immediately, he scrolled through his texts. Two were work related and could wait until tomorrow. The third was from Mallory. *Peter Lindstrom's party is tonight. 8pm at The Lofts. You should come.*

He sent a cursory reply. *Sorry. I'm at a conference in Texas.* Then he moved on to the last two messages. They were both from Gracie. The first one had been sent three hours previously. *Good luck with the speech. I bet everyone will love it. What's not to love about innovative insurance investments?* ☺

With a chuckle, he moved on to the last message, noting that it had come in soon afterward. *Boarding our flight. Dorcas says sleep is possible in first class, but I may prove her wrong. Hope your travels go well. Will watch for a text from you after your flight arrives in Venice.*

Quinn took a deep breath. This was it. Everything was about to change.

Using his phone to access his email, he pulled up two flight itineraries. The first one showed him leaving San Antonio at 6:13 a.m. tomorrow and arriving at JFK four hours later. He glanced at the second itinerary. His flight out of JFK and into Marco Polo Airport left at 5:10 p.m. With the travel time to and from the airport and the early check-in required for international flights, he'd be lucky if he had two hours at his apartment to do laundry and repack his suitcase. He hoped there'd be no delays in getting out of San Antonio and that once he was finally seated on the trans-atlantic flight, he would have time to think about what lay ahead.

During each of their phone calls, he and Gracie had somehow managed to avoid talking about their upcoming roles in Europe. It had seemed easier at the time; now it seemed foolish. He knew her favorite color, flower, foods, and music, but despite all his questioning, he didn't know what kind of engagement ring she preferred. Quinn ran his hand across the back of his neck. She obviously knew so much more about such things than he did. But maybe it didn't matter anyway. Once the cruise was over, they'd go their separate ways and the ring would be returned.

Coming to his feet, Quinn crossed the small room and opened the closet doors. Pulling his shirts off the hangers, he turned to face his waiting suitcase. He had no idea what next week would bring, but if the current pit in his stomach was any indication, he was in for a bumpy ride.

CHAPTER 10

Gracie was quite sure she would never tire of this view. She sat beside Dorcas at a small table outside one of the cafés on St. Mark's Square, watching the people milling around the historic plaza. Locals cut through the square with barely a glance at their surroundings. Tourists circled, their eyes raised to the incredible architecture all around. And children ran, chasing pigeons and squealing with delight when the large birds took to the air.

Immediately across the square from where they sat stood the magnificent St. Mark's Basilica. The enormous arched entrances drew her eyes upward to the brightly colored murals and the gold-winged lion on the walls above. A small crew of workers negotiated the scaffolding standing against one portion of the elaborately decorated building, a subtle reminder to the many visitors that these ancient buildings deserved their consideration and care.

Across the paved courtyard from the basilica stood the Campanile di San Marco. The tall bell tower rose over the other buildings in the square, providing those who rode the elevator to the top with a panoramic view of Venice. Dorcas had taken her there the evening before. They'd arrived at their hotel in the early afternoon, and after checking in, Dorcas had insisted on guiding Gracie through the narrow walkways to St. Mark's Square and up the bell tower so she could see the floating city from above.

The view had been spectacular—orange-tiled roofs for as far as the eye could see, waterways cutting through the buildings, and off in the distance, the Mediterranean Sea dotted with boats and ships of all sizes and shapes.

"That's where we board the cruise," Dorcas had said, pointing to a dock where three enormous ships were berthed. "Our ship won't come into port until tomorrow."

Gracie had almost asked Dorcas to pinch her. From their first-class transatlantic flight to their arrival at the five-star hotel on the Grand Canal by private water taxi, this trip had had such a dream-like quality, Gracie was starting to wonder if she truly might wake up and find it all a fantasy. And yet, after sleeping the night in the luxurious four-poster bed in a room that belonged to a palace, she'd woken up to another beautiful, sunshiny day in Venice.

This morning, she and Dorcas had walked the quaint alleys together, meandering through the many market stalls surrounding the Rialto Bridge and winding their way across numerous other bridges until they found themselves back at St. Mark's Square, where they could sit and watch the world go by.

A waiter wearing a white suit coat and bow tie over black pants and a vest approached their table. "May I get you more iced tea, signora? More lemonade for you, signorina? Something else to eat, perhaps?"

"No, thank you, Piero." Dorcas shook her head. "Everything was perfect. I shall certainly order one of your honey fagottinos again."

The dark-haired young man beamed happily, and Gracie guessed that not many of the customers at this expensive café took the time to learn his name or to compliment him on the food.

"Then I shall bring the ticket," he said in flawless English.

"*Grazie*," Dorcas said, which earned her another broad smile.

The waiter turned to go, and Gracie's phone vibrated in her pocket. Pulling it out, she glanced at the screen and read the text message there. Drawing an unsteady breath, she looked up and met Dorcas's eyes. "It's Quinn," Gracie said. "He's landed and is waiting for a water taxi to take him to the hotel."

Dorcas must have recognized her sudden nervousness because she reached over and placed her hand over one of Gracie's. "I appreciate what you're doing for me, my dear," she said. "You and Quinn."

Gracie shook her head. "If pretending to be engaged to Quinn for a week gets you your jewelry back, every minute of the charade will be worth it. Besides, being here . . . visiting all these incredible places . . . I think it's safe to say that you're doing far more for me than I'm doing for you."

"Having you with me is a treat," Dorcas said.

For a split second, Gracie caught a glimpse of the older lady's deep loneliness, but the moment was gone almost as quickly as it had appeared, covered up by one of Dorcas's ready smiles.

"Why don't you tell Quinn we'll meet him in the hotel lobby in an hour. That should give him enough time to check in and drop off his bags, and it will give us time to request another water taxi." Dorcas patted Gracie's hand, her eyes sparkling with anticipation. "Now that Quinn's arrived, we've got a jewelry show to go to."

💎💎💎

The water taxi pulled up to a tiny landing spot next to a wrought-iron gate. Quinn glanced through the decorative bars at the short path that led across a small lawn and paved patio to the doors of a tall, salmon-colored building.

"The Palazzo Venart?" he asked, wanting to be totally sure he was at the right place before disembarking.

"Si, si, signore." The gray-haired taxi driver nodded his head vigorously. "This the Palazzo Venart."

"*Grazie*," Quinn said, handing the man several euro notes before stepping onto the tiny dock and reaching back for his suitcase.

The old man waited only until Quinn had his luggage in hand before powering up the throttle on the small motorboat. "*Arrivederci*," he called as he pulled away.

Quinn raised his hand, watching the driver skillfully maneuver between two oncoming boats, before he turned to enter the grounds of the luxury hotel behind him. The path led directly to double glass doors topped by a large arched window. Quinn let himself in and entered the long lobby. The marble tile floor was polished to a shine. A dark wood table with a large flower display filled the center of the narrow room. Mirrors and oil paintings in ornate gilded frames hung on one wall, and opposite them, a white-railed staircase led to the rooms above.

He stepped over to the small desk, and a middle-aged man in a dark suit greeted him.

"*Benvenuto*, signore," the man said.

"Thank you," Quinn replied, immediately establishing himself as American and hoping the man could speak decent English. "My name's Quinn West. I have a reservation; it may be listed under Dorcas Katsaros."

"Of course, sir," the man said with a warm smile. "We have been expecting you." He turned to enter something into his computer. "You are just now arriving? From America?"

"Yes," Quinn said.

"You will be tired." He handed Quinn a key. "Your room is ready should you wish sleeping now. Then you shall be ready to see our beautiful city at night."

Quinn wished he had time for a nap. A day and a half of travel had left him feeling tired and grimy. But since he'd managed to doze for a few hours on the flight and he hadn't washed or shaved in longer than he cared to remember, he would prioritize a shower over sleep. He glanced at the antique clock on the wall. If he was fast, he could get cleaned up before meeting Dorcas and Gracie.

The concierge rang a bell, and seconds later, a young man appeared at his elbow. "Giovanni will carry your bags and show you to your room. Please say if there is anything more that you require."

"Thank you," Quinn said, already making for the stairs.

The hotel's aura of opulence was not limited to the lobby. Giovanni opened the door leading to Quinn's room to reveal a large white duvet-covered four-poster bed surrounded by furnishings that looked as though they had once belonged to European royalty. Quinn crossed the parquet wood floor, dropped his suitcase beside the bed, and walked into the adjoining bathroom. Twin marble sinks and a claw-foot bathtub continued the costly antique theme, but to his relief, in the opposite corner, there was a modern-looking glass-enclosed shower.

After accepting Quinn's thanks and a generous tip, Giovanni slipped out of the room, and Quinn opened his suitcase. He pulled out what he needed and headed for the bathroom. Exactly eighteen minutes later, he emerged newly shaven, dressed in clean khaki pants and a navy polo shirt, with his wet hair combed.

Transferring his wallet and phone from the jeans he'd been wearing when he'd arrived, he moved to stand by the window, pausing to admire the view. His window looked out over the busy Grand Canal, where traditional cream, apricot, yellow, and pale-turquoise buildings lined the water's edge. The buildings were adorned with shutters and window boxes full of flowers. Boats ranging from large waterbuses to small gondolas plied the waterways, each one vying for space on the busy canal.

Immediately below him, two men sat at a table on the patio in deep conversation. Across the lawn from them, a young woman stood next to the wrought-iron gate that opened to the hotel's small dock. Her long brown hair glinted in the sunlight, her pale-blue dress echoing the pastel colors of the buildings across from where she stood. He watched as she raised her hand to signal an oncoming water taxi, then he turned away from the window and walked out of the room.

Quinn spotted his aunt as soon as he descended the stairs. If her pure white hair hadn't been distinctive enough, her bright purple floral dress would have caught his attention.

She turned from admiring one of the paintings on the wall and saw him as he reached the bottom step. "Quinn," she said, smiling warmly. "I'm so glad you're here." She moved closer and kissed him on both cheeks before pulling back to study his face. "How was the journey?"

"Long," Quinn said. "But the first-class seat helped me get some sleep, so thanks for that."

"Good," Dorcas said, tucking her arm under his and steering him toward the main doors. "Because we need to get to the jewelry show, and you'll have to have your wits about you if you're going to pick out an engagement ring."

Quinn reached to open the door with his free hand, hoping Dorcas wouldn't feel the sudden increase in tension in the arm she held. "While we're on that subject," he said. "Where's Gracie?"

"We ordered a water taxi, so she offered to wait outside for it," Dorcas said. She pointed as the young woman Quinn had seen from the window turned and waved. "There she is, see?"

Quinn's footsteps faltered. He couldn't help it. Why was it that every time he saw this woman he was taken aback? First it had been because she'd been standing in Henry Hamley's office dripping wet and filthy, then because she'd unexpectedly appeared in his aunt's condo dressed in workout clothes, and now because she was walking toward him beside the Grand Canal in Venice, dry, clean, and beautiful.

"Hi, Quinn."

Gracie moved forward, and Dorcas released his arm.

What was he supposed to do? Shake her hand? Give her a token hug? He hadn't felt this awkward around a girl since middle school.

"Good to see you again, Gracie."

She gave him a hesitant smile, and he realized she was probably feeling as unsure as he was, but before he could come up with anything articulate to say, she turned to Dorcas. "The water taxi's here."

"Excellent," Dorcas said. "Let's go. The show opened at nine o'clock this morning, so we're getting a late start, but there'll still be plenty to see."

💎💎💎

Gracie sat under the motorboat's canopy, her fingers gripping the edge of her seat as their destination drew closer and her nervousness increased. Quinn was beside her, not touching her but close enough that she was aware of him there. On the opposite side of the boat, Dorcas sat looking forward, an expression of excited anticipation on her face. Gracie closed her eyes and took a few deep breaths of the sea air. To visit the Venetian Jewelry Show had been a goal ever since she'd started designing jewelry; she couldn't let her anxiety over what lay ahead ruin the experience.

"Look," Dorcas said.

Gracie opened her eyes in time to watch the taxi driver guide the boat into a narrow inlet bordered on either side by tall stone arches. He drew the motorboat up to a small dock in front of the widest arch and deftly tossed a rope around a mooring post.

"The Laguna Hotel Convention Center, signora," he said, cinching the rope tight.

"*Grazie*," Dorcas said, getting to her feet immediately.

The boat swayed, and she teetered.

"Steady," Quinn said, standing up and reaching for her elbow.

He walked her to the side of the boat and helped her onto the dock while the driver assisted Gracie. When they were all onshore, Dorcas handed the taxi driver the fare and then led Quinn and Gracie through the archway and into a tiny courtyard with a stone water fountain at its center and earthenware pots brimming with flowers in every corner. Gracie looked around in delight, captivated by the charm of the hidden piazza.

"This way," Dorcas called, already across the courtyard.

Reluctantly, Gracie hurried after her, catching up with Quinn as he reached the glass doors that opened into a vast lobby. A few yards from the door, a long table covered in a navy-blue cloth with a matching skirt stood beside a large white sign that read *Spettacolo di Gioielli Veneziani 2018*. Underneath, in smaller print, were the words Venetian Jewelry Show 2018.

A woman and two men were sitting at the table behind a couple of computer monitors, and when Dorcas, Quinn, and Gracie entered, one of the men rose.

"Mrs. Katsaros," he said in heavily accented English. "I am glad you are come."

"*Grazie*, Signor Ricci." Dorcas leaned over the table and accepted the Italian's kisses on her cheeks. "I have brought guests with me this time."

"So I see," he said. "They are registered?"

"Yes."

The man turned to the woman and spoke in Italian. Instantly, her fingers flew across the keypad.

"You will forgive me," the man said, "but I am required to ask for identification for all three."

"Of course," Dorcas said, reaching into her handbag.

Quinn drew his wallet out of his pocket as Gracie dug her own out of her purse. Dorcas handed the Italian her driver's license. He read the information on it to the woman, who nodded and typed some more.

"Your bank information is current, Mrs. Katsaros?"

"Yes," Dorcas said.

"Very good." He handed the license back to her and accepted Quinn's.

"Quinn West," the Italian read off Quinn's license.

"That's right," Quinn said.

The Italian stood at the woman's shoulder, watching the computer screen. "I see your banking information is already with us."

"I submitted it last week," Quinn said.

Gracie glanced at him with surprise. Was he using his own bank account to buy the ring? It made sense if Steve wanted this purchase to be completely separate from one Dorcas would make, but what if something went wrong? What if the ring was stolen too? Or even worse, what if she lost it while it was in her keeping?

"Signorina?"

Startled back to the present, Gracie presented the man with her driver's license. Her fingers trembled, making the card shake slightly, but he took it from her and read off the information to the woman at his side.

"Do you wish to register any banking information, Signorina Miller?" the Italian asked.

"No, thank you," Gracie said.

"You are simply here to look and admire, eh?" He smiled and handed back her card while the other man pulled preprinted name tags out of a box on the table and gave one to each of them. "I hope you will enjoy the show."

Dorcas slipped her name tag over her head and moved to the left, toward a door flanked on either side by armed security guards. She opened her purse. One of the guards poked through it with a short stick, then nodded her through. Gracie put on her name tag and glanced up at Quinn to find that he was watching her. He offered her a small smile before surprising her by reaching for her hand.

"Act I, Scene I, Gracie," he whispered. "We've got this."

Gracie gave his hand a slight squeeze. She may not be used to standing beside him, but over the last week, she'd come to consider this man her friend. Right now, she wasn't sure which of Quinn's gestures gave her more courage, the feel of his strong fingers around hers or his use of the word *we* instead of *you*. Either way, for the first time since Steve had outlined her role, she felt like she was embarking on this venture as part of a team.

CHAPTER 11

QUINN LED GRACIE PAST THE security guards and into the convention center's main hall. Booths had been set up all around the walls and down the center of the vast room. Most of them were divided from each other by curtains and had their own spotlighting systems. Glass display cases covered the tables and oversized screens projecting images of various facets of the jewelry industry were scattered around the room.

Large signs promoting some of the lesser-known exhibitors clamored for attention over the subtle signage of the world-renowned jewelers who had come to Venice from all over Europe. People were gathered in twos and threes around some tables and in large groups around others, and the sound of voices speaking multiple languages filled the hall.

"Oh, wow!" Gracie had come to a complete stop and was gazing in wonder at the sight.

Quinn chuckled. "You look like a kid on Christmas morning," he said.

"I feel like one. Everywhere I look, I see another name I recognize from industry magazines. Jewelers whose work is considered the standard for everyone else to imitate."

Dorcas, who'd been waiting inside the door for them, moved to stand beside them. "Where would you like to begin?"

"Is there someone you usually buy from?" Quinn asked.

"I have a few favorites," she said. "But the three pieces you're concerned about were purchased from three different jewelers. The only thing they have in common is that all the transactions occurred here."

Quinn nodded. "Then why don't we start with those three, and if Gracie has others she'd like to see, we'll do those afterward."

"Come along, then," Dorcas said, taking the lead again. "Let's start with Hugo Martin."

He felt Gracie's grip on his hand tighten.

"You okay?" he asked softly.

She nodded, and Quinn felt himself relax. The excitement humming through Gracie's fingers now was far removed from the anxiety-born tremors she'd been battling in the lobby. She was in her element, and he was ready to step back and let her shine.

They started down the nearest aisle, and it quickly became apparent that while Dorcas was drawn to the displays of radiant gemstones, Gracie's primary interest lay in the settings.

"Tell me what you look for in a design," Quinn said curiously. She was studying the contents of a case of white-, pink-, and black-pearl jewelry.

She looked at him. "Textbook answer or personal opinion?"

"Personal opinion," he said.

"It should be something that stands on its own as a work of art and enhances rather than distracts from the beauty of the stones it displays."

Quinn raised his eyebrows. "Pretty sure no textbook could put it better. And to a guy who has no artistic ability, that sounds virtually impossible."

"Challenging, for sure," she said with a smile. "But not impossible."

His gaze flitted across the booths in the vast hall. "And this is the place Dorcas can find something like that."

"Absolutely." Her blue eyes twinkled. "Especially if she has a little help."

An hour later, with a few well-placed and knowledgeable questions, Gracie had successfully discouraged some hard-selling salesmen and, with gentle diplomacy, had steered Dorcas away from a couple of expensive purchases that would have had questionable long-term value. Quinn watched her now as she and his aunt discussed the merits of a brooch that had caught Dorcas's eye.

"It's lovely, Dorcas," Gracie said. "And on those days when you may have to dress more formally than usual or wear a solid color, it will give everyone you meet a hint of the floral patterns you love."

Quinn stifled a smile. It hadn't taken long for Gracie to notice that his aunt's taste in clothing leaned toward bright, cheery, and flowery.

"That's an excellent point," Dorcas said.

"*Oui. Oui.*" The French jeweler was eager to agree. "And all zee colors, madame. Zis brooch vill alvays brighten your spirits."

"What do you think, Quinn?" Dorcas turned to include him in the decision.

He studied the brooch in his aunt's hand. Polished to a beautiful shine, the platinum had been skillfully worked to create a posy of delicate flowers. A narrow platinum bow around the flowers' stems was studded with diamonds, and a variety of gemstones decorated the centers of every flower. The result was a sparkling array of color.

He raised his eyes to meet Gracie's. She gave a barely discernable nod. He'd watched her ask the jeweler if she could look at the brooch through his loupe. It must have passed the test, and even he could see it was designed better than the garish bangles his aunt had been considering earlier at another booth. "It looks like it was made for you," he said.

Dorcas smiled happily. "That's just the kind of thing Alessandro would have said." She handed the brooch back to the jeweler. "I'll take it," she said. "If you'll package it for me, I'll call my bank to initiate the wire transfer."

"Splendid, madame." The Frenchman beamed and opened a drawer in a chest behind him to find a suitable box.

Dorcas took her phone out of her purse, and while she dialed her bank in New York, Quinn turned to thank Gracie for her help. But she wasn't watching Dorcas or the jeweler. Her attention was on something or someone beyond Quinn's vision. He watched a frown wrinkle her brow, and she leaned sideways, her eyes never losing their focus as she stepped toward the edge of the booth.

Quinn moved closer. "What's up?" he asked softly.

"There's a guy." She shook her head, her frown still in place. "It may be nothing, but I've noticed him hanging around at several of the booths we've visited. He hasn't gotten too close before now, but this time he brushed right past Dorcas when she was showing you the brooch."

"Can you describe him?" Quinn said, purposely not turning to look.

"Short, kind of chunky. Looks to be in his late twenties. Curly brown hair that touches his collar in the back. He's wearing jeans and a black button-down shirt."

"Where is he now?"

Gracie chewed her lip, turning her head to check the other side of the booth. "I don't know. A group of people walked between us, and he's disappeared."

Quinn swung around and scoured the area behind him, but he didn't see anyone who matched the man Gracie had described.

"Thanks for being observant," he said, kicking himself for not being the same. "Let me know if you see him again, okay?"

"Yeah," she said. "I'm probably overreacting." She scanned the vicinity one more time. "He doesn't seem to be sticking around anyway."

Having neglected to watch the people around him, Quinn kept a close eye on the French jeweler as he placed the brooch in a padded silver box and handed it to Dorcas. There'd been no time or opportunity to trade the brooch out for another.

“Now,” Dorcas said, “we’ve spent far too much time on my whims. I think it’s time you two did some ring shopping.”

Trying to ignore the implication behind his aunt’s words, Quinn focused on the woman at his side.

“Where would you like to start, Gracie?” he asked.

She gave him a startled look. “I . . . uh . . .”

“Have you seen anything you like as we’ve been wandering around?”

“Something that *I* like?”

“Yes.” He gave an amused shrug. “I haven’t had a lot of experience with this, but I’m pretty sure that’s how it’s done. You’re the one who’ll be wearing it, so it should be something you like.”

Color tinted her cheeks. “I haven’t thought . . . I mean . . . I didn’t think . . .”

“Sorry,” Quinn said, enjoying this far more than he should. “That’s not going to fly. There’s no way a jewelry designer hasn’t dreamed up her perfect ring.”

Gracie expelled a deep breath. “Fine,” she said, her eyes meeting his with a flash of defiance. “A platinum ring with a radiant-cut diamond in the center and a few smaller stones on either side.”

“Great,” he said. “And how about a designer. Who’s your favorite?”

“Louis Barnard,” she said without hesitation.

“Does he have a booth here?”

She nodded. “We haven’t been there yet, but I saw it on the left side of the entrance.”

“Then let’s start there.” He extended his hand, pleased when she willingly slipped her hand into his. “Are you ready, Dorcas?”

“You know, I think I might sit down for a bit.” She pointed to a couple of vacant chairs up against the nearest wall. “Would you mind if I waited for you there? I’ll be in plain sight if you need me.”

“I think that’s a great idea,” Quinn said. “We’ll meet up with you after we’ve checked out the Louise Barnard rings.”

“Perfect,” Dorcas said.

💎💎💎

An older couple stepped away from the booth as Quinn and Gracie approached. The woman was carrying a gold gift bag with the distinctive Louis Barnard logo in its center, and Gracie leaned closer to Quinn. "I can't believe I'm really here," she whispered.

"Tell me about it," Quinn said. "I barely know what city I'm in."

Up until now, she hadn't given any thought to how recently Quinn's flight had landed in Venice. The brain fog that always accompanied lack of sleep had to be affecting him. She gave his hand an encouraging squeeze. "We've got this, remember?"

He smiled. "Yeah. I have no idea what a radiant-cut diamond is, but as long as you do, I figure we're good."

Gracie laughed, and the Louis Barnard representative gave her a welcoming smile before greeting Quinn politely. "How may I help you, monsieur? Mademoiselle? You are searching for something in particular?"

"Actually, yes," Quinn said. "We'd like to look at your engagement rings."

Instantly, the man's expression lit up. "Congratulations to you both. I confess, when I saw you coming across the way, I hoped it was so." He beckoned them to the other side of the table. "Come see what I have for you."

Unnervingly aware of Quinn's hand on her back as she stepped forward, Gracie tried to focus on the contents of the display case in front of her. Diamonds, emeralds, rubies, sapphires, and opals. Stones of every size and shape and rings of every description glinted under the bright lights. "Do you have a preference, mademoiselle?"

She glanced at Quinn, who gave her an encouraging nod. "I had thought perhaps a radiant-cut diamond," she said.

"Ah! A woman of discerning taste," the man said, looking pleased. "Something like this, perhaps?" He handed her a narrow band with a radiant-cut solitaire set in a basic four-pronged head. Its very simplicity was eye catching, but she hesitated, and he noticed.

"It needs something a little extra, yes?"

He took back the ring and offered her another. This diamond was surrounded by a halo of smaller stones, with even more small diamonds running down the upper shank.

"It's beautiful," she said. The ring would be returned within two weeks; it shouldn't matter if it wasn't exactly to her taste.

"Do you have anything with a slightly wider band," Quinn said. "And instead of all the small diamonds, just a few stones—like sapphires maybe—to set off the solitaire."

Stunned, Gracie swung around to face him. "How did you . . . ?"

The man behind the counter looked thoughtful. "I have one," he said slowly. "The solitaire is a cushion-cut not radiant, but otherwise, it is as you describe." He withdrew a small tray from under the table. "It is a particular favorite of Monsieur Barnard."

Plucking a ring out of the tray, he held it out to Gracie. She stared at it, a lump forming in her throat. All the rough ring sketches she'd made during her teenage years and all the details she'd incorporated into those sketches after her training at school had been added to by a master craftsman to create the stunning ring before her now.

The solitaire looked to be about three carats and was flanked on either side by two sapphires and three diamonds alternately set in a tapered milgrain bright-cut setting. She reached for the ring, but the man gave her a knowing smile and shook his head.

"No, Mademoiselle. I believe this one is for another to give." Then he passed the ring to Quinn.

"Can I have your left hand, Gracie?" Quinn said.

Silently, she extended her hand to him, watching as he slipped the ring onto her fourth finger. It fit perfectly.

He held on to the tips of her fingers, bending them slightly so the ring caught the light. Then he raised his eyes to meet hers. "This is the one, isn't it?"

Blinking back the tears, she smiled and nodded. "Yes."

💎💎💎

Quinn went through the motions of calling his bank in New York and reciting the correct passwords to initiate the wire transfer, but all the while, his thoughts were spinning. What had just happened? He was supposed to buy a ring—any ring—to use as bait for thieves. But somehow, he'd become emotionally involved in the purchase. He'd wanted something that pleased Gracie. So much so that when he'd sensed her readiness to settle for something she didn't love, he'd volunteered suggestions.

With his phone still up to his ear, he bowed his head, waiting for the bank operator to give him the go-ahead. A wider band and sapphires? Where had that come from? He knew Gracie's favorite color was blue; she'd told him that during one of their phone calls. And the fact that sapphires would match the color of her eyes was a no-brainer. How he'd instinctively guessed that she'd considered them for an engagement ring, however, was beyond him. But she had. There was no doubt in his mind. Her reaction to his request, followed by her response to the ring, made that completely clear.

He glanced at her now. She was standing beside him, patiently waiting for him to finish his call. In one hand, she held a distinctive Louis Barnard gift bag containing an empty ring box; on her other hand, she wore the ring. His ring. He turned away, running his fingers through his hair. Placing that ring on her finger had felt far too much like the real deal. Jet lag was making him loopy. The sooner he caught up on sleep, the better.

"Your wire transfer has been sent, Mr. West." The American voice on the other end of the phone was composed and detached. Qualities he obviously needed to work on.

"Thank you. I appreciate your help," he said.

"No problem. Can I do anything more for you today?"

"No, thank you. I think that's everything."

"Excellent," she said. "Have a good day." And then she was gone.

Quinn lowered the phone.

"Everything okay?" Gracie asked. She'd visibly paled when the salesman had quoted him the ring's price, and even now, her coloring was not what it should be.

"Yes." He gave her what he hoped was an encouraging smile, grateful that the hefty bonus he'd received when he'd made partner at Anderson and Gough had enabled him to make the purchase without any ties to Dorcas's bank account. "Everything's great."

CHAPTER 12

It was barely daybreak. Gracie lay in bed, staring up at the decorative ceiling of her hotel room. There was just enough filtered light coming in through the sheer curtains at the windows to make out the swirls in the plaster and to pick out the glint of gold on the baroque-style furnishings. The night before, she'd left her windows ajar, and besides the sound of an occasional motorboat coming from the nearby canal, she heard the rhythmic lapping of the water against the side of the dock.

By the time she, Quinn, and Dorcas had returned from the jewelry show in the early evening, they'd all been exhausted. Quinn's fatigue had shown on his face, and as soon as they'd arrived back at the hotel, he'd excused himself. Not even the possibility of eating a gourmet Italian meal was a big enough incentive to postpone his getting some sleep.

Dorcas's short rest while Quinn and Gracie bought the engagement ring had given the older lady the stamina necessary to make the return trip by water taxi but not much more. Upon stepping out of the boat, she'd declared that she was going to have a bowl of soup and a sandwich delivered to her room, a long soak in a bubble bath, and then go directly to bed. She'd encouraged Gracie to do the same.

Gracie had needed no persuading. The jewelry show had been as incredible as she'd always imagined it would be, but picking out an engagement ring with Quinn had affected her far more than she could have ever anticipated. She'd needed time alone to process all she'd experienced. Of course, clear thinking would have been a whole lot easier if she hadn't had the diamond ring on her finger. Dorcas had disappeared so fast Gracie hadn't been able to give it to her to place in the safe, and she was scared to take something so valuable off her finger without a secure place to store it.

She felt the unaccustomed weight now and reached out to touch it. Dorcas had declared it to be perfect. That was exactly what Gracie thought too. But how Quinn had known what her dream ring should look like she couldn't fathom. She'd wanted to ask him on their way back to the hotel, but his drawn expression on the boat had discouraged any discussion between them. She could only hope his silence was due to tiredness rather than shock over the new and enormous hole in his bank account.

Slipping out from under the bedcovers, Gracie padded across the parquet floor to the window. She pulled back the curtain. Fingers of light were beginning to touch the rooftops on the other side of the Grand Canal. A bird trilled its morning call in a nearby tree and was answered almost immediately by another. A new day was dawning, and Gracie was filled with a sudden urgency to be part of it.

Hurrying to her suitcase, she pulled out her navy capris, white short-sleeved blouse, and sandals. As soon as she was dressed, she ran a brush through her hair and plaited it into a long single braid, tying it off with a hair elastic. Then she lifted her purse onto her shoulder, and making sure she had her room key safely in her pocket, she exited her room and headed for the stairs.

The lobby was empty, but through the glass doors that led to the restaurant, she could hear the clatter of dishes and a male voice raised in song. She smiled. It definitely wasn't Pavarotti, but there was something rather magical about waking up to the sun rising on the Grand Canal and an Italian singing his heart out in the kitchen. She opened the door to the patio and stepped outside. There was a slight nip to the air, and she paused, wondering if she should run back up to her room to grab a sweater.

"Uh-oh, it looks like jet lag's messing with you too."

Startled by the sound of Quinn's voice, Gracie turned to her right. He was sitting at a nearby table, dressed in tennis shoes, cargo shorts, and a Yankees T-shirt. Vaguely registering that she'd never seen him dressed casually before, she stepped closer. "I guess so. I woke up a little while ago and couldn't get back to sleep."

"Same," he said. "I came downstairs to get something to eat." He inclined his head in the direction of the kitchen, his lips twitching as though he was fighting a smile. "The opera star in there told me the bread's in the oven." He pointed to another chair at his table. "D'you want to join me?"

"Actually, I thought I'd go explore," she said. "It's my last day in Venice, and I wanted to see a little more before all the other tourists are out."

Interest flickered in his brown eyes. "That sounds like a great idea."

Gracie wasn't sure how Quinn felt about spending time with her when they weren't under scrutiny, but she knew it would be much more enjoyable to share her spontaneous outing with someone else than to experience it alone. "You're welcome to come with me if you want to."

"You really don't mind?" he asked.

She glanced at the hotel restaurant. "Maybe we can find a café owner who put his bread in the oven a little earlier than the opera singer did," she said.

"Sold." Quinn came to his feet immediately.

Gracie smiled. "Let's head toward St. Mark's Square and see what we can find."

"Sounds great." He pulled his phone out of his pocket. "And just in case Dorcas wakes up early too, I'll send her a text telling her where we've gone."

Grateful for the vague memory she had of the route she and Dorcas had taken the day before, Gracie led Quinn through the labyrinth of narrow alleys, across three old stone bridges, and past shuttered shops and restaurants. As the morning light slowly reached into the passageways, the sun turned the shadowy gray walls pink, cream, and blue and illuminated an occasional metal plaque nailed to some of those walls that pointed them toward the Piazza di San Marco.

For the most part, they walked in silence, content to soak in the ambiance of Venice, but every once in a while, one of them would point out a building's unique architecture or a quaint storefront. They paused along their route to watch a delivery boat unloading supplies and a group of gondoliers preparing their boats for a day full of tourists.

At first, their path was empty, but as they drew nearer to the square, other people began appearing. Most of them seemed to be locals on their way to work, and many of them were eating breakfast on the run. They turned another corner, and not more than a hundred yards away was a small bakery with a cluster of tables set up outside and a line of people coming out the door.

"Admit it," Quinn said. "Right now, that's the best sight in all of Venice."

Gracie laughed, and without waiting for a reply, Quinn grabbed her hand and towed her toward the end of the rapidly increasing line.

💎💎💎

Two cups of coffee, a slice of berry tart, a cheese-and-prosciutto-filled crusty roll, and three croissants later, Quinn thought he might live to see another day after all. He couldn't actually remember the last time he'd eaten a decent meal, and even though the food at the Venetian bakery didn't exactly qualify as nutritionally well balanced, everything had been delicious.

He glanced at Gracie. She was sitting across from him, smiling at a little boy who was chasing a pigeon. She'd finished her hot chocolate and croissants long before he emptied his plate, but she was content to sit and quietly wait. Her behavior was the antithesis of Mallory's constant need for action and attention and was one of the things he was coming to appreciate about her.

As though sensing his eyes upon her, Gracie turned and gave him a quizzical look. "Are you ready to go?"

"Yes," he said. "Sorry to slow you down."

She shook her head. "It's still early. Even now, I bet we're ahead of the crowds."

In his pocket, he felt his phone vibrate. He pulled it out and checked the caller ID. "It's Steve," he said.

"You'd better take it."

He nodded and pushed the accept button. "Hey, Steve."

"You're awake," Steve said. "I wondered if I'd have to leave a message."

"Yeah," Quinn said. "Jet lag is a powerful thing."

Steve groaned. "I'm planning on taking something to make me sleep on my flight; I've got to hit the ground running when I get there."

"When are you heading out?"

"Tomorrow. I fly straight in to Athens. I should get there a day before your cruise ship docks in Piraeus—enough time to do a little groundwork and make a few contacts." He paused. "Right now, the Greek jeweler, Nikos Antoniou, looks clean. His son, Damien, may be another story."

Quinn sat up a little. "Really?"

"Yeah. I'm still digging, but let's just say he hasn't been quite as honest in his business dealings as his father."

Quinn wanted to ask for details, but before he could get a word in, Steve had moved on to his next question.

"How did it go at the jewelry show?"

"Good," Quinn said. "Dorcas bought a brooch, and Gracie has an engagement ring." He glanced over at Gracie. Her hands were clasped tightly on the table, but she gave him a small smile. "Gracie checked both pieces before we left the show. They're the real deal."

"Great," Steve said. "So far, no problems, then?"

Quinn hesitated. Should he tell Steve about the man Gracie had seen? "I think we're good. Gracie noticed some guy hanging around when Dorcas was buying her brooch, but we haven't seen him since then."

Steve's voice lost its casual tone. "Did she give you a description?"

"Short, chunky, late twenties. Curly brown hair that reached his collar. Black button-down and jeans." Quinn recited the list from memory. He'd repeated it several times after Gracie had given it to him at the show, watching for anyone who matched it.

"If she sees him again, I want to know about it. A picture would be fantastic if you can pull it off without drawing any attention. I have a guy going onboard before your cruise ship leaves port to install a miniature camera to monitor the safe in Dorcas's stateroom. Make sure that if the jewelry isn't in that safe, the women are wearing it."

"Will do," Quinn said.

"And, Quinn," Steve added. "If you're being watched, it's vital that you and Gracie are seen together. A lot. If the thieves catch wind that your engagement's not real, they'll smell rat and run."

Out of the corner of his eye, Quinn could see the ring on Gracie's finger. He'd noticed it as soon as she'd walked out of the hotel this morning, and knowing that it was *his* ring had felt unaccountably right. He was still trying to come to terms with his unexpected response to placing it on her finger yesterday and had already determined that he would need to make an effort to keep things lighter between them today. "She's really difficult to be around, but I'll do my best to endure it," he said, giving Gracie a quick wink.

A slight blush rose on her cheeks, and he mentally chastised himself for teasing her. It had taken him less than half a day in Venice to realize that pretending to be Gracie's fiancé was not going to be a challenge. Remembering that the engagement wasn't real was going to be a much bigger problem.

"I'm assuming Gracie heard that," Steve said dryly.

"She did," Quinn said.

"Okay, well, I'll let you fill her in, then." Steve was back to business again. "I'll touch base with you as soon as I get to Athens."

"Sounds good. Travel safe."

Quinn lowered his phone, and Gracie looked at him expectantly. "Can you tell me what he said?"

He nodded, pushed his chair back, and got to his feet. "Let's talk while we walk to the piazza." It didn't take long to share Steve's news and instructions with Gracie.

"I wish I'd pointed out that guy at the jewelry show to you sooner," she said.

Quinn shook his head. "Don't beat yourself up about it. At least you noticed him. We'll both be on the lookout from now on, and if we see him again, we'll act on it. If we don't, chances are he's nothing to worry about."

"Okay."

He gave her an encouraging smile and offered her his hand. "How about we focus on the other part of Steve's message instead? The part about hanging out together and acting like we're engaged."

Gracie nodded and slipped her hand into his. "I'll try not to be too difficult," she said solemnly.

"It's going to be a strain, isn't it?"

"Terrible."

He caught the quirk of her lips and grinned. "Come on. Show me where they filmed *The Italian Job*."

She gasped. "They did do that here, didn't they?"

"Right on St Mark's Square," he said as they entered the piazza. "And based on how empty it was in the movie, it was probably filmed at about this time of day."

There was only a handful of people to be seen. Two men were setting up café tables and chairs at the far end of the square, a woman was unlocking the door of a glass shop, and five students with oversized backpacks were wandering around in front of the basilica.

Quinn and Gracie followed the arched walkway around the square, stopping to peer into a few store windows and to study the magnificent frescos on the basilica walls. They stood, silently watching as the bell tower tolled the seven o'clock hour, then they made their way to the water's edge. Waves lapped the cobbles, and a few yards out, rows of tightly packed wooden gondolas clacked against each other and their moorings. Beyond them, one of the nearby islands rose from the water, its multicolored buildings vying for brilliance with the color-streaked sky. Within an hour, the crowds would come and everything would change, but for now, it was quiet, and it was theirs.

"Gracie." Quinn kept his voice low.

"Hmm?" She continued to gaze at the view before them.

"Would you like to go out there? There are some gondoliers standing on the dock. We could see if one of them would . . . ?"

She turned to face him, her blue eyes bright. "Do you think we could?"

"Let's go find out."

One of the gondoliers saw them coming. He separated himself from his friends and approached them.

"You wish to ride?" he asked, gesturing at the closest boat.

"Yes," Quinn said. "Will you take us this early?"

"Psht! We open at eight, but if I am here, I go." He grinned. "It is the best time, no? Better even than sunset. We shall have the canals to ourselves." He stepped into the gondola and reached his hand out to Gracie. "Come, beautiful signorina."

Gracie gave the cavalier gondolier a hesitant smile, took his hand, and stepped onto the gondola. The boat swayed, but he guided her to a cushioned seat at one end of the boat. Quinn waited until she was seated, then he stepped onboard and sat beside her.

The gondolier took his place on the back of the boat and raised his pole. "You are from America?" he asked.

"Yes," Quinn said.

"And you are just now married?" he guessed.

"Not yet," Quinn said.

"Ah!" The gondolier pushed away from the dock and gave them what he obviously believed to be a knowing look. "Not yet, but soon." He wiggled his eyebrows. "I can see from your eyes it will be soon."

Quinn didn't dare look at Gracie, but as the gondola pulled away from the protection of the dock, the sea breeze picked up, and he felt her shiver. He put his arm around her and drew her closer. She moved willingly and leaned her head against him. The gondolier's thinking was off, but then again, so was his. Offering Gracie a gondola ride at sunrise was a spectacularly stupid idea if he really wanted to keep things lighter between them.

CHAPTER 13

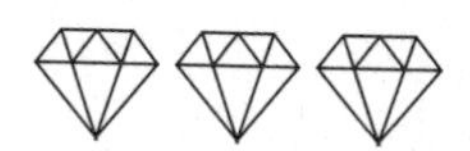

GRACIE STOOD AGAINST THE RAILING of the GCL *Fantasia*'s upper deck and watched Venice's terracotta skyline slowly shrink from view as the enormous ship left the port behind. From her position, seventeen floors up, she could barely feel the vibration of the ship's engines, but the cruise liner sliced through the water smoothly and effortlessly, picking up speed as it moved into the open sea. "This is incredible! It's like standing on top of a moving city."

Beside her, Dorcas smiled and nodded her agreement. "Complete with hotel, stores, restaurants, gym, swimming pools, dry-cleaning, and pretty much anything else you could want. There's even a library."

Tucking the wisps of hair blowing free from her braid behind her ears, Gracie looked out across the upper deck reserved for the cruise line's VIP guests. Comfortable deck chairs surrounded a private swimming pool, whirlpool, and bar. Attractive lamps were strategically placed for both practicality and ambiance, and sculptured dolphins and turtles decorated the walls. It was lovely, but she knew that it was a tiny fraction of what lay below deck.

"I should explore," Gracie said. "But I may get lost and never be seen again."

Dorcas laughed. "You'll get the hang of it in no time. The most important thing is to remember where your stateroom's located."

"Aurora floor. Room 16010. One door down from yours," Gracie recited.

"That's right," Dorcas said. "Do you remember where Quinn's room is?"

"Uh, room 12006. But I don't know what floor he's on."

"Incanto," she said. "The room number would get you there, but the name helps in the elevators." She frowned. "I wish his room were a little closer to ours, but booking as late as we did, I was lucky to get two on the same floor."

Gracie guessed that the cruise line had done everything possible to accommodate Dorcas's last-minute request. In the short time they'd been on board, she'd already witnessed the special treatment Dorcas received. They'd been allowed to board immediately, bypassing the incredibly long lines of passengers dropping off luggage, checking passports, and receiving the ID cards that gained them entry to their rooms and served as charge cards.

A pleasant woman sitting at a separate desk had completed their boarding procedure quickly and efficiently and had handed them off to three young men wearing Greek Cruise Line uniforms, who had carried their luggage directly to their respective rooms. Quinn had followed one young man to his stateroom while she and Dorcas had followed two others to their upper-deck suites.

Gracie had had a few moments to walk through her suite before joining Dorcas on deck, and she was still incredulous that such a luxurious room was to be hers for an entire week. It had every convenience, from a modern sitting area to a comfortable king-size bed, from marble appointed fixtures in the bathroom to her very own balcony. In fact, when the steward placed her slightly battered suitcase at the end of the bed, it appeared awkwardly out of keeping with the upscale décor.

Her phone rang, and she pulled it out of her pocket. "It's Quinn," she said to Dorcas.

"I wondered what had become of him," Dorcas said as Gracie accepted the call.

"Hey." Quinn's voice was loud enough that his aunt could hear him too. "Any chance one of you ladies of the elite Yacht Club would be willing to let someone from the lower echelon onto your deck? My card won't let me in."

"Oh, goodness," Dorcas said. "No wonder he didn't come join us up here. I'll talk to Henri, the head steward, about getting another card."

Gracie laughed. "I'll come open the door for you, and Dorcas will work her magic and find you a key."

"That would be great," he said. "I'm in the lobby opposite the elevators that lead to the Yacht Club decks."

"Okay. I'll be right there." Gracie disconnected the call and turned to Dorcas. "We'll join you soon."

"Thank you, dear. I'm going to spend a little time getting settled in my room before we go to dinner, so there's no hurry if you want to explore first."

Gracie gave her a quick hug. "I'll mention that to Quinn," she said. Then she hurried to the elevator.

The door opened immediately, but when she got in and faced the large panel of buttons, she realized she had no idea which floor to choose. She knew her suite was one floor below, so she pushed the button for two floors down. With a whoosh, the elevator dropped, and seconds later, the doors reopened. Gracie stepped out and looked around. She was in a small lobby, but there was no sign of Quinn.

Moving to her right, she peered down the corridor. It seemed to be the mirror image of hers and Dorcas's hall, but a glance at the closest door showed that the numbers started with 15000 rather than 16000. Perhaps there was another floor of Yacht Club member suites before the main level.

Not far away, a door opened, and a uniformed GCL employee exited a room carrying a pile of pillows and blankets. He started toward her, and Gracie hesitated, wondering if she might be better off asking for directions rather than trying every button on the elevator panel.

"Excuse me," she said.

Her voice obviously startled him, but he shifted his load slightly so he could see her. "*Buon pomeriggio*, signorina," he said politely. "How can I help you?"

Somehow, Gracie met the man's measured gaze without flinching. The man from the Venetian Jewelry Show recognized her. She was sure of it. But could he sense that she knew him too?

For a full three seconds, no words would come. Not in English, and certainly not in Italian. "Sorry," she finally managed. "I thought you were someone else." Then with a strained smile, she forced her feet to move down the hall. It didn't matter what direction it was or where it led, as long as it was away.

She made it as far as the first corner before turning around. When she did, the hallway was empty. Not willing to go back and run the risk of another encounter at the elevator, she continued forward, praying that at some point before she looped all the way around, she would find a stairwell. With her heart pounding, she scoured the doors for exit signs, finally spotting one at the far end of the hall. Another quick glance over her shoulder told her no one else was in the corridor, so she started running and kept on running all the way down the stairs.

When she reached the next stairwell, she stopped, leaned against the wall, pulled out her phone, and dialed Quinn.

He must have been holding his phone in his hand because he answered immediately. "Hi, Gracie."

"He's here," Gracie said. Her breath was coming out in short gasps. "The man from the jewelry show. I just ran into him."

"Where are you?" She could hear the worry in his voice. "Are you okay?"

"I'm in the stairwell. I didn't dare take the elevator because he was heading that way."

"Which floor are you on?"

Gracie faced the doors. "The sign above the exit says, 'Miraggio,'" she said. "Do you know where that is?"

"Yes," he said. "It's the main deck. I just need to figure out which stairwell you're in. What do you see from the doorway?"

Gracie moved closer to the door and peered through the small windows. "There's . . . there's a huge swimming pool with a big red tube slide and people everywhere."

"Do you see the gelato stand near the entrance to the slide? I passed it earlier."

She pushed open the door. People were milling around, but no one seemed to be watching the exit or her. She stepped outside and let the door close behind her. Shading her eyes from the bright sun, she studied the long, twisting waterslide until she spotted its base and the small structure at its entrance. "Does it look like a tiki hut?" she asked.

"Yes. D'you see it?"

"I think so. There's a big line of people standing there."

"Exactly," Quinn said. He was panting slightly, and she could hear the muffled sound of his footsteps hitting the deck hard and fast. "I'm getting close, but until I reach you, see if you can join the crowd. Right now, I think you're better off being around other people."

Recognizing the wisdom in Quinn's suggestion, Gracie started walking toward the gelato stand. She kept her phone to her ear but didn't look around. It was better not to know if someone was watching her. "I'm getting in line," she said, taking her place behind a father and his three young children.

The little girl and her brothers were talking rapidly, their faces wreathed in smiles. Not sure what language they were speaking, Gracie couldn't follow their conversation, but the children's excitement needed no translation. She took a shaky breath. Under half an hour ago, she'd shared their enthusiasm for being onboard this amazing cruise ship, but now her delight had dimmed. Her true purpose for being here, along with the accompanying risks, had suddenly become real.

💎💎💎

Quinn wasn't sure how long *Fantasia*'s main deck was—two or three football fields, at least—and he'd crossed most of it at a run. He was still several yards away when he saw Gracie take her place near the gelato stand, and he felt safe dropping his speed to a brisk walk. Seeing her in the distance and knowing that she was okay calmed his racing heart even more than slowing his pace could do, and by the time he reached her, his breathing was almost back to normal. "Gracie."

Lowering her phone, she swung around. "Quinn!"

He reached for her. She'd been standing in full sun, but she was shaking. "It's okay," he said, putting his arms around her.

"I'm so sorry." Her voice was muffled against his chest. "It was such a shock to see that guy in the hallway. I didn't think; I just reacted. I should've followed him, found out his name, what he's doing onboard." Her voice dropped. "I should have learned something that could've helped us figure out what he's up to."

Quinn leaned back so he could look her in the eyes. "If you ever meet him—or anyone else who may be involved in this crazy scheme—by yourself again, I want you to do exactly what you did this time," he said firmly. "Just get out of there."

"But Steve wants us to—"

"We're on this ship for a week, Gracie. We'll get another chance."

"We?" She shook her head. "I'm the one who messed up."

"*We*," he repeated. "You need to remember that word. We're a team."

She managed a wobbly smile. "Thanks," she said. "I needed to hear that."

He tightened his hold on her. "I'm happy to remind you anytime."

She smiled again, and this time, it reached her eyes. "Do you want some gelato, or should we get out of this line?"

He raised one eyebrow. "Is that a trick question?" She giggled, and his concern for her lifted a fraction. "I'm having pistachio and strawberry. What about you?"

Gracie ended up choosing chocolate and hazelnut. Then they found two chairs tucked behind one of the lifeboats where they could sit and watch the sea roll by. Despite the ongoing multilingual chatter around them, it was the rhythmic hum of the distant engines and the soothing swoosh of water against the ship's hull that dominated their tiny corner of the deck, and gradually, the strain on Gracie's face diminished. She licked the last bite of gelato off her spoon and set the cup on the small table between them.

"I don't understand how that guy could be working onboard this ship," she said. "The *Fantasia* hadn't even docked when we were at the jewelry show."

"I was thinking the same thing," Quinn said, grateful that she was ready to revisit the subject without his prodding. "But he was in uniform, right?"

"Yes. And he was coming out of some kind of linen closet, so he must have a crew key."

"Tell me exactly what happened, and don't leave anything out, no matter how insignificant it may seem."

Gracie leaned back in her seat and reviewed her experience from start to finish. "He knew me," she said. "I can't tell you how I know, but I do. Something to do with the look in his eyes." She frowned. "I don't know if he could tell that I recognized him too. I hope not, but I acted like such an idiot when he spoke to me, it's possible."

"Not an idiot, necessarily," Quinn said. "More like a lost and confused passenger."

"Maybe." She didn't seem very convinced. "Seeing as I am one of those, what should we do next?"

Quinn pulled his phone out of his pocket. "I'll call my aunt and see if she can figure out a way to get us a list of the crew members working this sailing. Then I'll send Steve a message to tell him you spotted the guy onboard and that we'll send him more information when we have it."

Dorcas answered her phone on the second ring, and when he explained what had happened, she offered a suggestion immediately.

"I'll talk to Henri when he brings me your key," she said. "As head steward, he should have access to a list of all those working hotel utility, housekeeping, or custodial. I'll tell him I want to see how many of my old friends are working this cruise."

"That might work," he said.

"If it doesn't, we'll come up with another plan," Dorcas said firmly. "We'll route out the weasel before he even knows we're on to him." Then her tone softened. "How's Gracie? Is she all right?"

Quinn glanced at the young woman sitting beside him. Her big blue eyes were watching him anxiously. "She's great," he said.

"Give her a tour of the ship," Dorcas said. "She'll feel more confident once she has her bearings, and seeing all *Fantasia* has to offer will take her mind off what just happened."

Quinn smothered a chuckle. It had been years since he'd lived in Dorcas's home, but that had yet to stop her from giving him instructions. "I will," he said. "Then we'll join you for dinner."

"Very good," Dorcas said. "And in the meantime, I'll talk to Henri."

CHAPTER 14

GRACIE TOOK QUINN'S EXTENDED HAND, and he guided her around the lifeboat and past the long row of deck chairs toward the forward side of the ship. She experienced a frisson of awareness whenever their fingers touched, but holding Quinn's hand was becoming natural. Too natural. She had to keep reminding herself that they were players in an elaborate charade and that within a week, their time together would be over. Unfortunately, the thought didn't fill her with the relief that it should have.

"How did Dorcas take the news that we have someone following us?" she asked.

Quinn grinned. "She called him a weasel, and believe me, that's never a good thing."

Gracie eyed him curiously. "It sounds like you're speaking from experience."

"Yeah," he said. "I'm afraid I wasn't the easiest kid to raise." He met her gaze, all trace of humor now gone. "After my parents' divorce, my mother and I moved in with Dorcas. My mother was the town librarian, and Dorcas ran a travel agency. Between them, they were able to work their shifts so that someone was always home when I got back from school. When I was fourteen, my mother died of cancer, and Dorcas stepped in full-time." He shrugged. "She's always felt more like a mother to me than an aunt."

Gracie remained silent for a moment, thinking of her own mother back home in Washington and how lost she'd feel without her love and support. "I can't imagine how hard that must have been," she said.

"I don't know where I'd be if I hadn't had Dorcas," he said. "She never gave up on me, and she made sure I worked hard and followed my dreams. I owe her big-time."

Gracie squeezed his hand. "Being here for her now is good payback."

"It's a start," he said, giving her a grateful smile. "Now, let's go check out this floating city, and if we're lucky, we'll spot weasel man while we're at it."

An hour later, they still hadn't seen the man from the jewelry show, but they'd explored the ship from bottom to top. They'd discovered half a dozen restaurants, several stores, a vast theater, a library, a spa, a children's center, and a gym. On the inner decks, the furnishings were sumptuous; on the outer decks, the lounge chairs stretched out as far as the eye could see.

Functional elevators sat at strategic locations throughout the ship, but three glass-walled elevators zipped up and down through the center of the cruise liner, taking passengers directly into the plush lobby, where a man in a tux was playing old show tunes on a grand piano while throngs of people stood in lines to sign up for shore excursions and transact currency exchange.

"Any idea what's on the agenda tomorrow?" Quinn asked, eyeing the posters behind the excursion desk as they walked past. "All I know about this cruise is that we have one stop in Athens and one stop in Santorini—and that's just because Dorcas mentioned them."

Gracie nodded. "Tomorrow's Bari. St. Nicholas's bones are supposed to be buried at the church there."

"Wait. St. Nicholas, as in Santa Claus?"

She laughed. "Yeah. That one. But judging by the lines at the excursion desk, not many people share your excitement for old St.

Nick. It looks like most people are taking buses to some of the other sights."

Quinn frowned. "I wonder what Dorcas plans to do."

"Are you thinking we should stick together?"

"It would probably be a good idea," he said. "But Dorcas won't want us limiting what we do because of her, so we'll have to make it out that whatever she's planning to do is what we wanted all along."

Gracie nodded in agreement. "We can do that."

"You really don't mind missing out on the excursions?"

"I've been to Venice and visited the Venetian Jewelry Show," Gracie said. "Anything else is frosting on the cake. Besides"—she gestured to the glittering spiral staircase in the center of the lobby—"staying onboard a ship like this is treat enough."

He glanced at the glitzy décor, then looked at her quizzically. "You're quite something, Gracie Miller," he said.

"I know," she said ruefully. "I'm an American farm girl who can barely find her way around New York City and is totally out of place on a fancy cruise ship in the Mediterranean."

"I was thinking more along the lines of unselfish and appreciative," he said.

"Or uncultured and awestruck."

Quinn laughed "Nope. Not that. Although maybe we'll get a glimpse of 'awestruck' when we reach the Greek ruins."

"I can guarantee it," Gracie said, hoping that the return of their easy banter covered her inevitable blush at Quinn's compliment. As much as she wanted to, she couldn't take his flattery to heart. Not when he had a girlfriend back home. She stepped closer to the elevators, suddenly needing a little distance. "Let's go see if Dorcas has had any success finding a crew list."

They rode the elevator as far as the main deck, then Gracie used her key card to access the Yacht Club suites. This time, she had no difficulty locating her cabin and Dorcas's, and as soon as they were outside number 16008, Quinn knocked on the door. Dorcas answered right away.

"Come in," she said. Dressed in a pearl-gray dress with a pink silk scarf attached to her shoulder with her new brooch, she led them into a suite identical to Gracie's, except the color scheme was purple rather than aqua-blue. She slid a card off the coffee table and handed it to Quinn. "Your Yacht Club access," she said.

"Thanks." He pocketed it. "Did you have any problems getting it?"

Dorcas waved her hand as though he'd asked a silly question. "Not at all." She picked up two pieces of paper that had been lying next to the card. "Henri didn't even blink when I asked for the crew list." She looked up, a twinkle in her eye. "I daresay he's used to fulfilling odd requests from eccentric, rich passengers."

"Have you looked at it?" Quinn asked, taking a seat and reaching for the papers.

"Yes." Dorcas sat and indicated that Gracie do the same. "Twenty-three fresh crew members came on board in Venice. They're the ones asterisked. Henri told me they're usually temp positions covering for someone who's ill or has a family emergency. Occasionally, it's a returning crew member taking up their position again."

Quinn studied the paper. "What about the ones who have been crossed out?"

"Those are all females," Dorcas said. "If we eliminate them, we narrow our search from twenty-three to thirteen."

"And would they all have access to linen closets?" Gracie asked.

Dorcas nodded. "This list includes housekeeping and hotel utility."

"What's hotel utility?" Quinn said.

"It basically covers everything from keeping the public areas clean to delivery of luggage to assisting the stewards with the staterooms or the barkeepers with cocktail parties."

Creases appeared across Quinn's forehead. "So they have free access to just about anywhere on the ship."

"Yes. I suppose so," Dorcas said.

He sighed. "All right. I'll get this list sent off to Steve so he can start checking the names on his end. Then we're going to have to start looking at name tags more closely and eliminating suspects after we've put a face to the name."

"I can keep a close eye out tomorrow," Dorcas said. "It's all hands on deck for the crew when the passengers are off on the excursions, so there'll be plenty of them around."

"Actually, Gracie and I were thinking of staying onboard tomorrow too," Quinn said.

Dorcas looked startled. "You're not going to visit the Sassi in Matera or Alberobello?"

"Don't be upset," Quinn said, raising his hands as though to ward off her ire. "But I need to spend a couple of hours doing some work. I was gone from the office for a week before getting here, and I need to check on a few things."

Dorcas frowned. "That is completely unvacation worthy."

"I know," he admitted, "and I won't do it every day. But Gracie suggested having a day onboard ship tomorrow, and it shouldn't take me too long." He glanced at Gracie, and she sensed his silent plea for backup.

"I thought it might be fun to have the swimming pool virtually to ourselves," Gracie said.

Dorcas gave an accepting nod. "Going to the pool while all the other passengers are on shore is one of the best kept secrets of cruising."

"Then it's settled," Quinn said. "And not having to go downstairs to stand in line for spots on a bus is an added bonus."

"All it would take is placing a phone call," Dorcas said.

"Oh, that's right." Mischief shone in Quinn's eyes. "I forgot I was traveling with *Mrs. Katsaros VIP*."

"Yes, you are, young man." Dorcas got up and moved toward the door. "And the three of us have been invited to sit at the captain's table for dinner tonight, so you'd better go get yourself cleaned up."

With a chuckle, Quinn rose and kissed his aunt lightly on both cheeks. "Give me fifteen minutes and I'll be ready."

💎💎💎

It was closer to twenty minutes later when Quinn arrived back at Dorcas's stateroom, and it was Gracie who answered the door.

While he'd been gone, she'd changed into a knee-length black dress and had pulled her hair up into an elegant twist. Simple pearl earrings matched the string of pearls around her neck, and a hint of perfume reached him as she stepped back.

"Wow!" he said. "You look stunning."

The slight blush he was coming to recognize touched her cheeks. "Thanks. You don't look so bad yourself."

He glanced down at his khaki pants and navy blazer and hoped it hadn't been a mistake to leave his suit at home. During his hasty packing session between flights in New York, the suit had seemed too businesslike for a cruise, but now he wasn't so sure.

"You look very nice, Quinn," his aunt said, coming up behind Gracie and giving him an approving smile.

"Thanks," he said. Then giving voice to his niggling concern, he added, "Will we need to dress up every evening?"

Dorcas shook her head. "No. I think there's one more formal dinner scheduled later in the week, but the other meals will be more casual."

Quinn worked to keep his relief from showing. "Sounds good."

Dorcas glanced at the clock. "We'd best be on our way. Dinner starts at seven thirty."

They took the elevator down one floor and walked the length of the hall until they reached a small atrium outside the restaurant reserved for Yacht Club members. Tall urns stood on either side of the swinging doors, and from within came the chink of silverware on china and the hum of voices.

"Please." A young woman with a camera slung around her neck approached them. "I shall take your picture before you eat."

Quinn glanced at his aunt. Was this normal?

She smiled at the woman as though she'd been expecting her request and positioned herself in front of a dark red curtain hanging to one side of the restaurant entrance. "Come along," Dorcas said, beckoning him and Gracie over. "This will be the first of many photos taken onboard."

Obediently, Quinn stood beside his aunt, with one arm around her and the other around Gracie. He watched as the woman adjusted her camera's wide lens to zoom in closer, then he tilted his head so he could whisper in Gracie's ear. "How detailed would photos need to be for the CAD program to produce a model?"

"This would be a good beginning," Gracie whispered back. "A camera like that would pick up important details, but you'd need close-up shots taken from several different angles to make a 3-D mold."

He gave a brief nod. Onboard photographers were something he hadn't considered before, and he wondered if Steve was even aware of their existence.

"Perfect," the photographer said, lowering her camera. "They will be ready for you tomorrow."

At that moment, the restaurant doors opened to reveal a short, wiry man with curly dark hair and a wide smile. "Ah, Mrs. Katsaros!" he said with a bow. "I heard we were to have the pleasure of your company tonight. Welcome back!"

"Good evening, Gustav," Dorcas said, giving him a warm smile. "It's good to be onboard once more."

"Of course," he said. "The *Fantasia* is a magical place, is it not?"

She laughed lightly. "It is indeed." She turned. "Gustav, this is my nephew, Quinn West, and his fiancée, Gracie Miller."

Gustav's head bobbed up and down. "Welcome, Mr. West and Miss Miller. We are very happy to have you with us." He gestured to the restaurant. "May I show you to your table?"

Gustav led the way to a round table at the far side of the room. There were eight place settings, and five of them were already taken.

The captain, immediately recognizable by the epaulettes on the shoulders of his jacket, stood as they approached. "Mrs. Katsaros," he said, leaning in to kiss Dorcas lightly on both cheeks. "It is good to see you again."

"And you, Captain Anastas," Dorcas said. She introduced him to Quinn and Gracie and smiled graciously as he introduced his chief engineer, Elek Drakos, who had risen to stand beside him, along with Don Juan de la Vega, a Spaniard who was apparently someone of importance in Barcelona, the don's wife, Maria, and his young son, Angelo.

When all the introductions were made, Dorcas, Quinn, and Gracie took their seats, and a waiter appeared with menus. Quinn made his selections quickly and lowered his menu to find Angelo staring wide-eyed at Gracie. The boy looked to be about five years old and was sitting at the table dressed in a miniature suit and bow tie. Oblivious to her audience across the table, Gracie was chewing her lower lip, studying the menu with intensity.

"Everything okay?" Quinn asked Gracie softly.

"How do you know what to order if you don't recognize a single dish?" she said.

Quinn fought back a smile. "You don't see mac and cheese?"

She eyed him over the top of the menu. "Go ahead and mock," she said. "But if you'd ever tasted my mom's homemade mac and cheese, that's what you'd want too."

Taking pity on her, he leaned closer and pointed to a couple of items. "If you're feeling like pasta, you might like this pelmeni dish. It's a stuffed pasta, kind of a cross between ravioli and a dumpling."

"Thanks," she whispered. "What are you having for dessert?"

"Gelato. Again."

She pointed to the chocolate hazelnut gateau. "I think I'll try that."

"It's like they knew you were coming or something," he said.

"I know." Her eyes twinkled, and even though the menu hid the lower half of her face, he knew she was smiling.

Quinn glanced over at Angelo again. The boy was still watching Gracie and appeared spellbound. "I think you've got a fan." He inclined his head slightly toward the other side of the table.

Gracie followed the motion, lowered her menu, and smiled at the boy. Angelo immediately dropped his head to study the tablecloth, but Quinn spotted the telltale redness creeping up his neck.

"What are you going to have for dinner, Angelo?" Gracie kept her voice low, as though she realized the boy didn't want the attention of all the adults at the table.

Slowly, Angelo raised his head. Dorcas was talking to the captain, and his parents were engrossed in a conversation with the chief engineer.

"Pasta," he said.

"Me too." Gracie gave him another smile, and this time, the boy reciprocated.

"*Y gelato*," Angelo added.

Gracie pointed at Quinn. "That's what he's having."

Angelo darted a nervous glance at Quinn before nodding his understanding.

"Gelato *es muy bueno*," he said.

"*Muy, muy bueno*," Quinn said, earning one of Angelo's smiles.

"Something to drink, sir?" The waiter had reappeared and was standing at Quinn's elbow, holding a bottle of wine. "I can recommend the merlot, but if you'd prefer white wine, we have an excellent Riesling."

"None for me, thank you," Quinn said. "I'll take water."

The well-trained server acknowledged his request without emotion. "Of course, sir. I'll bring it right out." He turned to Gracie. "And for you, ma'am?"

"I'd like water too," she said.

"Very good, ma'am." He reached between them and turned their wine glasses over, then he moved on to serve the other guests at the table.

As soon as the others' wine glasses were filled, the waiter took everyone's order, and within minutes, the first courses began appearing at their table. The photographer who'd taken their picture outside the restaurant floated through the room, snapping candid photos of the guests at their tables. She stopped at their table two or three times, the sound of her rapidly clicking shutter all the more disconcerting because Quinn couldn't tell exactly where the camera was focused.

Conversation ebbed and flowed around them as plates were emptied and disappeared and new ones arrived. Dorcas spent most of her meal reminiscing with Captain Anastas and receiving updates on each of his children. Chief Engineer Drakos asked about Quinn's work, but after learning that he was in the insurance business, he focused his attention on discussing Spanish politics with Don Juan and his wife.

Quinn listened in for a while, but soon discovered that watching Gracie and Angelo try to communicate in broken English was far more entertaining. Gracie's patience with the young boy amazed him, and before long, she was sketching animals on a brochure she'd found in her purse and Angelo was telling her what they were called in Spanish. Every once in a while, Maria would look over at her son and exchange a few words with him, but it was obvious that she was happy that for the time being, he was being entertained by someone else.

The meal was drawing to a close when the small band in the corner of the room switched from playing mellow classical music to familiar dance tunes. Within minutes, several couples had taken to the dance floor in the center of the restaurant. When the third dance was in full swing, Angelo tugged on his mother's arm and whispered something in her ear.

After a brief conversation with her son, Maria turned to Gracie with an apologetic look. "Angelo is wondering if you would be willing to dance with him, Gracie."

"I'd love to," Gracie said, pushing her chair back.

Angelo hopped off his seat and ran over to take her hand, leaving Quinn watching in bemusement as his so-called fiancée and her new young friend walked onto the dance floor together.

Their leaving seemed to trigger a mass exodus. Captain Anastas asked Dorcas to dance, and soon afterward, the de la Vegas joined them, which left Quinn and the chief engineer as the only ones at the table.

"It appears that you have some stiff competition, Mr. West," Chief Engineer Drakos said, pointing to Angelo, who was still holding Gracie's hands and was skipping in time to the music.

"Yes," Quinn said. "I'm trying to decide how long I let him go before I cut in."

The chief engineer laughed. "I hope he is familiar with that custom."

The upbeat song came to an end, and as the music changed and the tempo slowed, Quinn got to his feet. "Well, we're about to find out."

Chief Engineer Drakos gave him an approving look. "Good luck to you."

Gracie saw him coming. She bent down and said something to Angelo, pointing to Quinn as she spoke. The boy nodded and backed up a couple of paces.

"Any chance I can cut in?" Quinn said when he reached her.

"I told him it was your turn." Gracie gave her young partner an anxious look. "I hope he understands."

"Angelo." Behind him, Maria called to her son. She held out her arms, and Angelo ran into them.

"Looks like we're good," Quinn said.

"Yes." Gracie took his hand and slid her other arm around his neck. "I think we are."

The music swelled, and he drew her closer, leading her through the waltz steps Dorcas had forced him to learn as a reluctant youth. Gracie smiled up at him, and his breath caught. Her face was inches from his. It would be so easy to brush his lips against hers. And, heaven help him, he wanted to more than he'd wanted anything in a long time.

Then someone bumped his shoulder, and he missed his footing. "Pardon, monsieur." A tall, thin Frenchman offered a muttered apology as he attempted to guide his partner past them.

The interruption was fleeting but long enough for Quinn's head to clear. Kissing Gracie was a bad idea. A bad, bad idea. Over the last couple of days, they'd built on the friendship they'd developed over the phone, and if he wanted their ruse to flush out the jewelry thief to be successful, he couldn't do anything to jeopardize losing her trust. He took a deep breath. Kissing Gracie was a bad idea. Perhaps if he repeated the phrase over and over again, he'd actually come to believe it.

The first slow song rolled into a second, and he felt Gracie stir in his arms.

"Quinn?"

"Yes."

"You don't have to answer this if you'd rather not, but . . ." She paused as if plucking up courage to ask something difficult.

He looked down at her, experiencing a moment of disquiet when he saw the hesitation in her eyes. "I . . . I was wondering why you didn't have wine with your meal."

It was a question he'd fielded many times before, and he'd become quite adept at offering a glib reply followed by a change of subject. But he didn't want to do that with Gracie. For some reason, he felt safe sharing things with her; he'd already told her more about his growing-up years than he'd told most people.

"I don't drink because of my father," he said. Her gaze didn't falter, and with a sigh, he continued. "Not long after my parents were married, my father became an alcoholic." The music still played, and couples continued to swirl around them, but Quinn's feet slowed to a halt, and he forced himself to meet Gracie's eyes. "Alcohol destroyed my father's life and ended up killing him. No drink is worth that."

"That's not the answer you give most people, is it?" she said softly.

He frowned, slightly unnerved by how well she read him. "No. Not many people know about my father."

"You're a remarkable man, Quinn West," she said.

"Because I'm the only teetotaler in the room who's over the age of twenty-one?"

She shook her head, and he saw tears shimmering in her eyes. "No," she said. "Although, for the record, it's twenty-four, not twenty-one. I don't like the way alcohol makes me feel, so I don't drink it either."

He offered her a half smile. "I'm actually okay with that."

"Yeah," she said. "Me too."

The band played their final notes, and all around them, dancers parted, expressing their appreciation for the musicians through applause. Reluctantly, Quinn released his hold on Gracie. She took a step back, then reached for his hand. He wove his fingers between hers.

"Come on," he said. "I'll walk you and Dorcas back to your rooms."

CHAPTER 15

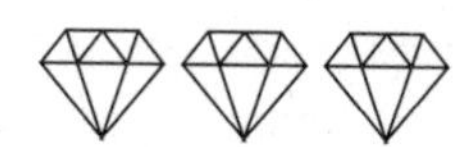

GRACIE STOOD ON THE BALCONY of her stateroom watching the Italian coastline on the distant horizon slowly take shape. According to the ship's itinerary that had been slipped under her door during the night, they would be making landfall at the port of Bari within a couple of hours. Her comfortable bed and the smooth sail from Venice should have guaranteed her a good night's rest. But sleep had been slow in coming, and instead, she'd lain awake reliving the day's tumultuous experiences. From her early morning gondola ride to running into the man from the jewelry show onboard ship to dancing in Quinn's arms, yesterday had been a roller coaster of emotions. And now, even though dawn was barely making its appearance, she was awake once more.

She sighed, placing her hands on the balcony railing. It had taken her months to get over the hurt Derek had caused when he walked away without looking back, but eventually she'd come to realize that his lack of interest in her hopes and aspirations was something she should have recognized earlier. For Derek, being with her had been convenient. Until it wasn't.

She'd hoped that all she'd learned from that painful experience would have prepared her for an engagement of convenience with

Quinn. But things were not turning out the way she'd imagined. Quinn seemed to genuinely value her opinions, and the companionship and trust between them felt real. Her concern that he was coming to mean more to her than merely a man playing a part beside her had been made all too apparent by her visceral response to his account of his father's battle with alcoholism.

When they'd arrived back at their staterooms last night, she and Dorcas had put their recently purchased jewelry in small boxes and placed them side-by-side in the safe in Dorcas's cabin, right in front of the boxes holding Dorcas's pink moissanite ring and composite sapphire pendant. She and Quinn had watched as Dorcas had reset the code on the safe and locked it securely. With Steve's miniature camera in place, the jewelry was doubly protected. There was little more they could do, but Gracie couldn't shake her feeling of unease.

With one more look at the view from the balcony, she reentered her cabin and dug her exercise clothes out of her case. Quickly changing into shorts, a T-shirt, and running shoes, she grabbed her phone, headphones, and key card and slipped out of the room. The corridor was quiet, the thick carpet deadening the sound of her footsteps as she hurried to the elevators.

Mentally reviewing the tour of the ship she'd taken with Quinn, she tried to work through her route to the gym. She got off the elevator when she reached the main deck, and circumventing the large swimming pool, she headed for the spa at the front of the ship. Even at this early hour, a handful of people were on deck. Some carried coffee cups and magazines, others stood beside the railings, admiring the view. Three people greeted Gracie—each in their own language—and she marveled again at the diverse cultures represented onboard.

The door to the spa was unlocked. Gracie pushed it open and smiled at the young woman standing at the desk. "I was hoping to use the gym," she said.

"Of course," the woman said, pointing to a pair of smoked-glass doors at her left. "You know the way?"

"Yes. Thank you."

Gracie cut across the small lobby and pushed open the doors. The gym was small but fully equipped. Four treadmills sat next to a couple of elliptical machines and three recumbent exercise bikes. Free weights and five different weight machines stood on the right side of the room; yoga balls and exercise mats were piled together on the left. Two baskets sat beside a water cooler. One of them was full of neatly folded clean towels; the other contained a handful of soiled ones. It appeared that she and the white-haired man using the nearest recumbent bike weren't the first people to use the gym this morning after all.

Gracie climbed onto the closest treadmill and studied the front panel. It didn't look too different from machines she'd used in the past. Straddling the running belt, she pushed a few buttons, and within seconds, the belt was moving. She set her phone on the stand and plugged in her headset. Starting the playlist she used for running, she stepped onto the moving belt and began a slow jog.

The wall in front of her was made entirely of glass. Windows stretched from the far left of the room to the far right, from the ceiling to the floor, and they were currently displaying a panoramic view of the ship's arrival into Bari. The gray smudge of land that Gracie had seen from her stateroom balcony was now a defined silhouette, showing the distant hills and the curvature of the coast. Keeping her eyes on the stunning seascape, Gracie increased the speed of the running belt and lost herself in her music.

Only vaguely aware of the sound of the gym door opening and closing, Gracie was startled back to reality with a gentle tug on her ponytail. Turning her head, she discovered Quinn standing beside her treadmill, also dressed in shorts, a T-shirt, and running shoes. But whereas her T-shirt was an old tie-dyed creation from her youth, his was a form-fitting black Nike shirt advertising the Rochester triathlon.

"I thought I recognized that swinging ponytail," he said.

"Hey," Gracie panted. She pushed a button to slow the running belt slightly. "Glad to know I'm not the only one still getting up too early."

Quinn rolled his eyes. "Nope. But the good news is the ship's breakfast buffet is already up and running."

Gracie managed a breathless laugh. "We shouldn't need to eat anything for days after last night's dinner."

"Which is why I'm here," Quinn said, climbing onto the treadmill next to hers. "I have to justify my next gelato."

Gracie was pretty sure his desire to exercise had more to do with missing his regular workouts than another scoop of dessert, but whatever the reason, she was glad for his company.

While Quinn adjusted the settings on his treadmill, Gracie glanced behind her. The white-haired man on the exercise bike was gone, and no one else was using any of the other equipment. In the far corner of the room, a crew member had just finished collecting the soiled towels from the hamper. Taking a spray bottle in one hand and a rag in the other, he began wiping down the handles of the nearest elliptical. His brown hair curled slightly over his collar, and when he turned so she could see his silhouette, Gracie's racing heart almost stopped.

Lowering the speed on her treadmill to a brisk walk, she looked straight ahead and forced herself to think. Beside her, the hum of Quinn's treadmill indicated that it was building up speed.

"Quinn. Wait." Without stopping her treadmill, she jumped off and stood beside his. "Before you start, we need to take a photo together."

Quinn pulled out his headphones. "What did you say?"

"We need a photo," she said.

He looked at her as though she'd lost her mind. "Right now?"

"Yes."

He slowed his machine and looked over his shoulder. "Are you going to ask that guy to take it?"

Gracie swallowed hard. "No. I'll take a selfie."

"Okay," he said, confusion evident in his face.

He stepped off his machine and came to stand beside her.

"Sorry. I'm kind of gross at the moment," she said, hoping he wouldn't actually reach out and touch her.

He raised his eyebrows questioningly. "We can come back and take a photo later."

She shook her head. Leaning toward him, she extended her arm so her phone was in position to take their picture, but instead of flipping the camera for a selfie, she zoomed in on the man who was now wiping down an exercise bike a few feet from them.

"Weasel," she muttered.

She sensed Quinn stiffen.

"Here," he said, reaching for her phone. "The lighting will be better on this side." He stepped around the treadmill so there was no equipment between him and the man wiping down the bike. Gracie followed him and forced a smile as Quinn pretended to take more selfies while capturing a series of shots of the man's profile.

Turning so his back was to the crewman, Quinn flipped through the photos on her phone screen. "Can you do something that will make him look this way?" he whispered.

"Hey," she said a little too loudly. "We're passing another ship. Take another photo now so it will show up in the background."

Curiosity got the better of the crewman, and he raised his head. At the sight of the unexciting, rusty red cargo ship steaming past *Fantasia*, his interest evaporated immediately and he returned his attention to the bike. But those few moments were all it had taken for Quinn to get the photograph they needed. Withdrawing his own phone from his pocket, he pulled up the settings.

"I'm going to airdrop the best ones to my phone," he said.

With his back to Weasel Man, Quinn zoomed in on one photograph that showed the crewman's metal name tag. Gracie read it. Vlasis. It sounded like a Greek name, but she wasn't sure. If they found it on the crew list Dorcas had given Quinn, they'd learn his last name, and Steve could really go to work. She waited until Quinn's phone showed that the airdrop was completed successfully, then she reached for her phone.

"I think I'll go back to my room and take a shower," she said.

Quinn nodded. She sensed the inner battle he was waging between his desire to leave the gym and send the information to

Steve and the risk he ran of raising the suspicions of Weasel Man if he left without doing any exercise at all. "I'll be right behind you," he said. "I'll lift a few weights and call it good."

She met his eyes and saw the conflict there. Quickly, she sent him a text. *Take as long as you need. He might change his plans if he thinks we're on to him. I'll wait for you in my room.*

His phone buzzed instantly. He read her message and sent a reply. *Be careful. I'll be there soon.*

Purposely taking the long way around the gym to avoid close contact with the crewman, Gracie made it all the way to the doors before she turned around. Quinn had already taken his place on the weight machine that gave him a clear view of the rest of the gym. She was sure that as soon as all the cleaning was complete and Weasel Man made his exit, Quinn would be right behind him.

💎💎💎

Quinn stared at his computer screen. There were 148 emails in his inbox, and not one of them was from Steve. It had been four hours since he'd emailed his friend copies of the photos he'd taken of the man in the gym, and he'd heard nothing. He'd tried calling and texting, with similar results. Admittedly, the ship's phone service and Wi-Fi weren't super reliable, but he'd had no problems connecting with Gracie by phone or with his New York office using the Wi-Fi. The most likely reason for Steve's silence was that his flight had been delayed and he was still en route to Athens.

Quinn scanned through the emails one more time. He'd responded to over a dozen work-related messages and had sent his senior partner the summaries he'd written regarding his meetings with colleagues from other insurance agencies at the conference in San Antonio. Nothing else seemed to be especially time sensitive, so he set up an automatic out-of-the-office reply for future emails and shut down his laptop. He was more than ready to step away from the computer and out of his cabin for a while.

By the time he'd escaped the gym and made it to Gracie's room, she'd showered and changed and checked on the jewelry in Dorcas's safe. Everything was accounted for, and Dorcas had suggested that they leave their valuables in the safe since they were planning to spend the day at the pool. It made sense. No one wore a valuable brooch to go swimming or risked losing an engagement ring in the deep end, but Quinn had already become accustomed to his ring being on Gracie's finger and found that he didn't particularly like seeing her finger bare.

They'd eaten a light breakfast at the buffet while most of *Fantasia*'s other passengers were disembarking for their various excursions, and when they'd finally left the restaurant, the halls were quiet, the elevators empty, and a feeling of calm had descended upon the ship. Quinn had seized the opportunity to return to his cabin and catch up on some work, and when he'd left the two women on the Yacht Club deck, Dorcas had been sweet-talking Gracie into joining her for a pedicure.

Quinn smiled as he slid his laptop into its protective case and locked it in his suitcase. Gracie didn't stand a chance. She'd be lucky if she made it through the pedicure without bright purple nail polish on every toenail. He glanced at the clock beside his bed. He'd been in his room for hours. The women had probably eaten lunch long ago and were already poolside. Filled with a strong desire to spend the rest of the afternoon with Gracie, Quinn opened his dresser drawer and pulled out his swim trunks.

It wasn't hard to locate Dorcas beside the Yacht Club pool. Her hot-pink floppy sunhat and matching sarong stood out against the rows of empty white lounge chairs. As Quinn drew closer, he noticed a small pile of books sitting on a table beside her, along with a tall glass of lemonade, complete with floating strawberries.

Dorcas's head was bent over the half-completed crossword puzzle in her hand, but she looked up as he approached. "There you are," she said. "We'd begun to think we were going to have to send out a search party."

"Sorry." Quinn grimaced. "Responding to emails always takes longer than I think it will."

"Then I recommend you don't open your computer again until you're back in New York," she said. She glanced at the lounge chair to her left. An eclectic collection of items, including a pair of flip-flops, a heap of white fabric, a faded baseball cap, a copy of Jane Austen's *Sense and Sensibility*, and a sketch pad and pencil lay on the seat. "Gracie was here a few minutes ago. Since she's left her shoes and cover-up behind, I'm guessing she's cooling off in the water."

The afternoon sun was beating down on the exposed deck, and the temperature had risen considerably since Quinn had gone to his cabin. Grateful that he was wearing his sunglasses and baseball cap, he scanned the nearby pool for any sign of Gracie. A small group of young children were playing in the shallow end, splashing each other with abandon. Three swimmers were crossing the pool with long, lazy strokes, and off to one side, a young woman in a navy swimsuit and large sunglasses was sitting at the pool's edge, her long, shapely legs only partially submerged in the water. She pulled at the elastic tied around the tight bun on her head, and when she shook her head and released a curtain of long brown hair, he recognized her.

Two men were standing at Gracie's side, talking and laughing, and Quinn felt a knot form in his stomach. How many times had he stood on the sidelines and watched Mallory entertain a string of suitors? At most functions, she barely acknowledged him, even if she'd begged him to be her escort and they'd arrived together.

"You'd better go rescue her," Dorcas said. "Those two have been hovering around her far too long."

It would be easier to take a seat on the other side of Dorcas, lower his cap, and catch up on some much-needed sleep. He knew that was what he'd do if it were Mallory sitting there with her usual entourage. But this wasn't Mallory. It was Gracie. And standing by while other men flirted with his fiancée was not going to happen. He took off his shirt, shoes, cap, and sunglasses and dropped them onto the chair beside Gracie's things.

He closed the gap between him and Gracie quickly. One of the men noticed his approach and gave him an acknowledging nod. Gracie turned, and when she saw him, she scrambled to her feet. Sliding her sunglasses to the top of her head, she smiled warmly, and the knot in Quinn's stomach loosened.

"Hey," she said. "I missed you."

They were the same words Mallory had used on him time and time again, but coming from Gracie, they sounded different. They sounded sincere. He slid his arm around her, and she moved closer.

"I'm sorry I was gone so long. Dorcas has banned me from doing any more computer work until I get home."

She laughed. Then she gestured to the two men who were now looking considerably less friendly than they had a few moments ago.

"Quinn, this is Paolo and Manuel," she said. "Paolo's from a small town outside Florence, and Manuel is from Rome. They've been telling me why I need to go visit those cities."

Quinn curbed his urge to tell both men that Gracie wouldn't be going either place without him tagging along. Instead, he managed an almost natural smile.

"Guys, this is my fiancé, Quinn," she said.

Out of habit, Quinn extended his hand. "Nice to meet you."

Paolo recovered first. He gave Quinn's hand a perfunctory shake. "Your fiancé?"

"Yes." Quinn gave him an unwavering look, and Paolo took a step back.

"You are a lucky man."

"I agree," Quinn said.

Manuel glanced at Gracie's ringless left hand, and with a quirk of one eyebrow, he shook Quinn's hand. "She will make a beautiful bride."

Quinn tightened his hold on Gracie. "Yes, she will."

Obviously ready to escape the mounting tension, Paolo offered Gracie a last dazzling smile. "It was good to meet you, Gracie," he said.

"And do not forget," Manuel added, ignoring Quinn completely. "Rome is always a good idea."

"Thanks," Gracie said. "I'll remember that."

The two Italians raised their hands in farewell and walked off toward the bar. As they disappeared, Quinn felt Gracie sag against him.

"You okay?" he asked.

"Yeah," she said. "I'm just glad you showed up when you did. There's only so much male machismo and bragging a girl can take, you know?"

At her words, any remains of the knot in Quinn's stomach dissolved, and he brought his other arm around to pull her close. "Wait," he said. "You mean, all self-respecting men are supposed to have a brag list they share with beautiful girls?"

She met his teasing look with one of her own. "Absolutely. And it seems to me that you've really dropped the ball in that area."

Quinn wrinkled his forehead as though deep in thought. "When I was nine, I won the fourth grade spelling bee at my elementary school."

He saw her lips twitch as she held back her smile. "Ooh. That is impressive."

"Are you making fun of my academic successes?"

"I'd never do that."

"Okay, how about this one?" He slid her sunglasses off her head and lowered them to the ground. "When I was twenty-eight, I singlehandedly dropped a girl into a swimming pool."

"When you were twenty—?" He swept her off her feet, and she gasped as she realized what he was about to do. "No! No, Quinn!"

"You can swim, right?"

"Yes, but . . ." She wrapped her arms around his neck, and her fate was sealed. He needed an immediate dose of cold water, and the fastest way was the pool.

"We're going in," he warned, and he stepped off the deck.

He released her as soon as they hit the water, and when she surfaced, she looked like a mermaid with her hair spread out in an enormous fan around her.

"You barely gave me time to take a breath!" she said, slapping the water so that he got a mouthful.

He laughed unrepentantly and watched while she deftly gathered and twisted her wet hair into a knot on her head and pinned it in place with the elastic on her wrist.

"Come on," he said. "I'll race you to the other side."

CHAPTER 16

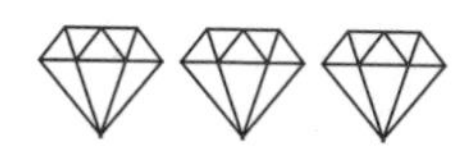

Gracie stood in front of the mirror in her stateroom and wrinkled her nose. Her skin felt tight, and she was pretty sure that despite her liberal use of sunscreen while she'd been poolside, she was going to be a few shades pinker by the end of the evening. Grateful that tonight's casual dinner meant she could wear a soft cotton tee and flowing floral skirt against her sensitive skin, she applied some lip balm and stepped into the sitting area just as a knock sounded.

When she opened the door, Quinn was standing in the hall, wearing gray pants and a sage-green button-down shirt. An evening shadow of stubble covered his chin, and his hair was still wet from the shower. He'd rolled up his sleeves to his elbows, exposing the tan already starting to develop on his arms. Gracie took an unsteady breath. She'd already had to smother her response to seeing him bare-chested at the swimming pool, and now she was faced with this.

"Hi," Quinn said. "Are you ready?"

"Yes." Gracie grabbed her purse and checked that her key card was inside. "Is Dorcas?"

"I stopped here first," he said, pulling the door closed behind her.

Gracie knocked on the next door down, and Dorcas answered it immediately.

"Perfect timing," Dorcas said. "I was just about to get your ring out of the safe."

She shut the door behind them, and they followed Dorcas into the bedroom and watched while she punched the code into the safe. The door opened, and Dorcas reached for the nearest jewelry box.

"Wait!"

Startled by Gracie's urgent voice, Dorcas pulled her hand back and turned to face her. "What is it?"

Aware of the puzzled expression on Quinn's face, Gracie stepped closer to the safe and studied the jewelry boxes inside. "They've been moved," she said.

Immediately, Quinn was at her side. "Are you sure?"

She nodded. "When we put the brooch box and the ring box next to each other, I noticed they were square to each other, with about an inch between them." She turned to face him, hoping he'd understand. "In my line of work, it's all about the little details—placement, symmetry, balance. I'm afraid it's rolled over into my everyday life." She shrugged, suddenly feeling self-conscious. "Some people would probably say I have OCD."

"Well, I'd say it makes you extremely good at what you do," Dorcas said.

Gracie gave her a grateful smile. The compliment meant more knowing that Dorcas had liked something Gracie had designed well enough to buy it.

"Without your observation skills, we wouldn't even be aware of the guy from the jewelry show," Quinn said. "So tell us what you're seeing now. What are Dorcas and I missing?"

She pointed at the two boxes at the front of the safe. "The box on the left is the brooch, and the one on the right is the ring. That's the order we put them into the safe. But do you see that the brooch box is now pushed up against the larger pendant box in the back of the safe? And it's not perpendicular to the ring box?"

"You mean the way it's crooked?" Dorcas asked.

"Yes. There are at least two inches between the boxes on one corner and less than one inch on the other."

"And you're sure they were square before?" Quinn said.

Gracie nodded. "Positive," she said.

"That's good enough for me." He turned and scanned the other side of the room. "I never asked Steve where his man placed the camera, only that it was supposed to pick up nothing more in the room than the front of the safe."

"I sincerely hope so," Dorcas said, suddenly looking a bit ruffled. "I don't want other people looking at pictures of me in my pajamas."

"Right now, I'm more concerned about whether we got pictures at all," Quinn said. He took out his phone and took a photo of the boxes in the open safe. "From now on, we need to take before and after photos whenever we open this thing."

"Shall we check inside the boxes too?" Dorcas asked.

Gracie's heart thumped as the older woman took out the brooch box and lifted the lid. Picking up the brooch, she handed it to Quinn, who held it while Gracie rooted through her purse until she found her loupe. Taking the magnifying glass out of its leather case, she put it to her eye and took the brooch from Quinn. She moved closer to the light and turned the brooch slowly, examining each jewel individually. "It's the real thing," she said, lowering the loupe. She stared at the safe. Had she imagined it? Would the movement of the ship cause the boxes to slide that much?

"Check the ring," Dorcas said, passing her the ring box.

Gracie pinched the beautiful engagement ring between her thumb and first finger and studied it through the loupe. "It's okay too," she said, unable to hide her relief.

Some lines on Quinn's forehead eased. "Put it on," he said.

She slipped it onto her finger and handed the box back to Quinn. "I don't understand," she said. "I could swear that someone moved things."

He studied the safe, his expression pensive. "Based on what's happened before, the brooch won't be stolen until the thief has a forgery to put in its place. And we're going on the premise that if he has access to the right CAD program, he can make a decent forgery from a few photographs. Up until this moment, we haven't been able to figure out how he takes those pictures without Dorcas knowing." He looked at her, the hint of a smile on his lips. "I think you may have just discovered the 'how,' 'when,' and 'where' of the thief's photo shoot."

Dorcas dropped into the nearest chair. "But the safe was locked, and there's no sign of forced entry."

Quinn paced across the room. "We may be dealing with a safe cracker," he said. "But if not, there has to be a way for the cruise line to override the codes. There are too many doddery old people with failing memories taking these cruises."

Gracie caught Dorcas's indignant expression and spoke up. "You're not one of them, Dorcas."

"Of course you're not," Quinn said as though the very idea were ludicrous.

Looking somewhat mollified, Dorcas picked at a piece of lint on her lime-green pants. "So do you want me to find out who—if anyone—has a master code to all the safes onboard?"

"If the camera picked up anything, we may not need to," Quinn said. "A clear video feed would tell us who opened the safe and how he did it."

"So how do we find out if the camera caught all that?" Dorcas asked.

He pulled his phone out of his pocket again and checked his screen. "There's only one person who can tell us," he said grimly. "And he's not responding to any of my emails, calls, or texts."

"Well then," Dorcas said, coming to her feet again. "I think the best thing we can do is go to dinner." She picked up her brooch and pinned it to her floral shirt, then she put both jewelry boxes back in the safe and closed it with a solid click. "Keep trying him, Quinn. He has to respond soon. His future supply of apple pie is on the line."

One look at Quinn's face told Gracie that apple pie would be the least of Steve's worries if he didn't reply soon. "Steve will contact you when he can," she said. "I bet he's stuck somewhere, feeling as frustrated as you are right now."

Quinn expelled a deep breath. "Yeah. You're probably right." He gave her a wry smile. "And it's never a good thing to be around a frustrated Steve. We're better off out at sea."

💎💎💎

Quinn's phone rang at 3:43 a.m. Cursing loud ringers, time zones, jet lag, and everything in between, he picked it up and accepted the call. "Hello."

"Yeah, you sound about the way I feel," Steve said.

Quinn sat up in bed, trying to shake off his sleepiness. "It's about time! Where have you been?"

"Remind me to never fly Aegean Airlines again," Steve said. "Being rerouted through Istanbul and waiting ten hours for another flight into Athens was not my idea of fun."

Steve was probably looking for sympathy, but Quinn had more important things on his mind. "Did you get my messages?"

"The three emails, six missed calls, and ten texts? Yeah. I just finished reading them."

"I need that backup you promised me, Steve," Quinn said. "If you can't do it, tell me now."

"The camera guy is already looking at the video feed," Steve said. "He'll let me know as soon as he's got something. Whenever I hear, I'll pass it on. I forwarded the photo of the crew member you sent to Interpol and the Hellenic Police to see if they can come up with a match. I have a buddy at the office in Philly checking on him too, along with the other names asterisked on the crew list." He paused, and Quinn wondered if he was running down a checklist. "If you're right about the safe being compromised yesterday afternoon, and if the safecracker was able to get photos sent to shore right away, there'd be just enough time to make a forgery before Dorcas visits the jewelry shop in Athens on Wednesday."

Quinn let that sink in for a minute. "You think that's where the switch is going to happen?"

"It's the most likely spot. But just because it makes sense doesn't always make it right."

It was the middle of the night, and Steve was talking in circles. Quinn closed his eyes. "Okay. I'm glad you made it to Athens. I'm glad you got back with me, and I'm glad your people are doing their thing with the information I sent you. But since I'm supposed to act like a relaxed guy on vacation tomorrow, I'm going to try to get some more sleep, and we can continue this conversation tomorrow." He opened his eyes again and glanced at the digital clock. "Later today," he amended.

"All right. Maybe there's an off chance I can get some sleep too."

"Good luck," Quinn said.

"Yeah. You too."

Quinn placed his phone on the bedside table and lay down, staring at the ceiling. He probably should have acted more relieved that Steve was safe and been more appreciative that despite his late arrival in Athens, he'd already started working on the leads Quinn had sent him. But it was four o'clock in the morning, and between trying to outthink a nameless, faceless jewelry thief and battle his growing feelings for Gracie, he hadn't fallen asleep until after 2:00 a.m. On top of that, they would be in Greece by morning and would lose another hour with the time change. He punched the pillow, hoping it would fluff up some more. If he could just get some more sleep, things would surely seem less complicated by daylight.

CHAPTER 17

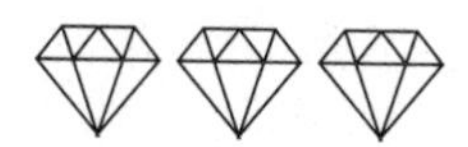

THE SHIP ARRIVED IN KATAKOLON, Greece, at eleven o'clock in the morning. Gracie stood at the railing of the upper deck beside Quinn and Dorcas watching the feverish activity on the dock below as the enormous vessel dropped anchor and lowered the walkways. Within minutes, streams of passengers flowed off the ship toward the waiting tour buses at the far end of the dock. Parked off to one side of the buses were half a dozen taxis.

"I'm sure Takis is here by now," Dorcas said. "He'll be waiting with the other drivers."

According to Dorcas, Takis was the best taxi driver on the island and would be their chauffeur for the day. The night before, Dorcas had decreed that Quinn and Gracie were not to miss seeing Olympia and had contacted Takis personally. Thankfully, she'd also agreed to accompany them on their trip to the ruins, so Quinn had been happy to fall in with her plans.

"Are you ready to head down there?" he asked.

His aunt gave a crisp nod. "The worst of the crowds will be gone by the time we reach the walkway."

Gracie slid the strap of her purse higher onto her shoulder and moved away from the railing, anticipation humming through her.

Quinn must have sensed her excitement because he raised one eyebrow in a teasing look.

"How are those 'uncultured and awestruck' feelings doing? Are you keeping them under control?"

"Barely," she said with a light laugh. She pointed to the nearby shoreline. "Just look at how beautiful it is."

The port of Katakolon, although capable of berthing enormous ocean liners, had retained its provincial feel. Tree-covered hills were the backdrop to the cluster of red-roofed buildings that spilled down to the waterfront. White sand fringed the shore, and the water was clear.

"Olympia is about twenty miles inland," Dorcas said, leading the way to the elevators. "But we'll drive through more pretty scenery en route."

Gracie wished she'd had more time to learn about the places they were visiting on this cruise. She knew Olympia was the home of the original Olympic Games, but she really had no idea what to expect once they got there. Truthfully, "uncultured and awestruck" accurately described her today.

Takis met them at the end of the dock. He was dark haired, olive skinned, and as round as a barrel. He greeted Dorcas warmly with a kiss on each cheek, then he did the same with Gracie before reaching for Quinn's hand.

"Welcome to Greece," he said. "This is your first stop in my country, correct?"

"Yes," Quinn said.

"Excellent," he said with enthusiasm. "Come, come." He opened the doors of his black Mercedes. "We shall go to Olympia, and you shall be amazed."

Dorcas had been right. The drive to the archeological ruins was a stunning combination of pristine coastline, picturesque small towns, and groves of olive and orange trees. Takis provided interesting commentary on the places they passed, and during the breaks in his tour spiel, he made sure Quinn was updated on the ongoing woes of the Greek economy. Secretly glad that Quinn had been the one assigned to sit next to their talkative driver, Gracie couldn't help but be impressed by Quinn's professional approach as he listened to Takis and expressed just the right amount of sympathy and understanding over his countrymen's financial difficulties without adding fuel to the Greek's frustrations.

Turning off the main highway, Takis followed a winding road and pulled up outside a large white building.

"This is the museum," he said. "We can take the car no farther, but you should go this way." He pointed down a sign-posted path. "Take the time you need visiting the ruins. I shall wait for you here."

He got out of the car and opened Dorcas's door. Now that they were miles from the moderating sea breeze and had suddenly lost the benefit of the Mercedes's air conditioning, the afternoon heat hit them in a merciless wave.

"Oh my." Dorcas stepped out of the car, already fanning herself with a brochure she'd found in the door. "This is a lot hotter than I remember."

Quinn joined Dorcas and Gracie on their side of the vehicle. The sun beat down on the parched ground, and from all around, the sound of cicadas filled the air.

"For this week, it has been more hot than usual," Takis said.

Dorcas studied the building in front of them, then gave the winding path a doubtful look. "I believe I'll spend time in the museum while you two explore the ruins. I can meet you inside when you get back."

"Are you sure?" Quinn asked.

"Yes." Dorcas said. "If you've never seen them, visiting the ruins is a must. But since I've visited them before, I'll excuse myself this time."

"Are you still up for it?" he asked Gracie.

"Yes." She could feel perspiration gathering along her hairline, but it wasn't enough to dampen her enthusiasm.

"Okay." He turned back to his aunt. "We won't be long."

"Don't worry," Dorcas said. "There's plenty for me to see inside. And Takis will be here."

"Of course. Of course," Takis said, smiling widely.

Gracie and Quinn waited until Dorcas had entered the museum, then set off down the meandering path that led between two rows of dusty olive trees. After a short distance, they reached a small gate that led up a slight rise, and when they reached the top, they looked out over a vast, open area.

"Whoa." Gracie stopped, the stifling heat momentarily forgotten. "It's so big."

For as far as the eye could see, the ground was littered with stone ruins. Ancient pillars stood in rows, reaching up to the sky, some of them still resting on solid stone bases and others holding up small portions of a roof. Some pillars lay on the ground, still intact but horizontal; others were broken, large chunks separated by a foot or two like a row of broken vertebrae.

Tourists wandered the dirt and gravel paths that wound between the building remains. Patches of grass defined the breaks between structures and gave a splash of color to an ancient, dusty world. Some of the stone blocks were little more than short retaining walls; others formed easily recognizable buildings with elaborate masonry work still visible around the windows and doors. There were circular pedestals and amphitheaters, stone cobbles and arched entrances—it was the footprint of a vibrant city worn down by weather and time.

"Let's get closer," Quinn said.

The nearest path led between two rows of pillars and took them toward a well-preserved wall. A stone arch hung over a break in the wall, creating a wide entrance. Grateful for a few moments of shade, they stepped beneath the arch and followed the passageway until it emerged at one end of a massive outdoor arena. All around them, the ground sloped upward, and in front of them, a long marble slab in the dirt marked the start of a wide oval path barely visible in the short grass.

"It's the Olympic track," Quinn said, his eyes alight. "This is where the athletes competed." He pointed to the arena's steep, sloping sides. "And that's where all the spectators sat."

Sightseers milled around them, their excited voices reminiscent of the crowds that would have filled the arena so long ago. Centuries of history surrounded them, and it was impossible not to feel something, some connection—no matter how tenuous—to the people who'd lived here when the city had been a bustling center.

"It's incredible," Gracie said. She pulled her phone out of her purse and took a couple photos.

"Hey there." A female American voice sounded behind them, and they each swung around. "Let me take a picture for you."

Without waiting for a response, a plump woman wearing a red visor that read *Texas A&M* broke away from a group following an umbrella-toting tour guide and approached them. She extended her hand for Gracie's phone.

"Photos mean so much more when there's people in them, don't ya think?" She backed up a few paces. "Stand right there by the stone marker. That way I can get the whole arena in the background."

Quinn put his arm around Gracie.

"That's it," the woman said. "Get in nice and close."

The camera sounded a few times.

"Thank you," Gracie said.

With a happy smile, the woman lowered the phone. "Absolutely," she said. "When I noticed your boyfriend's Yankees T-shirt, I guessed you were Americans." She lowered her voice a fraction. "And it's so much easier to help out when we speak the same language, isn't it?" She moved closer, and Gracie reached for her phone. "Oh my stars!" With a gasp, she grasped Gracie's hand and turned it so the engagement ring faced her. "That's one beautiful ring." She looked up at Gracie. "Tell me, did you pick it out, or did he?"

Gracie met Quinn's eyes. "He wanted me to have something I liked, so I was there when he bought it, but he didn't really need my help. He knew what to ask for."

The woman patted her hand and released it. "My group's leaving, so I must go, but take it from someone who's on her third husband," she said. "He's a keeper, so don't let him go." Then with a friendly wave, she hurried off to stand beside a timid-looking, gray-haired man at the back of the crowd that was now disappearing through the arena's entrance.

Gracie turned to face Quinn. He was looking slightly uncomfortable, but whether that was because of the temperature or the Texas A&M woman's comments, she couldn't tell. The heat was making the air shimmer behind him, but Gracie's thoughts were on the ring glistening on her finger. "How *did* you know?" she asked. "I wanted to ask you when we were on our way back from the jewelry show, but you seemed so tired I didn't want to bother you. How did you know what kind of ring I wanted?"

"I'm not sure," he said. "I could tell you didn't like the ones the guy had already shown you, and I knew your favorite color was blue. Maybe my subconscious made the transition to sapphires. For some reason, it just felt right."

"It just felt right?"

"Yeah." Quinn took her hand. "And when he took this one out of the tray, I knew. It wasn't so much that it physically fit; it was more that it fit *you*."

Gracie looked down at her hand in his. She'd never experienced anything like the connection she felt to Quinn. Certainly not with Derek, even though they'd known each other far longer. Did Quinn feel it too? Did he understand Mallory the way he did her?

"I . . . I've never asked you what Mallory thinks of our temporary engagement."

"Mallory?" He looked at her in confusion.

"Yes. I doubt she was too happy about Steve's plan."

"She doesn't know about it," he said. "She contacted me the day before I left San Antonio, and I told her I was at a conference in Texas." He shrugged. "She may think I'm still there."

Gracie stared at him. She'd had regular contact with Quinn every day for the last eleven days. Already, she knew that once their time together was over, she would miss that interaction. Even when it had only been by phone, talking to Quinn had been the highlight of her day. What kind of relationship did he have with Mallory if they spoke to each other so infrequently that they didn't even know what city the other was in? But she'd seen Mallory's lipstick on Quinn's lips when he'd arrived at Dorcas's condo, and she knew he was not the type of man to take kissing a woman lightly. It made no sense.

"Gracie," he said. "About me and Mallory. We—" His phone rang.

At first, he looked like he would ignore it. "It could be Steve," she said. She needed this interruption. The only way she could continue to play her part in their short-lived engagement was if she pretended Mallory didn't exist. Knowing more about her and her relationship with Quinn would make that virtually impossible.

Muttering something under his breath, Quinn pulled his phone out of his pocket and glanced at the screen. "It is Steve," he confirmed.

"You'd better take it."

He nodded. "Let's find somewhere a bit quieter, preferably with shade."

💎💎💎

Sometime in the near future, Quinn was going to tell Steve that the timing of his phone calls stank. But it couldn't be now, not with Gracie within earshot and not when he needed to know what his friend had uncovered. He accepted the call and followed Gracie under the arched arena entrance toward three broken pillars that stood beneath the outstretched arms of an old oak tree.

"Hey, Steve," Quinn said.

"Glad I caught you," Steve said. "Where are you now?"

"Olympia."

"Can you talk?"

"Yeah." Quinn checked his surroundings. Most of the tour groups were going directly from the arena to the remains of what looked to be some kind of temple a few hundred yards farther down the dirt path. The small corner of the ruins where he and Gracie stood was quiet.

"Gracie was right," Steve said.

Quinn's heart rate ratcheted up a notch. "Someone broke into the safe?"

Gracie swiveled around to face him, her eyes wide and questioning. He beckoned her closer and moved into the shade of the tallest pillar, making room for her beside him so she could hear Steve's voice.

"Yep. The camera picked up a man approaching the safe at 2:35 p.m. He had some kind of miniature screwdriver in his hand that he used to pop off the *Bohman* plaque on the door."

"Is that the name of the company that made the safe?"

"Yeah. And apparently, underneath their company plaque, they always have a small keyhole designed as a backdoor entry. The tumblers have to be rotated to the left and to the right, but for someone who has the right tool and knows what he's doing, it takes a matter of seconds."

"And this guy did."

"Oh yeah. He pulled a thick wire out of his pocket and had the door open in no time."

"Could you see what he did once the safe was open?" Quinn asked.

"He took out the brooch and took several photos of it, then he replaced it and did the same with the ring."

"So Gracie really nailed this operation," Quinn said. "They're using photos to make a mold."

"It sure looks that way," Steve said. "We've IDed the guy in the video. His name's Vlasis Galatas, and he's the man Gracie spotted at the jewelry show and later onboard ship. So far, all we have on him is that he grew up in Athens and had a run-in with the Hellenic police when he was a teenager. He was booked for petty theft. Since then, he's kept his record clean and has been working for the Greek Cruise Line on and off for six years."

"On and off?"

"Apparently, he worked four years straight, then put himself on the temp list," Steve said. "He came onboard in Venice to cover for a crew member who had a sudden family emergency."

Quinn's suspicions rose. "Was the emergency legitimate?"

"We're checking on that," Steve said. "Along with digging into what Vlasis does with his time when he's not working a cruise."

Quinn took a deep breath. "So what's next?"

"We keep with the plan," Steve said. "We have enough on this guy to book him, but if we do that now, it'll alert whoever's behind this. And to be honest, that's the person we want. We still don't know who received the photos. We're looking into all transmissions from the ship yesterday afternoon, but it will take awhile to sort through them since we don't know exactly what method Vlasis used to send his." He paused. "I'm banking on something happening once you arrive in Athens—either at Nikos's place or onboard ship afterward. Until then, it's a waiting and watching game."

Waiting and watching weren't exactly Quinn's top pick of activities for the next two days, but he recognized that he had little choice. "Okay," he said. "Let us know if there's anything new on your end, and we'll do the same."

"Will do," Steve said. "And tell Gracie thanks. If she ever wants a career change, she should consider law enforcement. The FBI could use someone with her observation skills."

Beside him, Gracie shifted slightly, but she didn't say anything.

"Thanks for the call, Steve."

"Yep. I'll be in touch."

Quinn lowered his phone. "You heard all that?" he asked.

Gracie nodded. "More waiting and watching," she said with a grimace.

"Yeah. That's about how I feel about it too." He put his phone in his pocket. "But on the flip side, it means we get to play being carefree sightseers for another day."

"That definitely sounds better," Gracie said. She moved out from the protection of the pillar's shadow and put her hand up to shade her eyes from the unrelenting sun. "How about we get out of this heat and head to the museum so we can act like tourists there instead?"

Quinn stepped off the large stone slab and onto the path. "Any suggestion that involves air conditioning or a cold drink has my vote," he said. "Let's go."

CHAPTER 18

Two days later, Gracie sat alone on her stateroom balcony and watched as the ship approached the port of Piraeus. Early-morning mist hung over the water, adding a gray hue to an already drab scene. Piraeus was an industrial terminal, a convenient link between the Greek capital and the sea but very different from the picturesque stops they'd experienced over the last two days, first in Katakolon and then in Corfu.

The pictures she'd taken at those stunning locations hadn't done them justice. She'd been fascinated by the artifacts on display at the museum in Olympia and had loaded her camera with photos of the statues, pottery, coins, and jewelry. Already, ideas of how she could incorporate the ancient art into designs of her own were filling her sketchbook.

Their visit to Corfu the next day had been a kaleidoscope of color. Cobbled streets, small shops with local merchandise spilling out onto the narrow thoroughfares, baskets of fruits, vegetables, and fresh-cut flowers at every turn, and the ancient fortress standing sentinel on the hill above the brilliant blue water of the Mediterranean. Meandering through the old town had been a delightful way to spend the day. She'd even picked up a few souvenirs.

But overlying all their activities was the uncertainty of what lay ahead. As nervous as she was to visit Nikos's jewelry shop in Athens today, Gracie was ready to put the waiting and watching behind her.

A horn sounded, muffled by the mist, and Gracie recognized the change in vibration and pitch of the ship's engines as the vessel slipped into its assigned berth. She heard shouts from the dock and answering cries from the crew somewhere below her. They had arrived.

Sliding open the french windows, Gracie left the balcony and entered her cabin. It would take at least an hour before passengers would be allowed to disembark, which meant she had time for breakfast before they headed to the city. She knew she should eat. She just wasn't sure if she could stomach anything.

On the coffee table, her phone buzzed. It was a text from Quinn. *I'm going for breakfast. Want to join me? Dorcas is having something delivered to her room.*

She picked up the phone and sent a reply. *Don't think I can eat right now.*

Pacing around the buffet tables will be more entertaining than pacing alone in your cabin.

It was disconcerting that Quinn could read her so well, but she knew he was right. Being among people who had nothing more to worry about than catching the train to the Acropolis would be good for her. *I'll meet you at the buffet doors in 5 mins,* she texted back.

Gracie walked briskly to the elevators. Neither she nor Quinn had seen any sign of Vlasis since their encounter at the gym, and now that Steve had confirmed her suspicions about the man, she hoped she could avoid running into him again—particularly on her own. Grateful when a family of four entered the elevator with her, she pushed the button for the lower floor, and the elevator sped downward to the buffet restaurant.

She spotted Quinn as soon as the elevator doors opened. He was standing near the opposite wall, watching people come and go through the busy lobby. As soon as he saw her, he stepped forward and smiled.

"Hey," he said, reaching out and putting his hand on her shoulder. "You look amazing, but how are you feeling?"

Gracie put on a brave face. "Fine." She'd hoped that wearing her favorite summer dress and taking the time to style her long hair would help bolster her confidence, but it didn't seem to be working.

"Pretty sure a cup of hot chocolate will help," he said, taking her cold hand. "If only to warm you up."

"Sorry," Gracie said. "My hands always give me away."

Quinn gave her an understanding smile. "Come on."

They walked into the restaurant. Tables and chairs lined both sides of the ship, and people were loading plates with food around the oval buffet islands running down the middle of the room.

"Here's a table," Quinn said, snagging a small one near a window just as an elderly couple got up to leave. "Why don't you sit here to save the spot, and I'll go get you a hot chocolate."

"You don't need to . . ." Gracie began, but he'd already disappeared.

Not wanting to risk losing the table to one of the other people circling the restaurant in search of seating, she stayed in her chair and watched the passengers milling around the serving tables. Across the room, she spotted Paolo and Manuel waiting in line for a made-to-order omelet, but before either of them noticed her, Quinn returned carrying a mug full of frothy hot chocolate and a small plate of pastries.

"I figured I couldn't go too far wrong with fresh croissants," he said, putting the plate down in front of her and handing her the mug.

"Thank you," Gracie said.

"No problem. You get started on those, and I'll be back in a couple minutes."

Gracie wrapped her hands around the mug. The heat was soothing. She took a sip. The drink was soothing too. With a sigh, Gracie leaned back in her chair, and for the first time since she'd woken up, she allowed herself to relax.

"*Buongiorno*, Gracie."

Startled, Gracie looked up to see Manuel smiling at her. "Good morning," she said.

"You are here by yourself?" he asked.

"No." Gracie mentally willed Quinn to hurry back. "Quinn's here."

She saw the flash of disappointment in his eyes. "Ah yes, the fiancé."

"That's right." Not sure what else to say, Gracie raised the cup of hot chocolate to her mouth and took another sip. Instantly, Manuel's gaze moved from her face to her hands, and the moment he saw her ring, his expression changed.

"Your ring," he said. "May I see?" He reached out his hand. Unwilling to take the ring off, Gracie extended her arm to him. He held her fingers and studied the jewels.

"*Molto bello*," he said, his voice almost reverent.

"Good morning, Manuel."

Manuel instantly released his hold and turned to face Quinn. "And to you," he said as Quinn took the seat across from Gracie. Manuel gave Gracie's ring a final glance before giving Quinn a nod of reluctant approval. "I hope you shall both have a good day today."

Quinn waited until Manuel was out of earshot. "What did he want?"

"I'm not sure," Gracie said. "At first I thought he was just saying hello, but then he wanted to see my ring."

Quinn watched the Italian disappear into the crowd. "Let's hope all he was doing was admiring it," he said.

◇◇◇

Quinn sat beside the taxi driver as he navigated the outskirts of Athens. This part of the city was run down. The gray concrete walls were covered with graffiti, and bars hung across many doors and windows. It had an atmosphere of neglect, and only the Greek lettering on the signage set it apart from too many other inner cities.

Behind him, Gracie and Dorcas sat watching the streets go by through the taxi windows. Dorcas was unusually quiet, but she wore a look of determination. Gracie still seemed paler than usual, but she'd finished her hot chocolate and one of the croissants, and her hands were no longer as cold as they'd been when she'd met him for breakfast, nor were they shaking the way they'd been at the entrance to the Venetian Jewelry Show. He knew that despite her nervousness, she'd play her part perfectly once they arrived at Nikos's place.

"Ermou Street," the taxi driver said. "They will not allow vehicles to go, but I can stop here."

Quinn studied the road at his right. They'd driven into Athens's shopping district, and the atmosphere here was very different from the one they'd just passed through. The stores lined up on either side of the cobblestoned street were bright and cheery. There was an eclectic mixture of big-name department stores and small, exclusive shops, but they all radiated affluence.

"This is perfect," Dorcas said from the back. "We can walk from here."

With a pleased grunt, the driver got out of his car and opened the door for the women. Quinn let himself out and reached the other side of the vehicle in time to see Dorcas hand the driver a generous wad of euros.

"Good day to you," the driver said. Then with a cheerful salute, he got back into the taxi and drove away.

Dorcas led Quinn and Gracie onto the pedestrian-only street. Large, colorful signs vied for the attention of the many shoppers who were toting their purchases in glossy carrier bags. The aura of wealth was a stark juxtaposition to the sense of hardship only a few streets away, and Quinn found himself uncomfortable with the disparity.

"Athens is a city of contrasts," Dorcas said as though she'd read his mind. "New concrete structures built around ancient ruins; economically depressed citizens living a mile from one of the most expensive shopping streets in the world."

"Can anything be done for the poorer areas?" Gracie asked. "To help the people living there?"

Dorcas shrugged. "I wish there were an easy solution, but the Greek government is in turmoil, and until that's resolved, not much can be fixed."

Quinn reflected on his conversation with the taxi driver in Olympia. Takis had bemoaned the Greek economy for at least half their journey. Now that Quinn had set foot in Athens, he thought he understood the Greek's grievances a little better.

Dorcas pointed down the street. "Look. Nikos's shop is next to Berto Lucci."

Even though Steve had sent Quinn a text this morning to tell him Nikos's jewelry shop would be under surveillance for twenty-four hours, Quinn found himself scanning the passersby, looking for a familiar face or someone who might have unusual interest in Dorcas and Gracie. No one appeared to give them any extra attention, however, and within minutes, they were standing outside a small storefront squeezed between two upscale retail giants.

It was one of the older buildings on the street. The walls were of cream stone worn smooth over the years. Gold lettering on a black sign above the solid wood door read Nikos Andonious Gold. In a slightly smaller font, the title was repeated beneath in Greek. There were two windows, each one showcasing half a dozen pieces of jewelry that had been placed on uneven blocks draped by black velvet and highlighted by individual spotlights.

Gracie immediately stepped up to the closest window and studied the display.

"Were these all made by Nikos?" she asked Dorcas.

"I believe so," Dorcas said. "I don't think he sells anything that's not original."

"What do you think?" Quinn asked.

"They're amazing." There was a hint of awe in her voice. "His workmanship is good, but his designs are incredible."

Dorcas gave a pleased smile. "I'm happy you think so," she said. "That's what Alessandro believed too." She pushed open the door, and somewhere in the back, a bell rang. "Let me introduce you to the master craftsman."

Quinn reached for Gracie's hand, glad that this time it was warm and tremor-free. "I've lost track of how many acts and scenes we've done together, but how about we call this, Act II scene I?" he whispered.

"Sounds good." she replied. Then with a half smile, she added, "We've got this, right?"

He squeezed her hand. "Absolutely."

The shop's showroom was lined on either side with glass cases. Tracking lights ran the length of the room, strategically angled to draw customers' eyes to the glittering jewelry beneath the glass. Framed pictures of necklaces, bracelets, and rings designed by Nikos decorated the walls, and an exotic Persian rug covered the central portion of the marble flooring.

As they walked in, a short man with a corona of silver hair around his otherwise bald head entered from the back room. "Dorcas," he said. "I have been watching the calendar, wondering if you would come. I was beginning to worry that you had chosen to forgo your visit with this old friend."

"Of course not," Dorcas said, accepting his kisses on her cheeks. "Visiting you is always one of the highlights of my time in Greece."

Nikos waved away her compliment. "Ah, you flatter me." He peered curiously at Quinn and Gracie through his thick-lensed glasses. "But tell me, who is it that you have brought to see me?"

Dorcas stepped aside. "Nikos, this is my nephew, Quinn West, and his fiancée, Gracie Miller. Quinn and Gracie, this is Nikos Andonious, one of the best jewelers in Europe—maybe the world."

Nikos rolled his eyes. "Psht. Always the compliments. Do not listen to her. I love my work, and I have been blessed with success in this crazy business, but believe me, I recognize a true craftsman's work when I see it." He pointed at Gracie's hand. "May I?"

She nodded, slipped the ring off her finger, and handed it to Nikos. Quinn stepped closer. He watched as Nikos studied the ring, turning it slowly under the nearest light before drawing a loupe from his pocket and placing it up against his glasses to study the ring in more detail.

"Who?" Nikos asked.

"Louis Barnard," Gracie said.

Nikos nodded, a knowing smile exposing his yellowing teeth. "If I had been asked to guess, I would have said either Louis Barnard or Etienne Perot. No one can equal them in style or quality of stones." He offered her the ring. "You are most fortunate, Gracie. A woman would have to be dearly loved to be given such a treasure."

A slight blush tinged Gracie's cheeks, and Quinn placed his hand on her back. "I am the fortunate one," he said.

Nikos chuckled. "I cannot disagree," he said. "You are undoubtedly the envy of many men." He turned back to Dorcas. "And you, my dear friend, show me what you found at the jewelry show."

Dorcas unpinned her brooch and handed it to Nikos.

He took it in his calloused fingers and studied it under his loupe. "Beautiful," he murmured. "Truly beautiful." He raised his eyes to Dorcas's. "And this one? Is it also Louis Bernard's?"

"No." Dorcas smiled. "But you are close. It's from Etienne Perot."

"Ah." He shook his head in disgust. "I should have known." He turned the brooch over and ran his work-worn finger along the platinum stem. "You see, Etienne always leaves his mark." He handed Dorcas his loupe. "Look at the tip of the stem."

Dorcas put the loupe to her eye and raised the brooch. "There's a tiny *E P* etched into the platinum." She looked up in astonishment. "How did he do that?"

"He uses a laser," Nikos said. "It is his way of certifying his work."

"Why would he not advertise something like that?" Gracie said. It was obvious from her puzzled expression that she'd never heard of it before.

Nikos shrugged. "Those he trusts in this business know. Those he does not trust are best left in the dark. A laser mark quickly loses its authority if it is easily copied."

Quinn forced himself to keep his breathing even. Would a thief speak this openly about the possibility of forgeries—especially if he were speaking with a potential target? Or was Nikos simply proving that he knew enough to make an exact replica?

"That's remarkable," Dorcas said. "I'm glad you showed me. I will keep Etienne's secret."

"As I knew you would," Nikos said.

The sound of the back-room door swinging open caused them all to look up. A dark-eyed young man with brown hair gelled into a trendy casual style stood at the doorway. He wore a leather apron over his T-shirt and jeans, and even from this distance Quinn could see that the tips of his fingers were stained gray.

"Damien," Nikos said. "Dorcas has come to visit. Come meet her nephew, Quinn, and his fiancée, Gracie."

The young man stepped forward, his lithe movement at odds with his solid build. "Welcome back, Dorcas," he said. He kissed her cheeks and shook Quinn's hand. Then he turned his attention to Gracie. Quinn watched with irritation as Damien gave her a head-to-toe appraisal, followed by an appreciative smile. "And welcome to your guests also."

"Thank you, Damien," Dorcas said. "I did not see you in Venice this time."

"No. I was needed here," he said vaguely.

"Damien has been working on an order from the queen," Nikos said. "She wishes to wear a new necklace for the king's speech to parliament next week." His aging eyes sparkled with excitement. "But as you shall not be here on that day, you may see it before anyone else. Bring it out, would you, Damien?"

Damien obediently disappeared through the back-room door and reappeared moments later carrying a thick, sparkling chain littered with diamonds. He set it on top of one of the glass cases.

"I am still mounting the gems," he said. "But you can see the traditional Hellenic pattern in the metalwork."

The jeweler's calloused and stained fingers suddenly made sense. To mold precious metal into a necklace so delicate and so intricate would take hours of painstaking effort, not to mention the refining and polishing required afterward.

"It's stunning," Dorcas said.

Gracie ran her fingers over the box-like links. "It reminds me of some of the jewelry in the museum at Olympia," she said.

"Well done," Nikos said, obviously impressed. "I modified an ancient pattern found on the Temple of Heres at Olympia. The queen will have something completely new that is closely connected to the past."

"I'm sure she will love it," Gracie said.

"Damien has worked long into the night for two weeks to finish it in time," Nikos said. "I still do the design work, but he has taken over the production of all our pieces."

"Which means I do all the hard work, and he gets the credit," Damien said, wiggling his eyebrows at Gracie.

Quinn sensed Gracie bristle and worked to hide his smile. If there was anything Damien could have said that would have been less well received by Gracie the jewelry designer, Quinn couldn't think of it. And he wasn't about to help the self-assured idiot out of the hole he'd stepped into either. "I wonder if that's how the people who work on Louis Bernard's and Etienne Perot's designs feel too?" he said.

For a split second, Damien looked uncomfortable, but his ego quickly came to his rescue. "I imagine it is. After all, without them, those designers would have nothing to show or to sell."

Whether Nikos sensed the negative undercurrents and intentionally threw his son a lifeline, Quinn wasn't sure, but the older man seized on Quinn's mention of the famous designers and brought the topic back to the primary reason for their visit. "You must see the jewelry Dorcas and Gracie purchased at the Venetian show, Damien," he said.

"Of course," Damien said. "That is why I am here."

"First, Gracie's ring." Nikos took the ring from Gracie again and handed it to his son. Damien studied it carefully under Nikos's loupe. Nodding with approval, he offered it back to her.

"A beautifully made ring," he said.

"Thank you." Gracie slipped it onto her finger, and Dorcas gave him her brooch.

Damien set the brooch on the palm of his hand and gently bounced it in his hand as though gauging the piece's weight and balance. Then he put the loupe to his eye and moved it slowly over the entire piece, front and back. When he was finished, he looked up, his expression pleased. "It is exquisite," he said.

"It is, isn't it?" Dorcas said. "The design is unique, and the gems are so bright and cheery."

"You wear it well," Nikos said. "Alessandro would be proud."

Sadness filled her eyes. "I miss him every day, but being in Greece without him is especially hard."

Nikos patted her hand. "I am sure he is happy that you continue to visit, even though it is difficult for you. He loved his homeland."

"Yes. Yes, he did." Dorcas managed a wobbly smile. "And I should share more of it with Quinn and Gracie. They cannot return to the ship without seeing The Acropolis."

"That would be unthinkable," Nikos said. "You must go now, before the day gets any hotter." He waited while Dorcas pinned her brooch back onto her silk scarf, then he kissed her cheeks. "I am glad you came today, and I shall watch for your return before too many months go by."

"Thank you, Nikos," Dorcas said. "It's always a pleasure."

CHAPTER 19

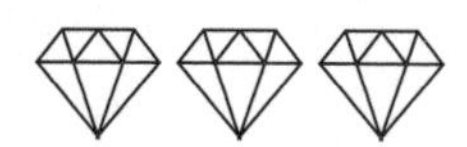

"It doesn't make any sense," Gracie said.

She, Quinn, and Dorcas were standing between the soaring pillars of the Parthenon with a breathtaking view of the city of Athens spread below them, but she couldn't fully appreciate it. Her thoughts remained on their experience in Nikos's jewelry shop.

"Nikos is obviously fond of Dorcas. The Queen of Greece has commissioned his work, so he's not looking for prestige. He owns a storefront on one of the ritziest streets in Europe, so he's not needing money." She frowned. "I just don't see what his motivation would be for stealing or making copies of another designer's work. His own designs are too good."

Quinn ran his fingers through his hair. Perspiration glistened on his forehead. "What about Damien?" he said.

She shrugged. "Remember when I told you the workmanship at Nikos's place is good but the designs are better? I stand by that."

Quinn raised one eyebrow, and his lips quirked upward. "You wouldn't be harboring any bad feelings about Damien's opinion of the worth of the designer, would you?"

Gracie glowered at him, and he laughed.

"But wouldn't his father's financing and prestige be enough to take Damien where he wants to go?" Dorcas asked. "Surely he wouldn't do anything that might put that in jeopardy."

"I don't know," Gracie said. "I guess he could be doing it for the power rush."

"Or he and his father may not be involved at all," Quinn said, the frustration in his voice an echo of Gracie's feelings. "I feel like we're groping around in the dark, looking for clues that might not even be there."

"What did Steve say when you called him?" Dorcas asked.

As soon as they'd walked far enough to be out of sight of Nikos's shop, Quinn had called his friend. Having placed himself on surveillance duty on Ermou Street, Steve had known exactly where they were and how long they'd been with the jewelers. What he didn't know, however, was what had happened while they'd been inside.

"He said he'd meet us at The Acropolis as soon as a colleague from Greek law enforcement got there to spell him. It was supposed to be within the hour."

Even though she was wearing sunglasses, Gracie shaded her eyes and scanned the ruins. Somehow, despite the deterioration brought on by age, the ancient structures remained majestic and reflected the sunlight with almost as much brilliance as did the white marble littering the ground.

Tourists wandered between the soaring pillars, lingering in the narrow slivers of shade, and over by the Temple of Athena Nike, she noticed a man break away from a tour group gathered around a woman holding a red flag. The man wore brown pants, a plaid short-sleeved shirt, and a gray bucket hat. Sunglasses obscured his face, but as he walked toward them, his long-limbed gait seemed familiar.

"Is that Steve coming this way?" she asked.

Quinn swung around. "That's him," he said with a grin. "I'd recognize that ugly hat anywhere. It used to be his grandpa's, and because he's colorblind, he thinks it matches everything he wears." Quinn stepped out into the sunlight and waited for Steve to reach him.

"Why haven't you melted already?" Steve said, not stopping until he reached the shade Quinn had vacated. He took off his sunglasses and wiped his glistening forehead with his sleeve. "This heat puts East Coast summers to shame."

"Good to see you too, Steve," Quinn said.

Steve looked momentarily sheepish. "Sorry. Blazing sun and I don't get along. And the Greek guy taking over surveillance at Nikos's place was late."

Gracie reached into her purse and pulled out a water bottle. "Here," she said. "Take a drink and see if it helps."

He accepted it gratefully and took a long swig. "Thanks," he said, offering her the bottle back. "I didn't take the time to go get mine from the car because I was running behind."

As she took the bottle from him, he twisted it so he had a better view of her fingers. Then he gave a low whistle. "Wow, you guys really know how to choose a ring."

"Yeah. That's what Nikos and Damien thought too," Quinn said dryly.

"I bet they did." Curiosity flickered in Steve's eyes. "How did they respond when you got there?"

Quinn gave him a detailed rundown of their experience at the jeweler's shop. Steve listened carefully, and when Quinn had finished, he shook his head, his expression troubled. "We're missing something," he said. "Something big."

"Like a motive?" Quinn said.

Steve frowned. "I don't think we're seeing the whole picture." He started to pace. "We've got Vlasis onboard ship supplying Nikos Antoniou Gold with photos of Dorcas's jewelry."

"Wait," Quinn said. "Do you know that for sure?"

"I got the report while you were in the shop," he said. "One of the computer guys from my office in Philly tracked an email sent from the *Fantasia* two days ago to a computer registered to *Nikos Antoniou Gold*. The email had an attachment that contained multiple photographs."

Dorcas gave a soft moan. "Why?" she said. "I don't understand."

Quinn stepped closer and put his arm around his aunt, giving her shoulder a comforting squeeze.

"That's just it, Dorcas," Steve said. "Why? If we can figure that out, I'm pretty sure everything else will fall into place." He resumed his pacing. "If Damien's our man and he's been working on making a forgery of Dorcas's brooch while his dad thinks he's been working on the queen's necklace, your visit today enabled him to compare his brooch with the real thing."

"He took more time examining the brooch than he did the ring," Gracie said. "At first I wondered if it was because the brooch is more intricate, but he seemed to be gauging its weight too."

Steve pondered that for a moment. "Then I think it's fairly safe to assume that he still has the forgery. He'll use this opportunity to make any necessary tweaks to his counterfeit, but he's going to have to work fast. They have to be traded out within the next forty-eight hours."

"Do you think he'll hand it off to Vlasis to make the trade?" Quinn asked.

Steve raised the front of his bucket hat and scratched his head. "That's the obvious answer," he said. "I have a guy watching the dock for any sign of Vlasis leaving the ship, but with limited manpower, we can't monitor all the supplies being loaded onboard right now. It's simpler for us to watch the shop for Vlasis or anyone who might be acting as his courier."

"But you're not convinced that's how it's going to happen," Quinn said.

Steve sighed. "It's never that easy," he said. "Something's off. I just can't put my finger on it."

"Is it possible there's another player?" Gracie asked. "Someone else who's orchestrating everything from a distance?"

The men looked at her.

"Keep talking," Steve said.

Suddenly feeling awkward, Gracie shrugged. "Maybe I'm underestimating his abilities," she said, "but even if Damien's dishonest enough to steal, he doesn't strike me as a mastermind. I honestly wonder if he's capable of coordinating a scheme as elaborate as this one.

"As far as we can tell, the thefts have occurred within a tiny window of time over multiple years. That would take meticulous planning, along with knowing pretty much everything about Dorcas's life—her schedule, her habits, her friends, and so on. I can't see Damien putting in that kind of research."

"Even if it nets him hundreds of thousands of dollars in stolen jewelry?" Steve said. "He undoubtedly has the skills to redo any piece and sell the gems and precious metal as something completely different."

"So help me, if he's melted down my jewelry . . ." Dorcas's dismay was giving way to anger.

Gracie wished that she could reassure Dorcas. The truth was the worth of her pieces would drop considerably if they'd been reworked—especially the ones from top designers. But realistically, no thief would risk trying to resell them as is. They were too recognizable.

"I'll have a tail put on Damien," Steve said. "We'll monitor the store for twenty-four hours after your ship sails, but we'll also keep track of where Damien goes and who he meets. There's going to be a handoff sometime soon, and if we catch it, the bigger picture may open up."

"And in the meantime Dorcas, Gracie, and I continue to act like nothing is wrong," Quinn guessed.

"Yes. That's critical," Steve said. "Make sure the jewelry's in the safe long enough to facilitate a trade if that's their plan, but monitor it even more carefully than before." He frowned. "I'm going to do some more digging into Damien's associates. If Gracie's right and there's someone else pulling the strings, we're not missing a piece of the puzzle; we're missing a massive chunk."

💎💎💎

Quinn knocked on the door of Dorcas's stateroom. It had been five hours since Steve had left him, Gracie, and Dorcas at The Acropolis. Not long afterward, Quinn had suggested that they head back to the cruise ship, and neither woman had objected. The heat had been so enervating and their lack of leads on the missing jewelry so discouraging, they were all ready to put Athens behind them.

They'd stopped at the bottom of the hill beneath the ancient citadel to buy gyros and carbonated orange juice from a street vendor. That simple taste of Greece had helped restore their flagging spirits, and Dorcas had instructed the taxi driver to take an indirect route back to the dock so Quinn and Gracie could see The Temple of Zeus and The Agora before they left.

Once they'd arrived at the waiting ship, however, his aunt had announced that she was going to take a much needed nap, and when Gracie then suggested that she'd be happy to do some quiet reading on the balcony of her stateroom, Quinn had seized the opportunity to return to his cabin to catch up on some work. It had been good for him to do something completely unrelated to Steve's investigation, and he hoped that both Dorcas and Gracie had benefited from the break.

The door to Dorcas's cabin opened, and his aunt stood in front of him dressed in a pink dress edged with embroidered daisies. She smiled, and he was relieved to see the sparkle back in her eyes.

"Come in, Quinn," she said, "You're just in time."

He entered the room, and she closed the door behind him. Gracie rose from the sofa. She'd changed into a pair of black pants and a cream-colored top that shimmered as she moved. Quinn was struck once again by her simple elegance.

"Hi, Quinn," she said. "We thought it might be best if we put the jewelry in the safe before we leave our cabins for the evening."

He thought it was a great idea for Dorcas to leave her brooch behind for a few hours, especially as her dress didn't need any further decoration, but thinking about Gracie going out without the engagement ring was considerably less appealing.

"Uh, sure," he said, knowing he had no choice. Both pieces needed to be put away together. He could only hope they didn't encounter Paolo or Manuel at dinner.

"I'll go open the safe," Dorcas said.

He and Gracie followed Dorcas into the bedroom, where she inputted the code and opened the safe. Dorcas handed Gracie the ring box, and Gracie slid the ring off her finger and put it inside. Then she gave it back to Dorcas, who set it right next to her brooch box.

"Go ahead and take a picture, Quinn," Dorcas said.

Quinn stepped around his aunt, pulled his phone from his pocket, and took a photo of the placement of the boxes. "Okay," he said. "We'll check them in a few hours."

After shutting the safe and ensuring that it was locked, Dorcas reached for the copy of the ship's daily itinerary on the dresser and handed it to him. "Have you decided what you'd like to do tonight?" she asked.

Quinn had spared a brief glance at the piece of paper that had been slid under his door, but he couldn't remember anything more than their arrival time in Piraeus. "Not really," he said.

"We've been invited to a cocktail hour with the captain, followed by dinner."

Quinn's heart sank. Cocktail hours were invariably a torturous mixture of small talk, bragging, and loud laughter made all the more uncomfortable because he didn't drink alcohol. "I accepted the invitation for myself," Dorcas continued. "It's expected that I attend, and I won't risk offending Captain Anastas. But I thought you and Gracie might prefer to do something else."

Hope for a reprieve flared. "What do you think, Gracie?" he asked.

"Right before you got here, Dorcas was telling me about tonight's variety show," she said. "It sounds like it might be fun."

"The cruise line hires singers, dancers, acrobats, and jugglers from all over the world," Dorcas said. "I've never seen the same show twice, but they're always entertaining."

"What time does it start?" he asked.

"They perform twice," Dorcas said. "There's an early show and a late show, so you can work dinner around either one."

Spending the evening with Gracie at dinner and a show sounded infinitely better than attending a cocktail hour with the captain and the other VIPs onboard, and Quinn suddenly wanted it very badly. "Would you go to the show and dinner with me, Gracie?" he asked.

She gave him a shy smile. "If Dorcas really doesn't mind going to the cocktail hour alone, I'd love to," she said.

"Goodness," Dorcas said. "I've monopolized your time all week, and I've been going to these things alone ever since Alessandro passed away. I'll be fine."

Quinn checked the times typed on the paper. "The first show starts in fifteen minutes," he said. "Do you want to do that, then go to dinner afterward, or are you too hungry to wait that long?"

"Let's go to the show first," Gracie said.

"Excellent," Dorcas said, already shooing them toward the door. "But you'd better hurry. It will take you almost that long to reach the theater."

Quinn leaned down and kissed his aunt's cheek. "Thanks, Dorcas," he said. "We'll meet you back here later."

The theater was at the other end of the ship and several decks down, and by the time Quinn and Gracie got there, it was nearly full. They found two seats on the mezzanine and sat down to wait. Three rows ahead of them, Quinn recognized the Spanish family who'd shared their table their first evening onboard ship. Angelo was sitting between his parents, wiggling with excitement, and when he turned to watch some latecomers arrive, he spotted Gracie sitting behind him. He tugged on his mother's sleeve, whispered something in her ear, and pointed at them. Maria turned and smiled; Angelo bounced up and down, waving furiously.

Grace smiled and waved in return.

"Our first official date, and I'm still competing with the other men in your life," Quinn teased.

She looked up at him with wide eyes. "*Is* this our first official date?"

"Well, I asked, you said yes, and we don't have my aunt chaperoning." He shrugged. "I think it might qualify."

She smiled then, and Quinn felt his heart stutter. But before either of them could say anything more, the lights dimmed, there was a drumroll, and a bright spotlight followed the cruise director onto the center of the stage. As the woman began her welcoming spiel in multiple languages, Quinn slid his arm around Gracie's shoulders. When she leaned her head against him and he caught the faint hint of her perfume, everything else faded into insignificance. For the moment, nothing mattered but being there with her.

💎💎💎

As Gracie and Quinn approached Dorcas's stateroom, Gracie's footsteps seemed to slow of their own accord. She didn't want the magical evening to end. The talent on display at the variety show had been impressive. She and Quinn had alternately gasped at the acrobats' daring, laughed at the comedians' routines, and cheered at the musicians' abilities. Then, when the performance was over, they'd eaten a delicious meal at the ship's French restaurant, L'Etoile.

The maître d' had managed to find them a small table for two tucked away in a quiet corner of the restaurant, and even though they'd talked for almost two hours, not once had they mentioned jewels, thieves, Mallory, or returning to real life. It had been a wonderful break from the pressure they'd been under, but Gracie knew that the moment they knocked on Dorcas's door, reality would return.

Quinn reached the stateroom and stood unmoving. "I had a good time tonight," he said.

"I did too." She offered him a small smile. "Thanks for asking me."

He took a step closer, his gaze not leaving hers. "Thanks for saying yes."

Behind him, the doorknob clicked. Quinn spun around, and Gracie shut her eyes and took an uneven breath.

"I thought I heard voices," Dorcas said, opening the door wide. "Come on in. How was the show?"

"Great," Quinn said, his enthusiasm sounding rather forced. "How was your evening?" He entered Dorcas's stateroom, and Gracie took two more calming breaths before following him inside.

"It was fine," Dorcas said. "The moussaka was very good, but otherwise, you didn't miss much." She led them to the safe and started inputting the code.

Wondering if she would ever again watch someone access the contents of a safe without her stress increasing, Gracie moved to stand beside Quinn. As though sensing her apprehension, he curled his fingers around hers, and as the door of the safe opened, he gave her fingers a reassuring squeeze.

"What do you think?" he said.

Gracie looked at the boxes lying side by side in the safe. "They don't look like they've been moved," she said.

"I agree."

Gracie dug through her purse and took out her loupe. "I can check them."

One by one, Dorcas passed her the jewelry, and within seconds, Gracie gave them her verdict.

"They're both fine," she said.

With a sigh that was one part relief and the other part frustration, the older woman put both pieces back in their respective boxes.

"I'll leave them in here until tomorrow morning," she said. "We'll want to wear them when we visit Theo."

"What are our plans tomorrow?" Quinn asked.

Dorcas locked the safe and turned to face him. "The ship will be anchored in Santorini Bay by the time we wake up in the morning," she said. "Most passengers will be transported by tender to the base of the cliffs, where they'll take a cable car, donkey, or walk 588 steps up to the town of Fira."

"Please tell me we're not doing the donkeys," Quinn said.

Gracie took one look at his alarmed expression and couldn't suppress a giggle.

Dorcas rolled her eyes. "No, dear. We're not even taking the tender." She patted his arm. "Theo will send his speedboat to pick us up as soon as the tenders have left. It will only take us about twelve minutes to reach Oia, and we'll spend the day there at Theo's house. The cruise ship isn't scheduled to leave the bay until after dark, so Theo will bring us back here soon after sunset."

"Isn't that cutting it a bit close?" Quinn asked.

Dorcas gave him a long-suffering look. "No one goes all the way to Santorini and misses seeing the sunset."

"Okay." Quinn accepted her reprimand good-naturedly. "What else should I know about this place?"

"The town is stunning. It's built on the side of a volcanic caldera," Dorcas said, "so be prepared for a lot of stairs. Oh, and don't forget your swimsuit."

"My swimsuit?"

Dorcas chuckled at his puzzled expression. "Yes. We all need to take one. I promise, you'll thank me."

Feeling as mystified as Quinn looked, Gracie put her loupe back into its case and dropped it into her purse.

"What time do we need to be ready to leave?" she asked.

"Our ride should be here about 10:00 a.m." Dorcas thought for a moment. "If we open the safe together at about nine, that will give us plenty of time to get down to the exit portal before it arrives."

"Sounds good," Quinn said. He glanced at the time on his phone. "It's getting late; I should go."

He started for the door and regret stabbed at Gracie. This abrupt, emotionless ending to their evening together was undoubtedly for the best, but it was not what she wanted.

"Thanks again, Quinn," she said, crossing the room and meeting him at the door.

For a split second, it seemed that he was going to reach for her, then he appeared to change his mind and grasped the doorknob instead. "We'll do it again," he promised.

She nodded and swallowed the lump in her throat. With only two more days before they headed home, it was very unlikely that they would have another evening alone.

CHAPTER 20

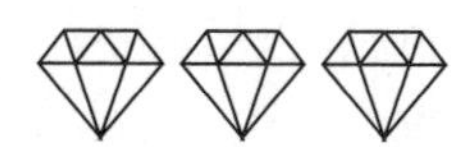

GRACIE STOOD AT THE OPEN portal and watched the final tender pull away from the side of the cruise ship with the last load of passengers headed for Fira. About twenty yards away, a sleek white speedboat with red and gray trim idled in place. As soon as the tender's wake subsided, the speedboat moved forward until it was adjacent to the portal. There was a slight bump as it grazed the rubber cushions that had been placed against the ship's hull, and one of *Fantasia*'s crewmen lowered a short gangplank onto its deck.

"Are you ready, Mrs. Katsaros?" A second crewman who was standing at the edge of the portal offered Dorcas his hand.

"Yes. Thank you." Dorcas took his hand and allowed him to help her onto the gangplank. She took three slow steps before reaching for the extended hand of another young man waiting on the speedboat.

As soon as Dorcas was safely onboard, Gracie stepped onto the gangplank. Keeping her eyes on the speedboat's deck and off the ocean water below, she crossed quickly. Quinn was right behind her, and as soon as he was off the gangplank, the crewman raised it and yelled something in Greek. The driver of the speedboat gave him an acknowledging shout and wave and pulled away.

"Welcome on the boat," the young man said with a broad smile. Gracie guessed he wasn't much more than fourteen or fifteen. He pointed to the closest seats. "You sit. We shall be in Oia in ten or twelve minutes, and there, Mr. Katsaros will meet you."

"Thank you, Gino," Dorcas said.

The boy's face lit up. "You remember."

"Of course. I remember you and your father, Petros. I was hoping you'd be the ones who came to pick us up." She smiled. "You've grown since I last saw you."

"Yes," he said, looking quite proud of the accomplishment. "My mother say I eat too much."

From the bow, Petros called out to his son. Gino replied in Greek and sat next to a coiled rope. Gracie heard the engines power up, and suddenly, they were skimming over the water, hurtling across the bay toward the towering cliffs at their left. They passed another enormous cruise ship, a couple of tenders loaded with tourists, and several small fishing boats. When they bumped across the whitewater left by another speedboat, Gracie flew upward a few inches, and feeling like a child again, she laughed into the wind.

Quinn glanced her way and grinned. Beyond the foaming water behind him, the brilliant blue sea was a reflection of the clear sky above and a perfect foil for the dark lava rock crags and the bright white buildings on the hillside.

Gracie's hair whipped across her cheek, and she leaned back in her seat, wanting nothing more than to soak in the beauty and exhilaration of this moment.

Petros throttled down the engine as a narrow dock came into view. Small stone buildings lined the shore, and some fishermen sat in the shade of a scraggly tree, working on their nets. Not far from the fishermen was a tiny square where a battered green truck was parked next to a black sports car. Petros maneuvered the speedboat into an empty mooring spot, and a man exited the sports car and started walking along the dock.

Gino tossed a rope at the nearest bollard and scrambled ashore. Petros cut the engine, and following Dorcas's lead, Gracie and Quinn rose to their feet.

Quinn leaned a little closer to Gracie and inclined his head toward the dock. "Theo Katsaros," he said softly.

"I wondered," she said, studying the man who was approaching them.

He looked to be in his early thirties. Of average height, he was broad shouldered and had thick, brown hair that curled around his ears and collar. He was wearing a white, short-sleeved, button-down shirt, with the top buttons open wide enough to reveal a heavy gold chain around his neck, and despite the humidity, his navy pants were crisp and wrinkle-free. When he reached Gino, he put his hand on the boy's shoulder and exchanged a few words with him. Gino nodded, gave the rope a final cinch, and then hurried back to straddle the dock and the boat and extend his arm to Dorcas.

As soon as she was onshore, Theo greeted Dorcas with a kiss on each cheek. "Welcome back to Santorini."

"Thank you, Theo," Dorcas said. "It's as beautiful as it was the last time I was here."

"But of course," he said. "Perhaps even more so." He turned as Gracie and Quinn stepped onto the dock. "Quinn," he said, extending his hand, "it has been a long time."

"It has," Quinn said, shaking Theo's hand. "Not since your father's funeral."

Theo clicked his tongue and shook his head. "Far too long." He gave an overly bright smile. "But you are here now, and you have brought someone else for me to meet."

"Yes." Quinn shifted slightly, drawing Gracie forward. "Theo, this is my fiancée, Gracie Miller. Gracie, Theo Katsaros."

"It is a pleasure to meet you, Gracie," Theo said.

After having spent a week with Dorcas, Gracie was becoming accustomed to being greeted with a light kiss on each cheek, but for some reason, Theo's traditional welcome seemed to last a few seconds too long. Perhaps Quinn thought so too because as soon as Theo stepped back, Quinn put his arm around her.

"Thank you," Gracie said. "I'm excited to be here."

"Ah, once you have truly seen it, you will lose your heart to Oia," Theo said. He wiggled his eyebrows. "And then you will have to return for a longer stay." He turned back to Dorcas. "Do you not agree, Dorcas?"

"It is a magical place," Dorcas said. "And your home is stunning."

Theo laughed. "And this is how she tells me that it is time to take you there." He raised his arm, indicating that they precede him down the dock. "Come."

The closer they got to the sports car, the fancier it appeared. It sat low to the ground, chrome detailing and hub cabs glistening in the sunlight, and even with the sunroof down, there appeared to be more room for the engine than the passengers.

"Of course Theo drives an Alfa Romeo," Quinn muttered under his breath.

Gracie glanced up at him. "Whatever that is. I'm just wondering how we're all going to fit in it."

He looked at her. "Thank you."

"Thank you?"

"For not knowing or caring about Alfa Romeos."

She gave him an impish smile. "Even if it proves that I'm uncultured?"

He chuckled. "Yes. And I hope you stay that way."

Theo moved to open the passenger side door. "I apologize that we will not be able to drive to the top together. One of my employees took the Mercedes to the airport to pick up Calista." He shrugged. "But taking you one at a time will give you a chance to see the view from the front seat, and if we do not meet any other traffic, it will only take five minutes each way."

"I didn't know Calista would be here," Dorcas said.

"She wanted to surprise you," Theo said. "She had to be at a photo shoot in Paris yesterday, so she took a flight into Athens late last night and should arrive in Santorini after lunch. It's a fast trip; she will leave again this evening. But she always wants to do things her way, no matter how crazy it is, and I am happy that she is coming."

"It's very good of her to go to so much trouble to see us," Dorcas said.

Theo waved off her appreciation. "Psht, Calista is always flying somewhere. Why not to Santorini to see her family?" He raised his eyebrows quizzically. "Now, which of you ladies wishes to ride first?"

Gracie glanced from the capacious bucket seats to Theo's inviting smile and made her decision. She'd rather take her chances on missing the view than drive with Theo alone.

"Dorcas and I can share a seat," she said, "and that will save you a trip."

"That's a marvelous idea," Dorcas said.

Theo's smile did not waver, but she caught the hint of annoyance in his eyes. "You are sure?"

"Absolutely." Dorcas was already getting into the vehicle. "Come on, Gracie. There's plenty of room for both of us."

Grateful for Dorcas's willingness to be unconventional, Gracie slipped in beside her. It was tight, but they fit, and by the time Theo took the driver's seat, they'd managed to secure the seat belt across them both. He turned on the ignition, and the engine roared to life. Quinn stepped away from the vehicle. Concern lined his face, but he didn't say anything.

"I shall return shortly," Theo shouted. Then he backed up, shifted into first gear, and peeled out of the square with a spray of gravel.

Gracie clutched the armrest, trying to anticipate Dorcas's movement as Theo took the hairpin bends at hair-raising speed. Alternately smashed against the car door and landing against the side of their crazed driver, they swayed back and forth with each turn. Her heart raced as the speed limit signs passed in a blur and Theo's foot stayed firmly on the accelerator.

A loud honk was her only warning that another vehicle was on the road. With a screech of brakes and smell of burnt rubber, Theo swerved to the right, narrowly missing the stone retaining wall as an orange VW bug met them on a bend. The other driver slammed on the brakes. Letting loose a string of Greek words that thankfully meant nothing to Gracie, Theo waited only for the bug to inch past before stomping on the gas again and sending a stray cat skittering out of the way after it came within inches of losing its life.

When the road eventually leveled off and they pulled into a large parking lot, Gracie was finally able to release her death grip on the armrest and look around. Cars, minibuses, and small delivery trucks took up most of the parking spots, and a stream of people were filing off a large bus in the corner.

"I shall meet you here with Quinn," Theo said, pulling up opposite a coffee shop.

"Very well," Dorcas said, releasing the seat belt.

As soon as she was free to move, Gracie opened the door. On shaky legs, she climbed out of the car. Dorcas followed more slowly, closing the door once she was on her feet again.

"You will not have to wait long," Theo said. "But should you want to sit, there are usually empty chairs at the coffee shop." Then he revved the engine, and with the eyes of almost all nearby pedestrians on him and his flashy car, he tore out of the parking lot and headed back down the hill.

"Well," Dorcas said, smoothing down her bright yellow dress. "That was an adventure, wasn't it?"

Gracie linked her arm through the older woman's. *Adventure* was a well-chosen euphemism, and since she couldn't say anything more positive than that, it was probably better to avoid the subject completely.

"How about we go check out the view we missed on the way up?"

Dorcas sighed. "I'd love to."

They walked over to a waist-high wall that formed the only barricade between the parking lot and the sheer drop below. From there, they could see the whole bay with the large ships anchored out at sea and the smaller craft flitting back and forth closer to shore. The craggy cliffs formed a crescent shape around the cove. To their right, the cliffs were wild and untamed; to their left, the town of Oia clung to the crags, spilling down to the water's edge in a tumble of whitewashed buildings and sky-blue roofs.

"It's beautiful," Gracie said.

"Isn't it?" At the sight, Dorcas's tension seemed to melt away. "Just look at how the houses hug the mountainside. It's as if the original settlers of this island needed a connection to something solid somewhere between the vastness of the ocean and the sky."

"They must have been remarkable people," Gracie said. "Even now, I don't know how a workman would get to those buildings."

"By stairs," Dorcas said. "The really heavy things are taken up and down by mule. There are a few community parking lots like this one where cars, buses, and trucks park. They all feed into the ancient walkway that runs along the cliff's edge. From there, people access their homes, hotels, or businesses by stairs."

The roar of the Alfa Romeo's engine coming back up the hill reached them, and Gracie turned to see the black car enter the parking lot. Theo swerved into a vacant spot beside a tree, and before he'd even cut the engine, the passenger door flew open and Quinn got out. Without a backward glance at the vehicle or its driver, he strode away, heading toward the coffee shop.

"Quinn must think we're waiting over there," Dorcas said.

"I'll go get him," Gracie said. "See if you can catch Theo's attention."

Weaving around three parked cars, Gracie hurried to intercept Quinn. His hands were clenched, his jaw rigid, and even from this distance, Gracie could tell fury was rolling off him in waves.

"Quinn," she called.

His rapid steps slowed, and he turned his head. She darted past a red minibus, emerging only a few feet behind him. The moment he saw her, his glowering expression moderated and he closed the gap between them.

"Are you okay?" he asked.

"Yes," she said. "Sorry. Dorcas and I were standing by the wall back there instead of at our designated meeting spot."

He pulled her into his arms. "When I saw the way that moron took off with you and Dorcas . . ." He closed his eyes, took a moment, then opened them again. "If anything had happened to you—to either one of you . . ." He was having a hard time finishing a sentence, and Gracie suddenly realized that not only had he had to endure his own nightmare ride, but he'd also had to watch the drive she and Dorcas had taken.

"We're both fine," she said. "It wasn't the most pleasant ride I've had, but we arrived in one piece."

He shook his head in frustration. "Promise me you'll never get in a car with Theo again," he said.

"I'd rather walk all the way down to the dock and swim to the ship than go through that again," Gracie said.

Relief filled his eyes, and he kissed her forehead. "If you hadn't agreed, I'd have been forced to take matters into my own hands."

She looked up at him, the spot where his lips had touched her skin still tingling. "Like taking the air out of his expensive tires?"

"I was thinking more along the lines of breaking his nose," he said.

Gracie wrinkled her own nose in sympathy. "That would have been awkward for Dorcas," she said.

He looked stern. "It still may happen if she doesn't make me the same promise."

His words were a good reality check. She needed to remember that she and Quinn were good friends. Nothing more. He cared about her wellbeing in the same way he cared about Dorcas's.

"Come on," she said, stepping away from him. "You need to see the view you missed. It will help you feel better."

CHAPTER 21

QUINN DIDN'T NEED TO TELL Dorcas how he was feeling when he met her at the wall. She'd always had an uncanny knack for reading his moods before he'd said a word.

"Try to understand, Quinn," she said. "Alessandro worked hard for everything he had, but his children did not. Affluence has made Theo arrogant; his willful spirit has made him foolhardy."

Quinn ran his fingers through his hair in exasperation. "Being arrogant and willful are not legitimate excuses for risking the lives of other people."

"I agree completely." Concern shone in her eyes, and she reached out and touched his face the way she'd done when he was young. "But for now, I ask you to let it go. We'll only be with Theo for a few hours. Let's make the best of it—for Alessandro's sake."

Quinn turned away. He had no doubt that he would have nightmares for weeks, reliving the images of the two women he cared most about hurtling toward a head-on collision on that mountain road. Not since he'd watched his mother take her last breath had he experienced that level of helplessness. He stared unseeingly at the view in front of him. Somehow, he had to look past Theo's behavior—if only for a few hours—and focus on the primary reason they were here.

He sensed Gracie's nearness before he felt it. Her fingers brushed his, and he opened his fist, weaving his fingers between hers. Taking her hand had been deliberate only a week ago; now it was instinctive. More than instinctive. It was something he sought.

"We've got this, remember?" she whispered.

He ran his other hand across his face and took a deep breath. "As long as you're on my team," he said.

She smiled. "I'm afraid you're stuck with me."

"Then I'm good," he said, and he meant it.

Gracie kept her hand in Quinn's as they followed Theo and Dorcas along the old walkway that ran the length of the cliffside. She was fairly sure the older woman was purposely keeping some distance between Theo and Quinn, allowing her nephew as much time as possible to regroup. The cobbled path was lined with unique restaurants, cozy cafés, colorful gift shops, and trendy art galleries, and for a few short minutes, Gracie allowed herself to pretend they were simply carefree tourists meandering in and out of the intriguing establishments.

Dorcas was drawn to the carousels of colorful scarfs that stood outside some of the gift shops, and Theo encouraged them all to have their feet massaged at a spa that specialized in kissing fish. To Gracie's amusement, however, one look at the people lined up with their feet in tanks of water full of tiny, nibbling fish was enough to discourage Quinn completely. And since Dorcas knew better than to press him right then, they opted to visit the art gallery next door instead.

Gracie was fascinated by the town's architecture. The ubiquitous whitewashed walls sparkled in the sunlight, making everything from the lowliest shed to the most elegant church look clean and bright. Doors and windows were arched and deeply recessed, as were the many stairwells that snaked down the hillside through breaks in the old walkway's low wall.

They reached the paved courtyard of a Greek orthodox church. A sign outside announced meeting times, and a gold cross reached heavenward atop the domed blue roof. Opposite the church gate was a staircase that led diagonally down the hillside.

"This way," Theo said.

After about a dozen steps, the stairway bent sharply to the right and continued downward until it reached a red gate set in an arched entryway. Theo opened the gate and led them into a small courtyard. Wooden boxes overflowing with hot-pink flowers lined the white walls, and up ahead, a solid wooden door marked the entrance of a large house.

Without giving the picturesque courtyard a second glance, Theo lifted the latch on the door, pushed it open, and ushered them inside. Gracie followed Dorcas and Quinn into an airy hall. An oval rug covered the center portion of the marble flooring, and a long, narrow table leaned against the opposite wall, displaying an impressive model of a multimast schooner.

On the walls, three oil paintings depicting Santorini Bay at different times of the day immediately caught Gracie's eye, and she stepped closer to examine them. "These are beautiful," she said, moving from the one that showed the muted shades of early morning to the one that was vivid with the bright colors of midday to the one that reflected the rosy hue of sunset.

"I have always liked them," Theo said. "My father bought them for my mother to celebrate the launching of his first cruise ship." He moved through a wide archway into a comfortable sitting room.

Here, the furnishings were surprisingly simple. A beige sofa and matching chairs were decorated with red-and-blue-striped throw pillows. Modern, stylistic lamps sat on two end tables, and a large terracotta urn in the corner housed a thriving fern. A shelving unit built into a recess on the far wall displayed a few books, a handful of framed photos, some trophies, and two more model sailing ships.

As interesting as the mementos on display were, however, it took only one glance for Gracie to realize the focal point of the room was not something on the shelves or anything hanging on the walls. In fact, what drew everyone's attention the moment they stepped into the room was not within the room at all; it was the scene through the open patio doors.

Stunned to silence, Gracie walked across the room and stood at the open glass doors. A paved patio ran from where she stood to the edge of the most incredible swimming pool she'd ever seen. Its surface was as white as all the walls in Oia, but its water was turquoise blue. A set of wide steps led into the water, and through its crystal-clear depths, it was possible to see ledges of different heights and the glowing circles of underwater lighting. Decorative lamps sat at each corner of the pool, and a black-and-white air mattress floated in its center.

Around the pool, flower barrels overflowed with a profusion of color, and four lounge chairs sat beneath the shade of two large umbrellas. On the other side of the patio, half a dozen white wicker chairs sat around a glass-topped table that had been set with plates, glasses, and silverware. As Theo stepped outside, a small woman wearing an apron and carrying a serving bowl exited another door and headed for the table.

Theo spoke to her in Greek. She lowered the bowl onto the table, and wiping her hands on her apron, she responded to Theo before offering Dorcas a shy nod and a smile.

"Hello, Desma," Dorcas said, stepping forward to greet the woman. "It's so good to see you again."

"Welcome to you, Mrs. Katsaros."

"Petros and Gino came to pick us up from the ship," Dorcas continued. "I can't believe how much Gino has grown since I last saw him."

Pride shone in Desma's eyes. "He is a good boy, but sometime I think he will never stop his growing. He eat all the time."

"Well, I'm not surprised. I remember how well you cook."

Desma beamed. "Today, I make the feta salad you like very much. Perhaps your family will like too."

"I'm sure they will love it," Dorcas said.

Theo spoke in Greek again, his tone as sharp as Dorcas's had been friendly.

Desma replied to him, then turned back to Dorcas. "The food, it is ready. I go for the bread."

"Thank you, Desma," Dorcas said.

Giving Dorcas a brief but grateful smile, Desma hurried off in the direction of the door she'd exited.

Dorcas turned to Quinn and Gracie and pointed to the pool. "And now you see why I told you to bring your swimsuits," she said.

Theo looked pleased. "Ah, so you came prepared. Then we shall all enjoy the pool this afternoon."

Quinn stood in the shade of one of the large umbrellas, waiting for Dorcas and Gracie to appear. Theo was already gliding lazily across the pool, and Quinn was thankful for the temporary respite from the man's endless self-aggrandizing. Spending lunch listening to him boast about his new villa in Southern France and how well the Greek Cruise Line was doing under his stewardship had been bad enough. But when the man had added flirting with Gracie to his repertoire, it had been all Quinn could do to not call him out for the braggart he was. Only the strain etched on Dorcas's face and Gracie's repeated rebuffs of Theo's advances had kept him from telling Theo exactly what he thought.

At the sound of voices coming from the patio doors, Quinn looked over to see Dorcas and Gracie step out of the sitting room together. Dorcas was wearing her big floppy hat and a purple floral-print sarong wrapped around her pink swimsuit. Gracie had pulled her hair into a high ponytail and was wearing a simple white cover-up over her navy swimsuit.

He watched as Gracie shaded her eyes from the bright sun and quickly scanned the patio. When she turned his direction, he raised his hand. She instantly smiled, and Quinn felt his heart lift. After Gracie pointed him out to Dorcas, the women headed his way and met him beneath the umbrella just as Theo surfaced from the pool.

"You are here at last," Theo said, pulling himself out of the water until his arms were resting on the edge of the pool. He nodded toward a hamper half hidden behind the lounge chairs. "Towels are in the basket. Take what you need."

Dorcas walked over to the hamper and pulled out three fluffy towels. "I'll leave them here for you," she said, dropping them on the end of one of the lounge chairs. "I'm going to sit for a while, but you two should get in."

"Dorcas is right," Theo said from the pool. "Come into the water, Gracie."

It wasn't lost on Quinn that Theo had singled Gracie out in his invitation. A quick look at Gracie's face told him she hadn't missed it either.

"Want to go in?" he asked softly. "Just so you know, if your answer's yes, you won't be going in alone."

The unease in her eyes morphed into relief. "Thanks. I appreciate the backup."

He raised one eyebrow. "Are we taking the stairs this time or going for the splashy cannonball approach we used before?"

"Stairs," she said, taking a quick step back. "Definitely the stairs."

He chuckled. "All right, but I'm not promising your hair will stay dry the whole time."

"Is that right?" She slipped out of her cover-up and met his teasing look with one of her own. "Funny thing is, I don't suppose yours will either."

Gracie was a good swimmer. It didn't take Quinn long to realize that even though his presence in the pool prevented Theo from completely monopolizing her attention, she was like a slippery eel in the water. Whenever Theo got too close, she dived out of reach or relocated to a different spot where she had more space to sit in the shallower water and rest.

At first, their self-assured host seemed to enjoy the challenge. It wasn't likely that he'd had too many women purposely try to avoid him, and Quinn guessed that he thought it was a game. But after about thirty minutes of unsuccessfully trying to corner Gracie, Quinn sensed that Theo's patience was wearing thin. He knew he was right when, a few minutes later, Theo turned away from Gracie, pulled himself out of the water, snatched one of the towels Dorcas had set out on the lounge chair, and rubbed himself down with a scowl.

Quinn swam over to the ledge where Gracie had retreated. "Are you ready to dry off for a bit too?"

"Sure," she said, coming to her feet. "We've left Dorcas on her own long enough."

He slid onto the ledge and stood up. The water level was to his knees, but for Gracie, it came higher. He reached for her hand to lead her to the stairs. Then he stopped so abruptly she ran into him. He lifted her hand and tried to calm his racing heart. "Where's your ring?"

"I didn't want to wear it in the pool," she said. She glanced behind her to check on Theo. He was talking to Dorcas. "I wrapped it in a tissue and put it in the toe of my shoe. It's hidden under my clothes in the bedroom where I changed." She bit her lip anxiously. "I didn't know where else to put it."

Unfortunately, relief that the ring wasn't at the bottom of the pool was nothing to his rising stress over their lapse in monitoring the jewelry. "Where's Dorcas's brooch?"

Gracie shrugged helplessly. "I don't know. We changed in different bedrooms and met up in the sitting room. I wanted to ask her, but Desma was with her, and when I saw that Theo was out here with you, I figured as long as he was with us he couldn't go looking for anything."

Quinn ran his fingers through his wet hair. "Heaven knows where Dorcas put it. I hope it's at least out of sight."

"I'll go check," Gracie said. "I think she was just one or two doors down from the room I used."

Quinn resumed towing Gracie to the stairs. "I'll keep Theo occupied," he said. "If you're fast, he may not miss you."

"If he does, tell him I had to use the bathroom," she said.

Quinn nodded. He hated to feed Theo's ego, but he was quite sure that a well-placed question about the role the Katsaros's cruise line was having on the Greek economy would keep Theo talking far longer than Gracie needed to check on the jewelry.

They stepped out of the pool, and Quinn handed Gracie a towel before using another one to wipe off his face and rub down his hair. Gracie had dried herself off enough to put on her cover-up when the insistent clacking of heels hitting the paving stones drew everyone's attention to the other side of the patio.

"Calista." Theo left Dorcas's side and extended his arms to his sister. "I was beginning to think you weren't coming after all."

"I sent you a text telling you my flight was delayed," she said. "But I should have guessed you were in the pool and nowhere near your phone. Lucky for me, Desma let me in."

Murmuring something placating in Greek, Theo kissed her cheeks, then stood back to enable Dorcas to greet her.

"Hello, Calista," Dorcas said. "Thank you for coming all this way to see us."

"But of course," Calista said. "Paris to Athens. It is not so far. And I have to make a visit to Santorini every once in a while or I risk insulting my brother." She tossed Theo a long-suffering glance, as though daring him to contradict her. When he said nothing, she continued. "And this time there is even more reason to come as I hear Quinn is with you."

Dropping his towel onto the chair, Quinn caught Dorcas's pleading look a split second before it was replaced by a smile. He got the message. She wanted him to be nice to both Katsaros siblings, no matter how insufferable they were. Quinn stifled a sigh. He had a sinking feeling that this difficult day was about to get worse.

CHAPTER 22

GRACIE WATCHED AS THE ELEGANT brunette approached Quinn. She wore a pale-blue sleeveless silk blouse with matching dress pants. The diamonds at her ears and in her tennis bracelet sparkled in the sunlight, and her heels were so high Gracie could see only the tips of her toes and the base of the stiletto beneath her pant legs. Her brown hair cascaded over her shoulders in a smooth curtain, and her perfectly shaped lips were curved in an inviting smile. From her eyelash extensions to her french-tipped nails, she was flawless.

A drop of water dripped off the end of Gracie's wet ponytail and trailed down her back. She couldn't ever remember feeling more like a piece of driftwood, but she stood her ground, waiting to see how Quinn would react to Calista's arrival.

"Welcome to Greece, Quinn," Calista said, expecting and receiving the customary kisses on her cheeks.

"Thank you," Quinn said. "It's good to see you again." He stepped back and reached out his arm, drawing Gracie forward. "I'd like you to meet my fiancée, Gracie Miller."

There was no hiding the skepticism in Calista's expression. "Your fiancée? Forgive me, but I thought you and Mallory were still seeing each other."

Quinn shook his head firmly. "Not anymore."

Calista raised her manicured eyebrows. "I see." She gave her full attention to Gracie. "And what do you do when you're not cruising the Mediterranean with Dorcas and Quinn, Gracie?" she asked.

Her tone was so condescending Gracie was tempted to tell her exactly what she did and whom she worked for. A position at Samuel Hamley carried enough weight in the fashion industry to knock Calista off her pedestal—albeit momentarily. But she wasn't in Santorini to defend herself to Calista Katsaros.

"I like to design things," she said, keeping her response vague.

"Design things?" Calista placed her hands on her hips and gave her a piercing look. "Like clothes?"

"No," Gracie said. "I usually work with metal."

"Hmm." Calista appeared unconvinced.

"Enough, Calista," Theo said. "Believe it or not, not everyone is looking for a personal introduction to the senior buyer for Louis Vuitton."

"Perhaps," Calista said. "But there are many who are." She placed her large designer handbag on the patio beside the closest lounge chair and lowered herself elegantly onto the seat. "Get me a drink, would you, Theo?"

"I think we could all use one," he said. "I will tell Desma to bring some out."

Gracie tensed. She didn't want Theo going back into the house before she'd located Dorcas's jewelry. "I'm going in," she said. "Can I give Desma a message for you?"

Theo frowned. "You are going inside?"

"Just to change," Gracie said. "I'll be right back."

His frown deepened. "You do not wish to swim longer?"

"Let her go, Theo," Calista said. "Believe it or not, not everyone is part fish." She gave her brother a mocking smile. Theo glared at her but conceded the point.

"Very well. If you would ask Desma for the drinks, that would be helpful," he said.

"Of course." Grateful that Theo's and Calista's personal spat had worked to her advantage, Gracie gave Quinn a small smile and made her escape.

She cut through the sitting room, but when she reached the hall, she paused. There was no sign of Theo's cook, and she had no idea which door led to the kitchen.

"Desma!" she called.

The clatter of dishes was her only reply, but it was a solid clue. Gracie followed the sound and walked through yet another arched entrance into a palatial kitchen.

"Desma?"

The small woman swung around, her hand on her heart. Muttering a few Greek words while she gazed heavenward, Desma took a ragged breath.

"I'm sorry I startled you," Gracie said. "Theo is asking if you would bring out some drinks."

"Yes, yes."

Desma lifted a basket off a shelf. It was already half full of glasses. Opening the nearby refrigerator, she took out some bottles and started stacking them around the glasses.

Gracie glanced at the clock above the stove. She wished she could offer to help, but she needed to hurry. "Thank you so much."

Desma smiled and waved her away. "I do this," she said. "You go."

Gracie ran up the steep stairs to the next floor. Now that she was in the cool house and out of the direct sun, her wet swimsuit felt clammy, and the water dripping down her neck was chilling. She paused at the door of the bedroom where she'd changed and studied the other doors on that floor. They were all closed. Hesitantly, she stepped up to the first one and gave a light knock. Turning the handle, she opened the door a crack and peeked in. It was a bathroom. Closing the door, she moved on to the next one. It was a linen closet.

With mounting frustration, Gracie hurried down the hall. She was raising her hand to knock again when she heard footsteps on the stairs behind her. Quickly and quietly, she retreated to the first door and leaned forward until she could see the top of the staircase. When a flash of purple and the wide brim of a floppy hat came into view, Gracie released the breath she'd been holding. "Dorcas."

The older woman stepped onto the landing. "Oh, hello, dear." She removed her floppy hat so she could see Gracie better. "You're shivering. Why are you still in those wet clothes?"

"I . . ." Gracie didn't want to take the time to explain. "What are you doing here?"

"Well, as much as I love this purple sarong, I thought it might be better if I wasn't the only woman wearing a swimsuit for dinner."

"You're getting changed?"

"I was planning on it." Dorcas looked at her curiously. "Is that okay?"

"It's m-more than okay," Gracie said. Her teeth were starting to chatter. "Where did you leave your c-clothes?"

Dorcas pointed to the third door down the hall. "In that bedroom."

Gracie lowered her voice. "What about your b-brooch?"

"Oh." Understanding replaced Dorcas's confusion. "I left it pinned to my dress," she said. "Then I folded the dress so nothing showed." She patted Gracie's shoulder. "Don't worry. No one uses these rooms unless Theo has company. His rooms are on the main level. And besides, Theo's been outside with us the whole time."

But his employees hadn't. She'd seen only Desma in the house. If she was Theo's cook, was there someone else who acted as housekeeper? And then there were Petros and Gino. Were they back from the dock?

Gracie forced a smile. "That's true, but I'll feel b-b-better once I know the b-brooch is safe."

"Come along, then," Dorcas said, already making for the bedroom.

She opened the door and led Gracie inside. A small pile of clothes was folded neatly on the corner of the bed, and on the floor beneath them were Dorcas's shoes.

"Here we are." Dorcas lifted the yellow dress, and as the fabric tumbled out of its folds, the brooch attached to the collar sparkled in the light.

Gracie stepped closer to examine it, but her shivering was becoming more violent, and when she extended her hand, she found that it was shaking too much to control.

"Gracie!" Dorcas noticed immediately. "The brooch is exactly where I left it. Now go get out of those wet clothes before you become ill."

As much as she hated to admit it, Gracie knew Dorcas was right. "I-I'll meet you d-d-downstairs," she stammered.

"Can you manage?" Worry filled Dorcas's voice.

Gracie nodded. "Yes. S-sorry. I don't do v-very well with c-c-cold."

"Because you've got no body fat on you." Dorcas untied her sarong and wrapped it around Gracie. "Now. Where are *your* clothes?"

Gracie clung to the purple fabric, soaking in the residual warmth left by Dorcas and the sun. "Th-three doors d-d-down."

Dorcas wrapped an arm around her and walked her to the other bedroom. Once the door was opened and the older woman saw Gracie's clothes on the bed, she took a step back and waggled her finger at Gracie. "Change. Right now. I'll be back to check on you as soon as I'm dressed."

"Th-thanks."

Gracie waited only until the door clicked shut. Then with numb fingers, she peeled off her wet cover-up and swimsuit.

Her shivering subsided as soon as she was wearing warm, dry clothes. She ran a brush through her hair and pinned it up into a bun so it wouldn't drip on her shirt. Then, when she could trust her fingers not to fumble, she pulled the tissue out of her shoe and unwrapped the ring. Its unique design, along with the clarity and cut of the stones, still took her breath away. And it was the original. She'd held it and worn it enough now that she knew it without using the loupe.

A knock sounded at the door, and she slipped the ring onto her finger. "Come in."

The door cracked opened, and Dorcas peeked around the gap. "How are you feeling?"

"Better," Gracie said. "And warmer."

Dorcas swung the door wide and gave Gracie's loose-fitting linen pants and wrap-around blouse an approving look. "And even lovelier."

Appreciation for Dorcas's kindness swelled within Gracie. She handed the older woman the folded sarong and gave into her impulse to give her a hug. "Thank you," she said. "For everything."

Dorcas squeezed her tightly. "I should say the same," she said. She pulled back. "Now, if you're feeling up to it, I think we've been inside long enough that we'd better go rescue Quinn."

💎💎💎

Quinn heard Dorcas's and Gracie's voices coming down the stairs and moved across the sitting room to watch their approach. The women had been gone far longer than he'd anticipated, and he didn't know what that meant. He and Theo had decided to change out of their swimsuits after Dorcas had followed Gracie inside, but they'd returned and had been talking with Calista for some time with no sign of either Dorcas or Gracie.

"Here they are at last," Calista said as the women made their appearance.

"I'm sorry," Dorcas said. "Have you been waiting for us?"

"Not a problem," Theo said. "Come and sit. Tell me about life in New York."

As Dorcas moved to take a seat on the sofa beside Theo, Quinn closed the gap between him and Gracie. Only too aware that they were currently under Calista's scrutiny, he pulled Gracie into his arms and dropped a kiss on her forehead. He'd already noted the presence of the brooch on his aunt's dress and the ring on Gracie's finger, but with Theo and Calista in the room, he couldn't ask about them.

"Everything okay?" he murmured.

She gave a slight nod. "But I'm guessing this warm reception is because Calista's not fully convinced we're a couple," she whispered in return.

"She's been grilling me about Mallory," he admitted. "I know she met her in New York last year, but I don't see why she cares."

"Sorry if that's been difficult," Gracie said.

Quinn stared at her. No catty remark or cross-examination. Simply an apology for something that wasn't her fault. His time with Mallory had truly jaded him; he hadn't believed women like Gracie still existed. "I'm glad you're here," he said. "Maybe she'll change the subject now."

Gracie gave him a small smile. "I guess it's my turn to do some socializing."

She pulled out of his arms and stepped toward Theo's sister. "Tell me about your work, Calista," she said. "What's a normal week like?"

Quinn watched the suspicion in Calista's eyes slowly fade as Gracie's attentiveness and follow-up questions proved her genuine interest in the fashion buyer's work. Calista was more than happy to talk about herself, and when their conversation moved on to a discussion of the ills of rayon, he opted to leave them to it. Walking slowly around the room, he stopped opposite the large shelving unit tucked into a recessed archway on the far wall. The two model ships on display were not as large as the one in the main hall, but the workmanship was superb. Quinn studied the model of a nineteenth-century clipper carefully.

"You've discovered one of my passions." Theo spoke from behind him. "Not many craftsmen capture the details of the old sailing ships as they should."

"They're impressive," Quinn said.

"I agree. And almost as valuable as this." Theo reached past him to lift a gold trophy off a higher shelf. He handed it to Quinn. "The Greek National Amateur Football Championship 2010." He stood a little taller. "I scored the winning goal in the final game, and the newspapers claimed we were good enough to take on some of the professional teams and win."

"Really, Theo! Are you still boasting about winning that football game after all these years?" Calista's voice cut across the room.

"Yes," Theo said. "And I shall continue to do so." He pulled down a couple of framed photographs. "You see how proud my father was."

Quinn looked at the first picture. It showed a smiling Alessandro standing next to Theo, who was dressed in a soccer uniform and was holding his trophy. Next to him stood Calista, then Damien, who was wearing an identical soccer uniform and holding a similar trophy, and on the end was Nikos.

"These are our good friends, Nikos and Damien Andonious. Perhaps you visited them when you were in Athens."

"Yes," Quinn said. "We stopped at their shop briefly."

"Damien and I played on the same football team from age six to twenty-six," Theo said. "We both retired after winning the championship game." He pulled the second photograph to the front. "Here's our winning team."

"Hey, Gracie," Quinn said, working to keep his voice even. "You should come see this."

Throwing Calista a triumphant look, Theo shifted slightly to make room for Gracie. Quinn handed her the team photograph.

"Theo's soccer team," he said. He watched her face, knowing that her attention to detail would catch what he'd spotted almost immediately.

"What a great achievement," she said. "You all look great."

Quinn noticed the slight shake in her hand as she handed the photograph back, and when she lowered her arm, he wound his fingers between hers. He knew the initial shock of seeing Theo, Damien, and Vlasis lined up side by side on the front row of the soccer team would wear off soon, but until then, he'd keep her trembling hand in his.

"How long did you all play together?" Quinn asked.

Theo shrugged. "It varied. Damien and I for twenty years; a few of them for only one or two. Most were somewhere in the middle."

"And this was when you were in Athens?"

"Yes." Theo replaced the photos on the shelf. "There were a few on the team who came from other cities, but at that time, we all lived and worked and practiced in Athens."

Calista groaned. "Enough talk of your football glory days," she said, coming to her feet. "I can smell Desma's *dolmadakia* cooking. She will have the table set on the patio by now, and if we do not go outside soon, we are in danger of missing the sunset."

Dorcas rose too. "Oh yes, we mustn't miss that. And afterward, I'm afraid we must be on our way."

"Of course," Theo said. "We shall eat, enjoy the sunset, and then Petros will take you down to Amoudi Bay and, from there, to the cruise ship. If you will forgive me, this time, I must drive my sister to the airport."

"Of course," Dorcas said. "Thank you for arranging everything for us."

Theo turned his dark eyes on Gracie, the hint of a smile on his lips. "It has been my pleasure."

Grateful to have avoided a confrontation with Theo about their return trip, Quinn opted to ignore the man's continued and blatant attempts to charm Gracie. From this point on, he simply needed to stay alert. As soon as he was able to use the phone freely, he would contact Steve. They'd known that Alessandro and Nikos had been friends for years, but Theo's long association, not only with Damien but also with Vlasis, was a new and potentially game-changing revelation.

CHAPTER 23

GRACIE LEANED AGAINST THE SHORT retaining wall at the edge of Theo's patio and watched the sun slowly sink below the water's edge. The glowing orange ball sent a beam of golden light across the ocean that stretched from the horizon in the distance to the shoreline below. Streaks of purple blended with pink, darkening to deep red where the sky touched the sea. It was stunning.

"I've never seen anything quite like a Santorini sunset," Dorcas said.

"I agree," Theo said. "No matter how long I am here, it never fails to impress."

They stood a little longer, watching as the last sliver of sun finally slipped below the horizon and the vivid array of colors darkened to midnight blue. All around them, decorative lights flickered to life.

Gracie heard the clack of Calista's heels crossing the paving stones toward the house, and Dorcas moved away from the wall.

"I'll go get my things," Dorcas said.

"I have my bag down here already," Gracie said.

Quinn patted the bulge in his cargo pants pocket. "I'm good to go too," he said. "We'll wait for you here."

"I won't be long," Dorcas said.

She started toward the patio doors, and Theo fell into step beside her, the murmur of their voices fading as they entered the house.

Beside her, Quinn's eyes were raised to the silver moon. "Incredible, isn't it?"

"Yes," Gracie said, her voice hushed.

From their position on the edge of Theo's patio, the houses seemed to spill down the mountainside beneath them, the distinctive blue roofs now shadowy gray, and the white walls glowing softly in the moonlight. Myriad lights illuminated the narrow staircases between the buildings, and out in the bay, twinkling lights marked the position of small boats and large cruise ships waiting at anchor.

With every minute that passed, the moon shone more brightly and stars filled the velvety blackness above. From somewhere to their right, Gracie heard the sound of voices and laughter. Splashes coming from a nearby swimming pool overwhelmed the distant rushing of the ocean's waves and reminded her that despite this moment of tranquility, they were not alone.

Behind her, a door opened and closed. Gracie turned her head. Theo was approaching. He caught her eye and saluted her with his recently refilled wine glass. Gracie tensed. Quinn noted the exchange and slipped his arm around her waist.

"I shall never understand American men," Theo said. Gracie wasn't sure if he was speaking to her or to Quinn. "A beautiful woman, a perfect backdrop, and the magic of moonlight—no Greek would let such an opportunity pass without stealing a kiss." He arched his eyebrow, and she caught the gleam in his dark eyes.

"I don't steal kisses, Theo." There was an edge to Quinn's voice.

"Then you are missing out," Theo said. "Let me show you how it is done."

He took a step closer, but Quinn blocked him. "I don't think so."

"Ah!" Theo said. "Perhaps you are concerned that after one kiss from me, Gracie will have no further interest in you." He shrugged. "I would be worried too. After this pathetic display, she must be ready to spend time in the moonlight with another man."

Quinn's hold around her waist tightened. Theo was goading him, and after all Quinn had been forced to endure from the man today, Gracie wasn't sure how much more he could take before he snapped or was forced to walk away. Neither scenario boded well for them, especially with the suspicions they now had about Theo's connection to Damian and Vlasis. She had to do something to make him back off.

"I'm sorry, Theo," she said. "There's only one person I'll be kissing tonight."

She turned so she was facing Quinn, and before she could talk herself out of it, she slid her arms around his neck. For a split second, his eyes registered his shock, then without a word, he drew her closer. He gazed down at her and slowly lowered his head. Tentatively, his lips traced hers, and as the heady aroma of his spicy cologne filled her senses, she returned his kisses. He murmured her name once before claiming her lips completely, and she melded into his arms.

When they finally drew apart, Theo was gone, and Quinn looked almost as stunned as she felt.

"I . . . uh . . ." Gracie wasn't sure how to begin.

"Petros is here!" Dorcas called from the sitting room.

Gracie took a step back.

"I guess that's our cue," Quinn said, but he didn't move.

"Yes." She took a shaky breath. "We should go." Forcing herself to look away, she turned to face the house.

"Come on," he said, placing a gentle hand on her back. "We'd better go say our goodbyes."

💎💎💎

Quinn sat on the idling speedboat, watching the lights of the tender up ahead. The last few passengers were disembarking, entering *Fantasia* through the open portal. He saw one of the crewmen signal the tender's captain, and the boat's engines roared to life. Seconds later, the tender moved away, leaving room for the speedboat to take its place against the bumpers.

Dorcas sat across from him, watching the crewmen orchestrate the boats' comings and goings with choreographed precision. Gracie was at his side, her face turned toward the bright lights of the cruise ship. The reflected shadows of the water rippled across her beautiful face, and for a fleeting moment, his eyes sought and found her lips. That kiss. He'd never experienced anything like it. Her reaction when they'd drawn apart told him it had affected her too. But how much? Was she feeling the heightened sense of awareness humming between them now?

He looked away. Somehow, he had to keep his focus. The jewels. The thieves. And what their next move might be. Was Theo the mastermind behind the heists? He had the money, the connections, and the power to place whomever he wanted on board the cruise ship. Quinn hoped Steve had more information for them. They had to find some answers soon.

Gino tossed a crewman a rope. Once the rope was cinched tightly, Gino offered Dorcas his hand.

"Thank you, Gino," she said. "I look forward to seeing how much you've grown the next time I visit."

The boy grinned. "I will keep making my mother crazy with my eating."

Dorcas laughed. "You do that." She stepped onto the short gangplank, and a crewman helped her onboard.

"Welcome back, Mrs. Katsaros."

"Thank you." She stepped aside, waiting for Gracie and Quinn to join her. Then, when the crewman tossed the rope back to Gino, she raised her hand to him and his father. "Thank you," she called again.

With an answering wave, they sped away.

Quinn, Gracie, and Dorcas headed for the elevator and Dorcas's stateroom. As soon as they were inside the cabin with the door locked behind them, Quinn pulled out his phone and dropped onto one of the chairs. "I'm calling Steve," he said.

"Good idea," Dorcas said.

Gracie remained silent. Quinn glanced at her. She was standing a couple of feet from Dorcas, staring at her brooch.

"Gracie?" Quinn asked.

She ignored him. "Dorcas, can I see your brooch?"

Quinn rose to his feet, a sick feeling settling into the pit of his stomach. Without a word, Dorcas unpinned her jewelry and handed it to Gracie. Gracie turned it over and ran her finger down the metal stem. He saw the worry lines appear on her forehead and waited silently while she fumbled in her bag for her loupe. Seconds later, she had it in her hand and was using it to examine the brooch.

"Gracie?" he asked again.

She looked up. There were tears in her eyes. "I'm so sorry," she said. "I should have checked it at the house. It was only now, when Dorcas was standing under the bright light, that I even suspected . . ."

Dorcas gripped the back of the chair, shock draining her face of color. "It's been switched?"

Gracie nodded. "Etienne Perot's mark is gone, and the stones are not the same."

"How?" Quinn balled his fists. "How on earth did this happen? I thought you checked them when you went in to change."

Gracie wiped the tears off her cheek with the tips of her fingers. "I was still hunting for the room Dorcas used when she met me upstairs. She showed me the brooch still pinned to her dress, exactly where she'd left it, and we both thought . . . I should have gone for my loupe anyway, but I . . ."

"Goodness me," Dorcas interrupted. "It's not your fault, Gracie. If I had to do it again, I'd do the exact same thing."

Quinn looked from one woman to the other. "What are you talking about?"

"Gracie had been searching that cool house in a wet swimsuit for too long," Dorcas said. "By the time I got to her, she was shivering so badly she could barely talk, let alone hold a loupe. I sent her back to her room to get dressed without letting her look at the brooch."

"But when you came into the sitting room and I asked if everything was okay, you said yes."

"I knew the ring hadn't been switched out, so I assumed . . ."

"And so did I." Dorcas came and stood next to Gracie, putting her arm protectively around her shoulders.

"Wait," Quinn said, seizing on her first words. "The ring's okay?"

Gracie slid it off her finger and looked at it through the loupe before meeting his anxious eyes. "It's the original."

Relief coursed through him, followed almost immediately by guilt. There was no place for relief over the safety of his ring when his aunt's brooch was gone. He scrolled down the contacts in his phone until he found Steve, then he pushed call.

Steve answered on the second ring. "Hey, Quinn. I was hoping you'd check in."

"Yeah," Quinn said, turning on the speakerphone. "I need to know how fast you can get a search warrant."

Steve's friendly tone was gone. "Why?"

"Dorcas's brooch was traded out at Theo's house."

There was a stunned silence. "How?"

"We still haven't got that figured out," Quinn said. "But at least we have a 'where,' and I think we can get pretty close on a 'when.'"

"Spill it," Steve said.

Quinn outlined the time line of their day in Santorini.

"So you're telling me Dorcas left her brooch pinned to her dress in a bedroom, and it was there, unmonitored, for a couple of hours."

"Yep." Put like that, Quinn understood why Steve might think they'd all taken stupid pills.

"But Theo was outside with us," Dorcas pointed out. "And I've done the same thing every time I've gone. That's why I told Quinn and Gracie to take their swimsuits. We always spend part of the afternoon in the pool."

On the other end of the phone, Steve remained silent, as though waiting for Dorcas to realize what she'd just said. Quinn watched his aunt, recognizing the change in her countenance the moment she made the connection.

"Oh my word!" Dorcas looked at him with wide eyes. "Every time. I change in the bedroom; I leave my clothes and jewelry on the bed. I do the same thing *every time*."

"You are certainly a creature of habit, Dorcas," Steve said dryly. "And it looks like Theo has made the most of it."

Dorcas's face crumpled. "But why? Why would he do something like that to me?"

Gracie wrapped her arms around Dorcas and continued to hold her as she quietly wept into her shoulder. Quinn watched, helpless and hating it. Perhaps it was a good thing that they hadn't discovered the theft while they were still at Theo's house after all. He would not have waited for Steve or the police to arrive before placing a well-aimed punch at Theo's face.

"I'm going to sign off, Steve," he said.

"Okay," Steve said. "Thanks for the lead on the soccer connection. I'll get a list of Theo's employees and start working on that too. I'll call you back after I've talked to the Hellenic police. We should have Theo in for questioning later tonight, and a search warrant issued for his house by morning. If I can coordinate it with the authorities over here, I'd like to have Damien and Vlasis brought in at about the same time."

"If Vlasis is onboard, you may have to wait until we dock in Dubrovnik for that," Quinn said. "I think we're supposed to get underway pretty soon."

"I'll check the schedule and make sure we have someone there when the ship arrives."

"Thanks," Quinn said. "Keep me in the loop."

The line went dead, and he looked over at Dorcas.

She'd raised her head from Gracie's shoulder and was using the tissues Gracie had passed her to mop her face. "You know," she said between sniffs. "Knowing that my jewelry had been stolen was bad. Thinking that I may have been singled out by the thieves because of my naiveté or because I'm a single woman was worse. But believing that the person who targeted me is a family member, someone who should care about me . . ." She dabbed at her eyes. "That's the cruelest thought of all."

"I really hope we have more answers by morning," Quinn said, "and that those answers help us understand all this." He slid his phone into his pocket, his chest aching at the sight of his aunt's tearstained face. "Will you be able to sleep tonight?"

"I don't know," she admitted. "But if not, I'll watch a movie or something."

"How about we both get in our pajamas and I come watch something with you for a while?" Gracie said.

Dorcas looked at her, her expression a mixture of incredulity and hope. "You'd do that?"

"I'd love to," Gracie smiled. "It'll be like a slumber party."

"Then I'm going to see if Henri can send us up some popcorn." She moved into the bedroom, picked up the ship's phone, and started talking.

"Thank you," Quinn said to Gracie.

"It's nothing," Gracie said. She looked back at Dorcas. "She doesn't deserve this."

"No." Quinn sighed. "She doesn't."

Dorcas replaced the phone's handset and came back into the sitting room. "I wasn't sure that they'd have something so wholly American," she said, "but they do. Henri said he'll have it here by ten fifteen."

Gracie smiled. "Then I'll go get changed, and I'll be back here in a few minutes."

"And I'm going to excuse myself from this girl fest," Quinn said. "I'll see you in the morning."

"Not too early," Dorcas warned. "This girl fest might go really late."

Quinn chuckled and shook his head. His aunt's resilience was something else. He reached for the cabin door and held it open for Gracie. She slipped into the hall and took her key out of her purse.

"Shoot me a text when you get up," he said.

"I will." She stood at the door, hesitating. "I'm really sorry for not catching the switch sooner."

"It was probably for the best. We couldn't have done anything about it at the house, and it would have made things messier with Theo."

A small smile played across her lips. "Ah yes, the broken nose."

"Right." He stepped closer.

Her clear blue eyes met his, and he paused. Telling himself that kissing Gracie was a bad idea wasn't going to fly anymore. Not after what had happened between them on the patio. But things with Dorcas and her brooch were complicated enough already. Was he capable of keeping his growing feelings for Gracie out of the mix until this jewelry case was behind them? Heaven help him. Until their engagement charade was over—until he could share his real feelings and discover hers without any hint of pretense lingering over them—he was going to have to wield greater self-control than he'd ever thought he possessed.

Leaning down, he lightly brushed his lips across hers and stepped back. "Good night, Gracie."

A slight pink touched her cheeks. "Good night," she said. Then she swiped her key, opened the door, and disappeared inside.

CHAPTER 24

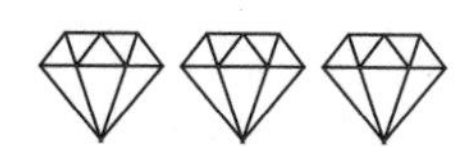

BRIGHT SUNLIGHT WAS STREAMING IN through the cracks in the curtains. Gracie blinked and rolled over in bed to look at the clock on the nightstand: 10:36 a.m. She stared at it, blinked again, then bolted upright. Her late night with Dorcas had truly gone late. When they'd started watching *My Fair Lady* at 10:30 p.m., she'd had no idea the movie would last almost three hours or that it would fill her head with songs that wouldn't leave even after she'd lain down to sleep.

Tearing back the covers, she got out of bed and hurried across the room. Picking up her phone, she sent a one-word text to Quinn.

Awake.

Then she pulled a T-shirt and a pair of capris out of the dresser drawer and raced for the bathroom. Unfortunately, she wasn't fast enough. She'd only just reached the door when her phone started to ring. Doubling back, she picked it up. It was Quinn. "Hello."

"I was beginning to think I was going to have to send in a recovery team."

Gracie groaned. "I was with Dorcas until after one thirty, but I had no idea I'd sleep this late."

"How was she when you left her?"

"Still a little sad, but I think the movie took her mind off things for a while. And hopefully, she was so exhausted by the time we finished, she was able to sleep regardless of yesterday's discoveries." Gracie paused. "Is she doing any better this morning?"

"Uh, I wouldn't know."

"You haven't heard from her?"

"Did I tell you it's been a very lonely morning?"

Gracie giggled. "I'm sorry. But I do feel better knowing I'm not the only lazy one."

There was a click, a pause, and then Quinn's voice came back on the line. "Hey, Gracie, Steve's calling. Can I call you back?"

"Yes," she said. "I'll hop in the shower while you take his call."

Gracie set her phone on the dresser and headed for the bathroom and the fastest shower she'd ever taken. She was dressed and running a brush through her wet hair when Quinn called back.

"Hey," she said. "What's the update?"

"Theo's in custody but is refusing to talk without his lawyer. His lawyer's based in Athens, but it sounds like he's now en route to Santorini to meet with Theo. The search warrant just went through, so the Hellenic Police are expected to be at Theo's house by lunchtime. They've already searched Nikos's shop."

"Did they find anything?"

"The mold for the brooch replica was in the trash."

Gracie dropped onto the nearest chair. "So Damien really did pull it off."

"It looks that way. He's been taken in, but he's not talking either. There's an IT guy working to access Damien's CAD program right now. So far, he's found the files for the brooch and the pink diamond ring."

Her ring. The one she'd designed. A lump formed in Gracie's throat. "I . . . I can't believe it . . ."

"Once they've identified them, they'll make sure the files can never be used again."

Gracie tightened her grip on the phone, hoping she could do the same for her emotions. "Have they figured out how Damien got the fake brooch to Theo?"

"Not yet. The men watching the store said that every customer checked out clean—with a legitimate reason for visiting. The guy tailing Damien said he left the store twice after our visit: once to pick up something from the dry-cleaner and another time to pick up the store's mail from the post office. The next morning, he made his regular stop at the local coffee shop on his way to work and didn't leave the jewelry shop until evening—by which time, the switch had been made."

"Could he have sent something off at the post office, along with picking up the mail? An overnight package would have reached Theo in time."

"They're looking into all registered packages leaving that branch of the Hellenic Post, along with anything that went by special delivery. So far, they've come up empty."

Gracie got to her feet and paced across the small room. "He could have passed it off to someone at the dry-cleaner or the coffee shop."

"Apparently, the dry-cleaning shop is owned by a Chinese family and an interpreter went in with the officer to question the owner. The officer is pretty sure the guy doesn't know anything."

"And the coffee shop?"

"They're working on that too. The waitress on duty yesterday was off today, but an officer is going to her home to see if she remembers Damien meeting anyone there."

Gracie made another circuit around the coffee table. They were so close. She could feel it. But the missing pieces of the puzzle were leaving gaping holes in the big picture.

"What about Vlasis?"

"Steve contacted Captain Anastas about an hour ago. He gave him the condensed version of the story and explained that they have video footage of Vlasis breaking into Dorcas's safe. Apparently, the captain about came unglued, and it was all Steve could do to persuade him to wait until law enforcement arrives to make an official arrest. Captain Anastas has agreed to personally escort the officer onboard and accompany him to Vlasis."

"When's the officer supposed to arrive?"

"He should be here within the hour."

Gracie stared out the balcony doors. It was far more disconcerting to anticipate an arrest being made on their ship than it was to hear of the ones happening back in Santorini and Athens. Her stateroom door was locked, but she suddenly felt unexpectedly vulnerable—and she guessed she wouldn't be the only one to feel that way.

"Maybe we should meet up with Dorcas before that happens," Gracie said.

"I think so too," he said. "How soon can you be ready?"

Gracie wasn't sure why the thought of running into Vlasis unnerved her so much; she only knew she would feel a whole lot better if she was with Quinn. "Can you come right now?"

"I'm on my way," he said.

💎💎💎

Most passengers had already set off on their excursions into Dubrovnik, so the elevators and hallways were unusually empty. Quinn walked across the Miraggio deck, past the vacant bar, the quiet swimming pool, and the distinctive red waterslide. On the raised platform beyond the pool, two members of the crew were prepping a sound system. Amplified squeaks and whistles came and went as a handful of workers set up props around them. Preparation was already underway for the party tonight that would spell the end of the cruise.

A couple of teenagers waited at the gelato stand, and the memory of meeting up with Gracie there after her first encounter with Vlasis flooded back. There'd been something in her voice at the end of their recent phone call that had hinted at a lingering fear of that man, and Quinn picked up his pace. He didn't think Vlasis was likely to be roaming the Yacht Club deck now that the theft of Dorcas's jewelry was complete, but he wasn't going to leave anything to chance.

He took the stairs two at a time, exchanging greetings with a steward in one stairwell and two waiters who were headed to the nearest restaurant in another. When he reached Dorcas and Gracie's hall, a man and woman exited one of the staterooms, hats, bags, and a guidebook in hand.

"*Guten morgen*," the man said as he passed.

"Good morning," Quinn replied.

He waited until the couple had turned the corner, then he knocked on Gracie's door.

She opened it immediately. "I thought I heard your voice," she said. "Come in."

Despite the tan she'd developed after spending a week in the Mediterranean sun, she looked pale.

"Are you okay?" He stepped inside.

She shut the door and turned the lock behind him. "Yeah. I'll just be glad when all these arrests are over. I keep telling myself that Steve deals with this kind of stuff all the time and that I shouldn't let it get to me. But it doesn't seem to be helping very much."

He moved closer and pulled her into his arms. "It'll be behind us soon."

She leaned her head against his chest. Her hair was still damp, and the faint smell of her shampoo lingered in the air. He closed his eyes, realizing at that moment how much he'd needed to simply hold her.

"There still seems to be a lot of loose ends," she said, raising her head to look up at him.

She was right. And he desperately didn't want her to be one of them. "Gracie, when this cruise is over, when we're back to our normal, everyday lives—" His phone started ringing.

Startled, Gracie broke eye contact and pulled away. "It's all right," she said. "I understand."

Understand what? That he needed to answer the phone? So help him, if this was Steve again, he was going to ring his so-called friend's neck. He pulled his phone out of his pocket. "It's Dorcas," he said, forcing down his frustration and accepting the call. "Hello."

"Quinn? I haven't heard from either you or Gracie this morning, so I thought I'd better check in."

"I didn't want to risk waking you," he said. "But now that I know you're up, can Gracie and I come over? Steve's been on the phone, and we have quite a lot to tell you."

"That would be great."

"Okay. I just arrived at Gracie's stateroom, so we'll be right there."

He hung up. "Dorcas is ready for us."

Gracie picked up her purse. "Let's go."

The hall was empty, and Dorcas answered her door as soon as Quinn knocked. She was wearing her purple butterfly dress—a sure sign that she wanted to face the new day cheerfully.

"Come sit on the balcony," she said. "I ate my breakfast out there, and there's a wonderful view of the coastline."

She led the way through the sitting room and the sliding glass doors and took a seat outside. The table next to her held a tray on which sat a small breadbasket, an individual-sized coffee pot, a mug, and an empty plate covered in crumbs. Quinn and Gracie took the two chairs opposite Dorcas, and for a few moments, they sat quietly, appreciating the view.

The *Fantasia* was berthed right up against the harbor wall. From their position near the top of the ship, they could look onto the road that led down a slope and out of sight around a curve in the shoreline. The ancient walled city of Dubrovnik was hidden a few miles farther down the coast, but tightly packed red-roofed houses covered the tree-topped rolling hills that surrounded the harbor, and vessels of all shapes and sizes lined the wharf. Seagulls soared across the water, their raucous cries exceeding any sounds from the people or vehicles on shore.

"Walking through Dubrovnik is like stepping back in time," Dorcas said. "We really should visit the old town, even if it's only for an hour or two."

"I hope we can," Quinn said. "But for now, I'm afraid we're going to have to stay put. At least until we get word from Steve or Captain Anastas."

"Captain Anastas?"

Quinn exchanged a glance with Gracie. "He's helping with the arrest of Vlasis."

Dorcas blanched. "Right now?"

"As soon as the police officer arrives."

His aunt clasped her hands tightly. "I think you'd better start at the beginning and tell me everything Steve said when he called."

By the time Quinn finished recounting his conversation with Steve, Dorcas looked numb.

"It's really happening, then," she said.

"Yes."

"But what about Theo?"

"Theo will get what he deserves," Quinn said.

"I still can't believe he'd do something like this. I know he's thoughtless and arrogant, but he's never been unkind to me." Deep sadness filled her eyes. "I didn't meet Alessandro's children until the day before our wedding, so I became their stepmother before we had a chance to get to know one another. Perhaps even after all these years, I still don't really know them."

"Give the authorities time to get to the bottom of it," Quinn said. "Maybe then we'll understand things better."

She gave an unhappy nod. "Very well."

A loud knock sounded at the door, and Dorcas tensed.

"I'll get it," Quinn said, coming to his feet straightaway.

He walked into the cabin and across the sitting room. Pausing long enough to check the peephole, he unlocked the door. "Good morning, Captain," he said.

Captain Anastas was standing in the hall, his hat tucked under his arm, his expression grave. "Not one of my best, Mr. West," the captain said, "but I am hoping it will improve." He paused. "Is Mrs. Katsaros available?"

"She is." Quinn stepped aside. "Come in."

The captain entered the stateroom, and Quinn closed the door behind him. Dorcas and Gracie must have seen him enter because they rose from their seats on the balcony and walked into the sitting room to greet him.

"Mrs. Katsaros." Captain Anastas gave her a small bow. "I am here to offer my great apologies for what has happened to you aboard my ship. It is beyond shocking. It is inexcusable.

"As of ten minutes ago, Vlasis Galatas has been removed from the vessel, and I will personally see to it that he never sets foot on this ship or any other ship in the GCL fleet again."

Beads of perspiration were appearing along the captain's hairline, and Quinn realized what a crushing situation this was for the man. To have a member of his crew break into the personal safe of any passenger would be bad enough; to have it happen to the wife of the cruise line's founder was infinitely worse. Dorcas obviously recognized the man's difficult position too.

"Thank you for coming to see me, Captain," she said. "I'm grateful to know that you've taken care of the matter and that Vlasis is no longer onboard." She gave the man a reassuring smile. "This whole unfortunate incident was not of your doing, so please don't be too hard on yourself."

He shook his head. "I am the captain, Mrs. Katsaros. Like it or not, I am responsible. When we reach Venice, I will file a full report, and I will be ordering a new screening on each member of our crew." He straightened his shoulders. "Today's black mark will not go unnoticed, but perhaps it will make GCL work even harder for our passengers' safety and security."

"I will be in contact with GCL too," Dorcas said. "I'll make sure they know of your willingness to work fully with the authorities and the professional manner with which you fulfilled your duties."

Relief shone in Captain Anastas's eyes. "Thank you, Mrs. Katsaros."

"Thank *you*, Captain Anastas. I look forward to seeing you again the next time I sail."

The captain shook her hand and managed a small smile. "I shall hope for that also."

CHAPTER 25

DUSK WAS FALLING AS THE *Fantasia* pulled out of port. Gracie stood at the railing on the upper deck, watching the Croatian harbor lights shrink. She'd liked Dubrovnik. After Captain Anastas left Dorcas's cabin, Gracie, Dorcas, and Quinn had eaten lunch together and had then taken a taxi to the old town. They'd walked the ancient city walls and the cobblestoned streets, soaking in the sunshine and the ambiance of the old maritime town.

A large well still stood in the center of the town square, its decorative pillars and unique gargoyles a reminder of a bygone era. Gracie had refilled her water bottle there, marveling at how far removed the Croatian well was from the utilitarian stainless-steel drinking water fountains at home. Stepping into the past had helped take her mind off the events of the last twenty-four hours. Now that she was back onboard ship, however, she found herself looking to the future.

It was the last night of the cruise. By the time they awoke in the morning, they'd be docked in Venice, and from there, it would be a short boat ride to the Marco Polo airport, followed by a long flight home. Despite the pressure brought on by their goal to uncover the jewelry thieves, it had been a magical trip, and she knew the memories she'd made here would stay with her forever.

From the Miraggio deck below, the upbeat rhythm of a popular song reached her. The farewell party had begun. According to Dorcas, the crew members would provide games and entertainment, followed by a dance. It sounded like fun, but for now, she was happy to spend a few minutes of calm enjoying the sea breeze against her skin.

Footsteps sounded behind her, and she turned. Quinn had just exited the elevator and was crossing the Yacht Club deck toward her. He stopped at the lounge chair where Dorcas sat reading her Kindle.

"When I got your text, I guessed this was another one of your best-kept secrets of cruising," he said.

"It's too perfect out here to be inside our cabins," she said, giving him a welcoming smile. "We're enjoying the quiet while everyone else is down on the main deck."

"Yeah. I walked through that craziness on the way up here. This is definitely the place to be."

The lone waiter on duty approached him from the bar. "May I get you something to drink, sir?"

Quinn glanced at the glass of iced tea on the table next to Dorcas and shook his head. "Not right now, thanks. But I'll come find you if I change my mind."

"Very good, sir."

The waiter wove through a few lounge chairs to approach the two people sitting on the opposite side of the deck. Quinn stepped closer to Gracie, and with a content smile, Dorcas took a sip of her iced tea and returned to reading her Kindle.

"How are you doing?" Quinn asked Gracie, leaning his elbows on the railing and gazing out to sea.

"Good," she said. "Dorcas was right. It's pretty much perfect out here right now."

He nodded and stood beside her, silently watching the ship cut through the dark water. She wondered what he was thinking.

"Any update from Steve?" she finally asked.

When they'd finished dinner, Quinn had left to call his friend. He shook his head. "Nothing yet."

Gracie's grip on the railing relaxed, and she gave him a sidelong look. "I'm glad. That's totally selfish, I know, but I was really hoping our last evening wouldn't be spoiled by more unpleasant news."

"If that means you're selfish, then I'm selfish too," he said. "I'm okay letting Steve do the stressing for a while."

She smiled. "I like that idea." She looked up into the darkened sky. It was like a velvet blanket dusted with sparkling sequins. "Can you find any of the constellations?"

Facing heavenward, he turned in a slow semicircle. "Well, it's been a long time since Cub Scouts, but I still recognize a few of them. How about you?"

"You're talking to a country girl, remember? On clear nights in the summer, my brother and I used to lie on the trampoline in our backyard and have competitions to see who could spot them the fastest."

"Will you show me?"

"The easiest is the big dipper," she said, pointing slightly to her right. "See the row of three stars that makes up the handle and four more that make up the bowl?"

"Yeah," he said. "I see them."

"The two stars on the outside of the bowl point to Polaris."

"That's the North Star, right?"

"Yes." She smiled. "Good remembering."

Quinn rolled his eyes. "How about the great bear and the little bear? Aren't those close to the big dipper?"

"Ursa Major and Ursa Minor," she said, scouring the sky. "The dipper's handle is the great bear's tail, so we should be able to find it." She leaned toward Quinn and pointed again. "See it there?"

When he didn't respond, she turned her head. She hadn't realized how close he was. Or that he wasn't looking at the sky anymore. In the shadowy light, she sensed rather than saw him move one arm until it encircled her.

"Dance with me?" he said, taking her right hand in his left.

"Here?"

"Yes. We have the whole floor to ourselves."

Gracie glanced over her shoulder. Darkness covered the deck. Decorative lights flickered around the private swimming pool and whirlpool, and a few yards away, a faint white glow emanated from Dorcas's Kindle. On the other side of the deck, the bartender stood quietly talking to the waiter; the other couple had disappeared. Strains of the song she and Quinn had danced to at the captain's dinner floated on the air from the party on the lower deck.

Ignoring the whispered warnings in her head and sudden increase in her heart rate, she slid her free arm across Quinn's shoulder. His eyes held hers, and he pulled her closer as he wordlessly guided her through the familiar waltz steps.

The first dance led to a second and then a third. When the music finally stopped and the sound of distant applause reached them, they were standing just outside the flickering light of a tiki torch.

With one arm around her still, Quinn released her right hand and gently ran his fingers across her cheek and through her hair. "You and the moonlight are a lethal combination, Gracie Miller," he said softly. "A man doesn't stand a chance." Then he lowered his head and kissed her.

When they drew apart, Gracie took a shaky step back, hoping her legs would hold her as she tried to come to grips with what had just happened.

A chair scraped against the wooden deck, and Gracie jumped. In her current, befuddled state, she'd completely forgotten that Dorcas was nearby. Quinn's aunt couldn't have helped but see her in Quinn's arms. Gracie covered her warm cheeks with her hands, grateful for the concealing darkness as Dorcas stepped into the light of the tiki torch.

"Well, Quinn," Dorcas said. "If you and Gracie are still acting, you both deserve Oscars. From where I was sitting, that was about as real as emotion gets." She patted his arm. "I'm going to bed. But you think about that as you head back to that emotionless world you live in back home."

Panic welled up in Gracie. No. Dorcas was not leaving her alone with Quinn after giving a speech like that. She didn't want to hear about moonlight or Mallory or mistakes. Her feelings were too real, and she would rather wait until she no longer had to see Quinn all day, every day before she had them crushed. "I'll come with you, Dorcas," she said.

Dorcas looked at her quizzically. "Are you sure? I don't want to rush you."

"Yes. I still need to pack."

Quinn ran his fingers through his hair, and she could see the confusion in his eyes. "Gracie, if I was out of line, I apologize. I thought . . ."

Gracie needed to leave before she started crying. She wanted the last few moments with Quinn to remain enchanted. Not awkward and embarrassing. "Good night, Quinn," she said. She leaned over and brushed her lips across his bristly cheek. "Thank you for the dance. I'll never forget it." Then she slipped her arm through Dorcas's and started toward the elevator.

Dorcas walked silently beside her. When the elevator doors opened, they stepped inside and turned around. Quinn was facing the sea, his head down, his hands in his pockets.

"He's fallen in love with you, Gracie," Dorcas said. "Admittedly, I don't know you as well as I know Quinn, but it seems to me that you've developed some feelings for him too. And if that's the case, why are you in this elevator with me instead of out there with him?"

Gracie let the tears she'd been holding back fall. "He may think he's in love with me when he's standing on a cruise ship in the moonlight," she said, "but he's been committed to Mallory for a long time. She's the special person in his high-powered New York life, and he'll be back in that world tomorrow."

Dorcas frowned. "Mallory has nothing to do with your feelings for Quinn or Quinn's for you."

"Mallory has everything to do with those things," Gracie said. "You saw her lipstick on Quinn's lips, and you know even better than I do how long they've been seeing each other. I can't compete with that. And I shouldn't."

The elevator pinged, and the doors opened. This time, it was Dorcas who took Gracie's arm. They walked together to Gracie's stateroom door.

"You're good for him, Gracie." Dorcas raised her eyebrows. "And maybe he's good for you too. Don't give up on that because of Mallory." She patted the hand she held in the crook of her arm. "A little hope and faith in the future never go amiss."

Gracie gave her a watery smile. "Thanks, Dorcas."

"Anytime. And I really mean that. Now go get your packing done, and I'll see you in the morning."

Gracie nodded, swiped her key card, and opened her stateroom door. "Good night."

"Good night, dear," Dorcas said and moved on down the hall.

Gracie shut the door and leaned against it. Closing her eyes, she could still see Quinn standing alone on the upper deck. Her heart ached. Was Dorcas right? Were Quinn's feelings for her more long-lasting than she'd allowed herself to believe? Or was it foolish to hope that Quinn would want her in his life when the time for acting was over? She walked over to the closet and pulled out her suitcase. Setting it on the bed, she opened the lid and started transferring the contents of the dresser's drawers into it. At the risk of breaking her heart more fully, she'd hold on to hope—at least until they reached New York.

CHAPTER 26

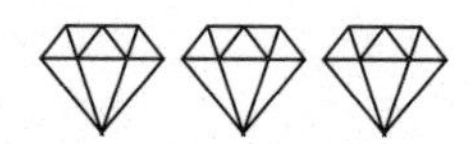

There were too many people, and they all had too much luggage. Quinn navigated his way through a crowd of Japanese tourists, wheeling his and Dorcas's cases behind him. Gracie followed, pulling her own luggage, and Dorcas brought up the rear, holding her smaller carry-on bag. It had been a long journey, and they were all exhausted, but they'd made it through customs and immigration at JFK, and all that remained was to drive home and collapse into bed.

"I've called Brent," Dorcas said, catching up to him as they entered the vast terminal lobby. "He's parking the car, then he's coming in to help with the bags. We'll drop Gracie off at her apartment on our way home."

"Sounds good," Quinn said. "I'm parked out in the boonies, so you'll get out of here long before me."

He glanced at Gracie. There were circles under her eyes, and she was leaning against her case. It wasn't surprising that she was exhausted. It was past 2:00 a.m. in Italy, and they were all feeling it. After her abrupt departure from the Yacht Club deck the night before, he hadn't known what to expect when they met up again for breakfast. But she'd been her usual self—considerate and warm. She'd been extra mindful of Dorcas during their multistage journey, had willingly held his hand, and had even laughed at his teasing. But the unique spark that drew everyone to her was missing, and he was afraid he was responsible for dousing it.

"Are you doing okay, Gracie?" he asked.

She gave him a tired smile. "Yes, but I'll be happy to see my bed."

"We all will," Dorcas said. She gazed out over the milling throng. "Let's hope Brent gets here soon."

Quinn barely had time to register movement to his left when a body came hurtling out of the crowd toward him.

"Quinn!" Mallory shrieked. She launched herself at him, throwing her arms around his neck, and planting her lips on his.

Quinn let go of the luggage and staggered back two paces before putting his hands on her waist and forcibly pushing her off. "What are you doing here?" He was so furious with her over-the-top display he could barely see straight.

"Welcoming you home," she said, patting her hair back into place.

"Welcoming me home?" He looked at her incredulously. "You didn't even know I was gone. How did you know when I was coming back?"

Her pout was back. "Why didn't you tell me you were going to Europe? I would have gone with you—even with last-minute notice."

"You haven't answered my question," he said. "How did you know my flight?"

"Calista told me."

"Calista?" Quinn was beginning to feel like he'd entered another dimension.

Mallory's eyes narrowed. "Yes. Calista. You know, the one you saw in Santorini when you were pretending that another girl was your fiancée."

Quinn stared at her, his mouth suddenly dry. "What do you mean?"

Mallory put her hands on her hips. "There's no point in acting innocent, Quinn. Calista called me because she wanted to know when we'd broken up. I told her we hadn't, and when I asked her why she'd ask something like that, she told me about the cruise you were taking with your aunt and someone called Gracie Miller. It didn't take me long to figure out that the girl you were introducing to everyone as your fiancée was the same person you were talking to outside my building when I got back from Vince's party." Her green eyes flashed. "I looked her up. A junior jewelry designer from Washington State." She spoke the words with as much distaste as she would have if she'd said, "A June bug from under a rock."

Pushing past his anger at Mallory's spiteful remarks, he tried to focus on what she'd shared with Calista. "I didn't know you and Calista were such good friends," he said.

"Why wouldn't we be?" she said defensively. "We hit it off when she came to New York for a fashion show awhile back, and we've kept in touch ever since. She gives me a heads-up when something new is about to hit the fashion world, and I tell her about Dorcas's new jewelry."

Quinn stared at her. "Why would Calista want to know about Dorcas's jewelry?"

Mallory shrugged. "Beats me. It's nothing like the trendy stuff they're coming out with in Paris. She says she has a boyfriend who designs jewelry and that Dorcas's pieces are so classic he likes to imitate them."

Quinn's heart was beating so hard he felt as though he'd just run a sprint. Calista and Damien. The soccer picture Theo had shown him had had Calista standing between Theo and Damien, but it was Damien's arm around her, not Theo's. And when she flew into Santorini, it was via Athens. She'd probably picked up the fake brooch from Damien herself. She'd already been inside Theo's house when she'd met them at the pool. The brooch exchange had been made before they'd even known she was there, and the real brooch had probably been sitting in that ridiculous designer purse she'd placed at her feet beside the lounge chair.

Out of the corner of his eye, Quinn had noticed Brent take Dorcas's suitcase from its position beside him, and now both Dorcas and Gracie were gone. He wanted to leave too, but Mallory had suddenly become the key to unlocking the mystery of the jewelry thefts. He had to keep her talking. "It doesn't make any sense," he said. "How could Calista's boyfriend imitate a piece of jewelry from a description you give her over the phone?"

"I'm not that stupid, Quinn," she said, a familiar bite to her tone. "I send her photos. Dorcas loves that I'm interested in her jewelry, so she always lets me know when she has something new. I go admire the new bauble and take a few pictures. I've even taken photos of some of her old favorites, like the sapphire pendant Alessandro gave her." She gave an indignant sniff. "She's always happy to have me come by."

Had Mallory's name been on the list Dorcas had provided for Steve? Or had the photo shoots been so casual, so neighborly, that Dorcas hadn't even considered them?

Mallory slid her arm through his. "Enough talk about Dorcas and her jewelry. What we should be discussing is why you went on a cruise with Gracie Miller and told everyone you're engaged to her."

Gracie. An unexpected frisson of fear shot through him at the thought of Gracie returning to her home alone. If Calista knew she was a professional in the jewelry business, would she attach the blame for the arrest of her boyfriend and brother on Gracie? Would she retaliate?

He pulled his arm out from Mallory's and stepped away. "That question has an easy answer," he said. "I love Gracie, and if I'm very lucky, one day she'll marry me."

"Don't lie to me, Quinn." Fury filled Mallory's face. "You barely know the woman."

"I'm not lying," he said.

She must have seen something in his eyes—something that confirmed his sincerity—because she took a step back. "She's just after your money," she hissed. "Don't you see that? It doesn't take a genius to realize who will inherit Dorcas Katsaros's fortune."

Finally, Quinn understood. "That's why you kept me around all this time, isn't it? You were never really interested in me. From our very first date, we both knew we had almost nothing in common." He raised a cynical eyebrow. "I guess Dorcas's 'baubles' must have more appeal than you've been willing to let on."

Mallory swung her arm back and slapped him across the face. Then she turned on her six-inch heels and marched out of the lobby.

Quinn raised his hand and gingerly touched his stinging cheek. Drops of blood coated his fingertips where the prongs of Mallory's oversized ruby ring had caught his skin.

A young man walked past and offered him a chagrined look. "Rough luck, dude," he said.

Quinn moved his jaw up and down, working out the soreness. "It's been a long time coming." He reached for his phone and the young man took his cue.

"Later," he said.

"Yeah," Quinn replied absently. He was already dialing Steve.

"Hello." Steve sounded faint and far away.

"Steve, this is Quinn."

"You remember what time it is in Athens, right?"

"Don't even . . ." Quinn warned. "Calista's behind the jewelry thefts."

Immediately, all trace of sleep was gone from Steve's voice. "Tell me what you've got."

Quinn rehearsed his conversation with Mallory.

When he'd finished, Steve let out a low whistle. "Sorry you had to take some physical abuse for that information," he said. "But it may have been worth the cost."

"It's a relief to have it behind me," Quinn said. "I'm okay never seeing Mallory again."

"Gracie, on the other hand . . ."

Quinn interrupted him. "Is she safe?"

"She should be fine," Steve said. "You're half a world away from Calista now. Give me an hour or two. As soon as she's been located, we'll take her in for questioning, and I'll call you."

"Okay. And, Steve, I don't care what time it is there; get on it right now."

"Will do," he said. And then he was gone.

Quinn dragged his suitcase through the lobby, following the arrows pointing to the long-term parking lot. As he walked, he pulled up Gracie's number and hit dial. It rang several times, but she didn't answer. The niggling worry that something wasn't right wouldn't leave, and by the time he'd ridden the shuttle and walked what felt like a full mile to reclaim his car, he'd unsuccessfully tried calling her three times. Still feeling unsettled, he loaded his suitcase into the trunk and drove out of the parking lot and into the New York traffic.

Forty-five minutes later, he pulled into his parking garage. As soon as he'd hauled his luggage into his apartment, he tried Gracie again. When she didn't answer, he called Dorcas.

"Hello."

"Hi, Dorcas," Quinn said. "Is Gracie still with you?"

"No. Brent dropped her off first. She's been home at least thirty minutes."

Surely she wouldn't have gone to bed that fast. And she certainly wouldn't have been asleep when he'd tried calling her from the airport.

"She's not answering her phone," he said, starting to pace across his small kitchen.

"Frankly, I'm not surprised."

Quinn stopped pacing midstride. "Why do you say that?"

Dorcas sighed. "Are you truly that dense, Quinn?"

"Obviously," he said, trying not to be irritated by his aunt's tone. "Because I don't know what you're talking about."

"Do you want to know why Gracie left you on the Yacht Club deck last night?" she asked.

His aunt knew the answer to the question that had been haunting him for over twenty-four hours? Why hadn't she told him sooner? "Of course I do."

"She was convinced that any feelings you had for her were brought on by the romantic ambience of the location and that once you returned to your life in New York, you'd also return to your long-time girlfriend, Mallory. Gracie cares for you, Quinn, but she believed that if she allowed herself to think that she meant more to you than a brief summer fling, she would end up hurt. She walked away so you could return to Mallory without looking back."

Quinn felt sick. "But I haven't had any interest in Mallory for months."

"That's what I thought," Dorcas said. "Even though you offered us plenty of evidence to the contrary when you showed up at my condo with Mallory's lipstick on your lips."

"Mallory kissed me after I walked her to her door. It meant nothing."

"Just like that exhibition in the airport lobby today, I suppose," Dorcas said. "Last night, I persuaded Gracie to give you a chance to prove yourself before she wrote off having any future with you. I should have saved my breath. The moment you put your feet on New York soil, you had Mallory in your arms and you were kissing her like there was no tomorrow."

"Dorcas, it wasn't like that," Quinn began.

"I don't know what was worse," she said. "Seeing you with that minx at the airport or watching Gracie fight back her tears in the car."

Quinn had never experienced such a torturous combination of frustration and anguish. "Mallory literally threw herself at me," he said. "I had no idea she was going to be there, and if I hadn't let go of the cases, I'd have been flat on my back. Grabbing on to her was the only way to push her off."

"Well, that's one explanation, I suppose, but I'm not the one you need to convince. I've said my piece, Quinn; you're on your own now. Good night."

There was a click, and she was gone. Quinn lowered his phone from his ear and stared at it. He couldn't remember the last time his aunt had hung up on him. Not since he was a teenager, he was sure. To say that she was upset right now would be an understatement—and he hadn't even had a chance to tell her about Calista.

Slowly, he sank into the nearest chair and tentatively touched his cheek. The bleeding had stopped, but there'd be a colorful bruise there by morning. He closed his eyes against the pain that Mallory's actions had inflicted on Gracie. That injury was far more serious and so brutally unfair. And at this late hour, there was nothing he could do to fix it. If Gracie wouldn't answer her phone, she surely wouldn't answer her door.

He dragged himself out of the chair, walked into his bedroom, and dropped onto the bed. Taking off his shoes, he tossed them across the room and lay down on top of the quilt with one arm over his eyes. If he was lucky, this day would end before it got any worse.

CHAPTER 27

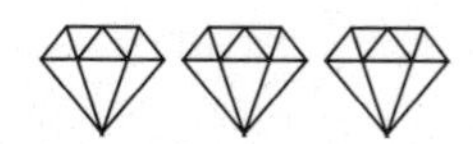

THE INSISTENT RINGING OF THE telephone woke Quinn from his fitful sleep. After a few frantic seconds of groping around his bed in the dark, he located the source of the noise under his pillow. "Hello."

"Quinn, it's Steve."

Quinn pulled himself up onto one elbow. "What have you found?"

"I have good news and bad news," Steve said. He didn't wait for Quinn to choose between them. "The good news is the waitress at Damien's favorite coffee shop IDed Calista from a photo the police officer showed her. She said Calista met Damien at the coffee shop the morning you guys arrived in Santorini and that he gave her a small box."

"So now we know how the fake brooch made it to Theo's house," Quinn said.

"Yeah, things are finally coming together." Steve paused. "The bad news is we've hit a minor setback in questioning Calista."

"What do you mean?"

"I've had officers trying to locate her for the last four hours. We just learned that she boarded a flight out of Paris late last night. She landed in JFK half an hour ago."

Quinn bolted upright. "You call that a minor setback?"

"Yes." Steve's voice was calm. "It just means that we'll arrest her in the U.S. instead of France or Greece."

"And when's that going to happen?" Quinn's stress was rising exponentially. "Before or after she's tracked down Gracie or Dorcas?"

"She's given us no indication that she's going to do that, and her alleged crimes have all been nonviolent."

"Well, she's not coming to New York on fashion business," Quinn said, already on his feet.

"I've just boarded my flight in Athens. I should be in New York tonight. Call Dorcas and tell her to stay put today. Her building has decent security. If Calista tries to see her, she'll have to call through from the front desk." Steve paused. "I daresay Gracie was planning on going back to work this morning. She's probably as safe at Samuel Hamley as anywhere else. They have their own security guards. But you should give her a heads-up about Calista."

"Yeah, well, there's a problem with that plan," Quinn said. "She's not taking my calls."

In the background, Quinn heard the distinctive sound of an overhead announcement.

"We're pulling away from the gate, so I've got to go," Steve said. "I don't know what your hang-up is with Gracie, but I can't call anyone else right now, so you'll have to figure out a way to get a message to her. I'll see you tonight." The line went dead.

With exasperation, Quinn dropped his phone onto the bed and walked out of the room. He was beginning to think he was better off without the annoying instrument that woke him up at all hours, interrupted him at the worst possible moments, didn't connect him with the people he wanted to talk to most, and broadcast messages he didn't want to hear.

Opening his refrigerator, he stared at the almost empty shelves. Dill pickles and mustard were not high on his list of preferred snacks. He glanced at the clock: 5:43 a.m. In another forty-five minutes, the deli down the street would open and he could pick up something there. In the meantime, he'd take a shower, put on some clean, unwrinkled clothes, and figure out how to contact Gracie without the help of Dorcas or Steve.

💎💎💎

Gracie stood in front of the mirror and gave her appearance a critical look. On the up side, her gray pencil skirt and rose-colored blouse were clean and pressed, her hair had not yet escaped the loose chignon she'd styled this morning, and her newly acquired tan had not faded overnight. On the down side, her eyes were still red from the many tears she'd shed, and no amount of makeup could conceal the dark circles beneath them. In short, her aura of sadness and general weariness was the antithesis of what everyone would expect of someone returning from a Mediterranean cruise. She was going to have to draw heavily on the acting skills she'd been honing all week if she was to make it through her workday without a grilling from Kelly.

Straightening her slumped shoulders, she walked into the kitchen and picked up her purse. Quinn's ring sparkled on her finger. He'd asked her to wear it on their journey home because it was safer on her finger than packed in a bag. Unfortunately, the same reasoning applied now. As much as Gracie wanted to remove the constant reminder of the man she'd fallen in love with, she had no personal safe, and her fear of losing something so valuable in her apartment was too real. Her safest option was to wear it to work, place it in a bag labeled with Quinn's name, and put it in the Samuel Hamley vault until he had an opportunity to stop by the store and pick it up. She could only hope none of her coworkers would notice the ring before it was securely hidden.

She glanced at the clock. It was already after eight, and if she wanted to arrive at work by nine, she needed to be on her way. Grabbing a granola bar from the cupboard, she dropped it into her purse and walked out of her apartment. Locking the door behind her, she headed down the shadowy stairwell and exited the brownstone house into the bright morning sunlight.

Huge, old sycamore trees lined the sidewalk, and a solid row of cars parked end to end extended down both sides of the residential street. Pedestrians dressed in everything from business attire to casual wear were walking in the direction of the subway station. Gracie increased her speed, heading for the crosswalk halfway down the block.

Somewhere behind her, a car door slammed. Across the street, a red car pulled out of a parking spot, and a green car hugged the side of the road, waiting to take its place. Reaching the crosswalk, Gracie waited for a white delivery truck to pass, then glanced both ways to make sure the road was clear before stepping out into the street.

She'd taken only three steps when a chain of events happened in such close succession it was as though they occurred simultaneously. The driver of the red car slammed on the accelerator. The engine roared, and the car leaped toward her. Someone yelled her name, and a woman on the other side of the road screamed.

Before Gracie could do anything more than check her forward motion, the red car reached the crosswalk. As though from a distance, Gracie heard the resounding thud as the vehicle hit her, and then she was on the ground, the pain so terrible she could barely breath. She heard more screams and running feet.

"Call 911!" someone yelled.

There were people moving all around her.

"Gracie! Gracie! Can you hear me?"

She opened her eyes. Quinn. He was kneeling beside her on the road. She hadn't thought she had any tears left to cry, but she felt the moisture running down her cheeks.

"Hang on, sweetheart," he said, clasping her hand.

She gripped his hand tightly and closed her eyes against another wave of pain. In the distance, she heard the wail of sirens. Then everything slowly faded away.

Quinn stood at the open doors of the ambulance as the paramedics lifted the stretcher carrying Gracie's inert body into the vehicle. The crowd that had gathered immediately after the accident was beginning to disperse, but a few people still stood, watching silently from the sidewalk. Three men were talking to the police officer who'd been taking eye-witness accounts. One of them pointed to the bloodstain on the asphalt. Quinn averted his eyes and tightened his grip on Gracie's purse.

A patrol car was parked perpendicular to the road at one end of the block, its lights flashing. On the other end, a row of orange cones had successfully closed the lanes to through traffic, even though it appeared that on one side, there was a gap wide enough to allow the ambulance through.

"All right, Mike?" The paramedic standing beside Quinn called up to the one inside the ambulance.

"Almost." Mike cinched a strap around Gracie and checked her connection to the cardiac monitor and IV fluid. "Okay. We're good."

Quinn grabbed ahold of the side of the door and pulled himself up.

"Hey, where d'you think you're going?" The paramedic grabbed his sleeve.

"With you," Quinn said grimly. "And don't even try to tell me I can't."

The man glanced at his clipboard. "You're the fiancé?"

"Yeah. And I've already given the cop my contact information."

"Get a belt on," he said.

The moment Quinn was through the doors, the paramedic slammed them shut, and within seconds, he'd started the engine. A short peal of the siren signaled their departure, and with a lurch, the vehicle set off down the street.

Strapping himself into the folding seat across from Gracie, Quinn watched the steady movement of her chest. Through the gap in the connecting window, he heard the driver call in the trauma alert to the hospital. His message was full of medical acronyms, but the sense of urgency didn't need translation. Quinn hoped the messages going out on the police bands were equally insistent. They had to find the driver of the red car. He turned to the paramedic riding in the back with him. "Is she going to be okay?"

"She's got a compound fracture of her right tibia, along with some nasty road burn, but her vitals are steady. I'd say she was pretty lucky. If she'd been another six inches into the road, we'd probably be looking at a very different story."

Quinn gazed down at his bloodstained pants, knowing that the paramedic was right. He'd driven to Gracie's apartment, hoping to talk to her before she left for work, but it had been so hard to find a parking spot, he'd almost missed her. She'd been walking down the sidewalk by the time he'd gotten out of the car, and he'd needed to run to catch her. He'd seen the red car pull out, heard the engine rev, and in that moment of pure panic, he'd shouted her name. The last few seconds it had taken him to reach Gracie's crumpled body had been the worst of his life, and he wondered if he'd ever again see a red car drive by without terror seizing him.

Pushing the vivid images out of his mind, he focused on the regular drip, drip, drip of the IV bag.

"We're hitting traffic," the driver called.

The ambulance slowed, and Mike leaned forward to look out the rear windows. "Rush hour," he said with a grimace. "Brace yourself. It looks like we're in for a noisy ride."

Up front, the driver flipped a switch. The unnerving wail of sirens filled the air, and slowly the cars parted to let them through.

💎💎💎

Quinn had been in the waiting room for two and a half hours. He'd taken off his suit coat and loosened his tie a long time ago, and his pacing back and forth across the room had almost worn a path in the industrial-strength carpet. He knew every crack in the waiting room ceiling, every stain on the floor, and was close to having memorized every notice posted on the bulletin board. He'd seen other patients and their worried family members come and go, but his interminable wait continued.

He'd purposely not called Dorcas. With Calista in New York, it was vital that she stay safely inside her condo, and if his aunt knew what had happened to Gracie, nothing would prevent her from coming to the hospital. He'd tried calling her earlier this morning with Steve's update on Calista, but there'd been no reply. Whether that was by choice or because she was still asleep, he didn't know, but he'd left her a vague message, urging her not to leave home or to allow anyone—particularly Calista—entry into the condo until either he or Steve had talked to her. He could only hope that she would comply.

Since Steve was in flight and contact with him was impossible, Quinn had had plenty of time to think. He hadn't gotten a good look at the driver of the red car, but he knew it had been a woman with long, dark hair. His gut told him it was Calista. And if that were true, the crimes on her résumé had just risen to a new level and it was impossible to guess her next move.

He had no way of knowing whether the police had had any luck finding the hit-and-run driver or if they'd identified the car. Maybe one of the eyewitnesses had made note of the car's license plate. He'd been too consumed with Gracie's wellbeing to think of anything else, and even now that she was receiving the medical care she needed, it was hard to think past the sight of her bloody, misshapen leg and her grazed, pale face.

Forty-five minutes after their arrival at the hospital, the head of the trauma team had sought him out to inform him that Gracie had regained consciousness and that her only serious injury appeared to be her broken leg. Sometime after that, a radiology tech had arrived to tell him the orthopedic surgeon had reviewed Gracie's X-rays and was preparing for immediate surgery. An hour later, a nurse had brought Quinn a steaming cup of insipid coffee and had told him Gracie was out of surgery and in the recovery room.

He was studying the slowly moving hand on the clock on the wall, wondering how much longer it would be before he received another update on Gracie's condition when the doors that led into the surgery wing swung open. Quinn looked up from his seat to see a man dressed in scrubs, surgical cap, and booties approaching.

"Mr. West," the man said as Quinn came to his feet. "My name's Tyler Reynolds. I'm the PA who assisted with Miss Miller's surgery."

Quinn shook the man's hand. "How did it go?"

"Very well," Tyler said. "The surgeon, Dr. Lamb, inserted a pin and a small plate to stabilize the bone, and she'll need to be in a cast for six to eight weeks. Because of her open wound, we'll keep her on IV antibiotics for the next twenty-four hours, but we don't anticipate any serious complications."

"How soon can she go home?" Quinn asked.

"That depends on her situation," Tyler said. "At first, she's going to need a lot of help. She can't put any weight on that leg for several weeks."

A vision of the narrow brownstone house where Gracie lived filled Quinn's mind. He was sure there were no elevators in that old building. There was no way she'd be able to manage the stairs.

"What if she were staying in a wheelchair accessible condo and my aunt was there to take care of her?" Until Calista was in custody, it would be much easier to keep Gracie safe if she were with Dorcas than if she were in one of hundreds of rooms at this hospital.

Tyler inclined his head. "I'll check on her in the morning. If she's doing well and you're able to get something suitable set up for her, tomorrow afternoon is a possibility." He glanced at his watch. "She's coming out of the anesthetic right now. As soon as she's awake, one of the nurses will come get you."

Finally.

"Thank you," Quinn said, shaking the man's hand again. "I really appreciate what you and the doctors have done."

CHAPTER 28

"THERE NOW," THE GRAY-HAIRED nurse said, sliding the stand holding the IV bag out of the way and smoothing down the bedcovers. "I think you're ready for a visitor."

"A visitor?" Gracie's voice was little more than a croak. She reached for the cup of ice water on the nearby table and took a sip.

"Yes, that handsome fiancé of yours. He came in the ambulance with you and hasn't stepped out of the waiting room since."

"Quinn?" Gracie put her hand to her head, wishing her brain didn't feel quite so fuzzy. Was Quinn still her fiancé? No, of course not. She was back in New York, and he was back with Mallory.

"Is that his name?" the nurse said. "It suits him."

"Yes, but . . ."

"My name's Edna. Give me two minutes, and I'll bring him in," she said, gathering up the empty water pitcher and bustling out.

Gracie gazed around. She was lying in a hospital bed, her right leg cast and elevated. Other than a small sink, some cupboards, and an ugly green reclining chair, medical equipment and monitors filled the small room. It was a sterile, uninviting place, and to Gracie's dismay, she had no recollection of getting there. She had vague, wispy memories of leaving her apartment, walking down the street toward the subway station, and seeing a red car coming toward her too fast. She remembered debilitating pain, many voices, men and women in scrubs, and being wheeled from one place to another, but no memory was distinct, and even now, she was struggling to think clearly.

At the sound of footsteps, she looked up. Quinn was standing in the doorway. He carried his suit coat folded over his arm. A purple bruise and a small cut marked his left cheek. His blue tie was askew; blood and dirt were smeared across his white shirt and suit pants, and in his hand, he held her purse.

"Hey," he said, his voice gentle. "How are you feeling?"

"Confused," she said.

His lips quirked into a half smile. "Confused?"

"Yes," she said. "Over just about everything—what happened to me, how I got here, and why you told the nurse you're my fiancé."

He stepped into the room and placed her purse on the floor beside the IV stand. Then walking over to the green chair, he pushed it closer to the bed and took a seat. "What do you remember?"

"Leaving my apartment for work and a red car," she said.

He nodded. "Yeah. That was how it began." He told her how the red car had hit her in the crosswalk and that the emergency responders had arrived soon afterward. She'd ridden to the hospital in an ambulance, and after an evaluation by the trauma team and some X-rays, she'd been whisked into surgery for a broken tibia.

"But why were you there when the accident happened?" she asked.

"Since you wouldn't answer my phone calls, I'd come to your apartment hoping to catch you before you went to work," he said. "Last night, we figured out that Calista is the mastermind behind the jewelry thefts, and early this morning, Steve called to say that before the French police could arrest her, she'd gotten on a plane headed to New York City." He looked at her, his expression haggard. "I was trying to warn you, but I was too late."

Gracie gripped the blanket. "You think Calista was driving the red car?"

"I haven't heard anything from the police since the accident, so I don't know if they've had any success in finding the car or the driver, but the person behind the wheel was definitely a woman." He paused, then said, "I'm sure the arrest of Theo, Damien, and Vlasis didn't go over well with Calista, and since she now knows you work in the jewelry business, she probably thinks you're the one who exposed them."

"How does she know about my work?" This conversation seemed to be following the uncomfortable pattern of her asking one stunned question after another.

"Mallory told her."

There was an awkward pause. "Maybe I'm still not thinking clearly," she said, "but I feel like I'm missing something."

Quinn ran his fingers across his bruised cheek. "Yeah. I should probably fill you in on my conversation with Mallory at the airport."

Gracie may have been having a hard time remembering the events surrounding the accident, but she needed no help recalling what had happened at the airport or her misery afterward. She had no desire to revisit that. "You don't need to."

Quinn leaned forward. Very gently, he lifted her arm off the covers, and working around the IV line, he rested her hand in his. "Yes, I do."

Stuck in a hospital bed with no way to escape, Gracie steeled herself against further hurt until Quinn told her of his bewilderment at Mallory's appearance at the airport and his subsequent shock and disgust over her startling confessions.

"Everything I learned at the airport about Mallory and Calista's interactions was helpful to Steve," Quinn said, "but there's something much more important that *you* need to know." He curled his fingers around hers, and Gracie's heart rate responded. "I have never been in love with Mallory. When I first arrived in New York, I was flattered that she showed interest in me, and I invited her to be my partner at some of the dinners and parties I had to attend for Anderson and Gough.

"It didn't take me long to realize that our interests and goals in life were miles apart, and I stopped asking her to go with me. But that didn't fit in with her plans." He scowled. "Mallory played the clingy, doting girlfriend whenever it suited her—and in front of you and Dorcas, it suited her just fine."

He sighed. "I hope you'll believe me, Gracie. It was Mallory's lipstick that you saw on my lips after the Guggenheim exhibition, but I didn't kiss her. When she literally threw herself at me yesterday, I pushed her off as soon as I had my feet under me. But it wasn't fast enough to prevent you from being hurt by what she did."

He hung his head, and Gracie waited, her heart pounding. When he looked up again, there was anguish in his eyes. "You asked me why I told the medics that you were my fiancée. The risk-free answer is that I'm taking your advice and I'm applying life skills learned from movies like *While You Were Sleeping*."

"Did . . . did you watch that movie again after I told you it was one of my favorites?"

He managed a ghost of a smile. "I know the heroine wanted to get into the ICU, not an ambulance, but I figured it was close enough."

She swallowed the lump in her throat. "If that's the risk-free answer, what's the other one?"

"It's the one where I tell you how I really feel," he said, his eyes not leaving hers. "I told everyone you were my fiancée because I love you."

Gracie stared at him. Her head was foggy, her thinking fuzzy, but it had sounded like Quinn had said he loved her. "You . . . you do?"

"Yes, sweet Gracie, I do." He ran his thumb back and forth across the top of her hand. "I'm sorry for all the misunderstanding about Mallory. It didn't even occur to me that she'd be a stumbling block between us."

"She does come across as an intimidating stumbling block."

"For some, maybe," he said. "But I think I started falling in love with you the night you faced her down wearing your brother's old T-shirt."

Color tinted Gracie's cheeks. "It really was more grungy than vintage, wasn't it?"

He grinned and then winced.

"Is it your face?" she asked.

"Uh-huh. I need to remember not to smile too widely."

"How did you hurt it?

"Mallory's hand and ring," he said. "It was her parting shot."

Gracie leaned forward and softly touched his bruised cheek. "I'm sorry."

"Don't be," he said, covering her hand with his.

"Quinn." He met her gaze, and suddenly it was hard to find her voice. "I . . . I think I started falling in love with you when you described the paintings in the Guggenheim as bicycle tracks and food spills."

The look in his dark eyes conveyed his feelings far better than words could. Slipping his other hand into his pocket, he pulled out the diamond-and-sapphire ring.

"The nurse brought this out to me before you went into surgery," he said. "Can I put it back where it belongs?"

Fighting back tears, she nodded, and he slid it onto her finger. Then rising to his feet, he leaned across the bed, and as Gracie sank farther into the pillows, he pressed his lips to hers.

"You're kinda dirty to be kissing my patient like that, Mr. Fiancé."

Quinn pulled back, gave Gracie a wink, and resumed his seat. Edna was standing at the door, her hands on her hips. Quinn gave his stained knees a brief look and shook his head unrepentantly. "I'd agree with you, but it's her blood."

"Thinking of sending her the dry-cleaning bill, are you?" Edna said. She moved to stand at the head of the bed and swiped Gracie's forehead with a thermometer before putting on the blood-pressure cuff. She waggled a finger at Quinn. "If I find that you're making her blood pressure go up, you're out of here." Edna checked the monitor, grunted, and wrote the figures on Gracie's chart. "Are you experiencing any pain yet?" she asked.

"No," Gracie said.

Edna nodded and slid her pen into her pocket. "Let me know when you start to feel uncomfortable. And in the meantime, would you like me to get you something to eat?"

At the mention of food, Gracie realized she was hungry. "That would be great."

Edna looked pleased. "We're between meals right now, but I'll call down to the cafeteria and see what they can do." She lowered her voice. "Maybe I could persuade them to send up an extra sandwich for your young man if he'd be willing to let you get some rest."

"I think I can convince him," Gracie whispered. "Food is a great motivator."

Quinn, who'd obviously heard the entire exchange, rolled his eyes.

The nurse laughed. "I'll be back," she said.

◆◆◆

"Quinn." Someone put a hand on his arm and gave it a shake. "Quinn."

Quinn opened his eyes to find Steve standing beside him. Jet lag had finally caught up with him, and he'd fallen asleep on the green chair in Gracie's hospital room. He glanced at the bed. Gracie was lying still, hopefully asleep.

"Can we go somewhere and talk?" Steve whispered.

Quinn nodded and got to his feet. Rolling his shoulders, he followed Steve out of the room. Farther down the hallway, two chairs had been positioned near a drinking fountain.

Steve claimed one of the seats. "You look worse than I feel," he said as Quinn sat next to him.

"It's been a rough few hours," Quinn said.

"I got your text as soon as I landed," Steve said. "Tell me about the accident."

Quinn was beginning to feel like he'd repeated the same story twenty times. It was actually closer to three, but he still had to remind himself that Steve needed all the details.

Steve listened carefully, and when Quinn finished his account, Steve shook his head. "That was too close."

"Tell me about it," Quinn said. "Have you talked to the cops? What are they saying?"

"The red Civic was checked back in at the Avis desk this morning. The renter, listed as Calista Katsaros, then turned around and rented another vehicle. A black Mustang."

"She didn't cover her tracks very well."

"Nope. But this was a spur-of-the-moment thing, and she probably didn't think anyone would ID her. A quick hit-and-run, get rid of the car, and be back on a plane before anyone even knew she'd been in the country."

"But she hasn't gotten back on a plane," Quinn said.

"It doesn't look like it."

Quinn didn't like the way this conversation was going. "Can you bring in extra security at Dorcas's place?"

Steve nodded. "Yeah. And we should probably have someone at the hospital too."

"I'm staying here until Gracie's released," Quinn said. "And I'll talk to Dorcas about having Gracie go stay at the condo afterward."

"Good." He gave Quinn a critical look. "But do yourself a favor and go get cleaned up first."

"I told you I'm not leaving Gracie here alone."

Steve held out a set of car keys. "It's a blue Ford Escort, and it's parked in the visitor lot right next to the dumpster. I'll stay with Gracie until you get back, then I'll head over to see Dorcas." Quinn frowned at Steve, but his friend jingled the keys. "Take them."

Quinn snatched the keys out of Steve's hand. "I'll be back in less than an hour."

"All right." Steve looked pleased. "I'm going to take over your napping spot till then."

CHAPTER 29

The taxi pulled up outside Dorcas's building. Quinn jumped out and ran around to the other side of the vehicle while the driver opened the trunk. He waited until Gracie had scooted to the edge of the seat and the driver had positioned the wheelchair next to the passenger door, then he reached into the vehicle. Placing her uninjured leg on the sidewalk and leaning heavily on Quinn's arm, Gracie pulled herself out of the car.

As soon as Gracie had found her balance, the driver maneuvered the wheelchair until it touched her leg, and Quinn helped lower her into the seat.

"Sheesh," she said breathlessly. "If it takes me that long to get out of a car, I can't imagine how slow I'll be at everything else."

"You'll speed up," Quinn said. He handed the cab driver some money and grasped the wheelchair handles. "This was your first time. You'll be a pro at getting in and out within a couple of weeks."

She looked worried. "Maybe Walter would be willing to help me when I go back to work."

"I'm sure he will."

He knew Gracie was concerned about being gone so long from Samuel Hamley. She'd called Kelly from the hospital to explain why she hadn't shown up for work on Monday morning. Kelly had been shocked to learn of Gracie's accident, and after talking to Mr. Hamley, Kelly had called Gracie back and told her to take the rest of the week off. She'd shown up at the hospital a few hours later with a colorful bouquet of balloons.

It had been a little harder for Quinn to explain to his secretary why he wouldn't be back in the office until tomorrow, especially since he'd already been gone for over a week. But he'd pulled the family emergency card and hoped he wouldn't have to use it again.

Gracie settled her purse on her knee, and Quinn pushed the wheelchair toward the building's large glass doors. The doorman saw them coming and held the doors open.

"Thanks, Bill," Quinn said. He was already scouring the lobby for the additional security Steve had promised.

Ted, the evening security guard, was sitting at his normal spot behind the front desk. He looked up as they entered.

"'Evening, Mr. West," he said.

"Hi, Ted," Quinn said. He moved a little closer. "Do you have any extra help tonight?"

Ted tilted his head toward a man standing not far from the elevators. He looked to be in his early thirties, and at first glance, he seemed to be watching the people crossing the lobby with casual indifference. Only the distinctive bulge under his slightly-too-tight suit coat and his alert stance suggested anything different.

"Thanks," Quinn said. He wheeled Gracie toward the elevator doors and the man who was monitoring them.

"Quinn West," he said, extending his hand to the FBI agent. "And this is Gracie Miller."

"James Greer," he said, shaking Quinn's hand. "Steve told me to expect you."

"I'm taking Gracie up to Dorcas's condo, then I'll be heading out."

James seemed to grasp the unspoken message. "My relief shift gets here at midnight, but until then, I'll make sure no one goes up who shouldn't be there."

"I appreciate that," Quinn said, his grip tightening on the wheelchair handles. Delegating responsibility was much easier when it involved insurance portfolios, not the lives of people he loved.

The elevator pinged, and the gold doors swooshed open. Quinn pushed Gracie inside, and she leaned forward to press the button for the penthouse suite.

"Have a good night," James said. Then the doors closed.

Gracie was nervous. She'd spent the last week with Dorcas, but moving into her home for an indefinite period of time was different. It felt like an imposition. "Are you sure this is okay?"

Quinn stood at the door to the penthouse suite. "Are you kidding me? When I suggested it to Dorcas, she acted like she'd just won the lottery."

"Pretty sure she doesn't need to win the lottery," Gracie said.

He chuckled. "No, but she loves having someone to fuss over."

Gracie tightened her grip on her purse. Maybe Quinn was right. Dorcas never complained about her single life, but over the last week, Gracie had caught occasional glimpses of the older woman's loneliness. She studied the bulky cast that extended half way up her leg and gave a resigned nod. "I guess I'm a pretty good candidate for that."

Quinn gave her a sympathetic smile and knocked on the door.

Within seconds, Dorcas opened it. "Oh, you poor dear," she said, ushering them inside. "You must be worn out after that ride from the hospital, but I have your bedroom all ready, and Steve brought over your suitcase. Such a good thing you hadn't unpacked from our trip." She started leading them toward the bedrooms. "Now, you be sure to let me know if you're missing anything or if you need help putting things away or doing laundry."

"See?" Quinn whispered. "She's already in full fussing mode."

Gracie bit back a smile. "Thank you for letting me stay with you, Dorcas."

"I couldn't be happier." She moved aside so Quinn could wheel Gracie into the bedroom. Then she frowned. "Well, that didn't come out quite right. I'd rather you hadn't been hurt, but I'm very glad you're here."

Touched by the older woman's kindness, Gracie gazed around the room. There was a built-in closet and dresser, a small desk, complete with a chair and lamp, a rocking chair, and a queen-size bed with a white eyelet bedcover and a scattering of multicolored pillows. Two of the walls were painted orange, and large framed prints of bright wildflowers hung on the other walls. It reflected Dorcas's cheery disposition perfectly.

"It's lovely," Gracie said.

Dorcas looked pleased. "You have your own bathroom right across the hall," she said, pointing to the door behind them. "I don't think you'll have any problem getting the wheelchair in and out."

"I'll pick up your crutches tomorrow and bring them over after work," Quinn said.

Her injury and surgery, staying in this luxurious but unfamiliar place, learning to live life in a wheelchair and on crutches—it was suddenly terribly overwhelming. "Thank you," she said, blinking back the tears. "Both of you."

Quinn crouched down beside her. "Hey, we've got this."

"We do?" For some reason, the long, painful recovery ahead seemed more daunting than the other challenges they'd faced together.

"Absolutely." He kissed her gently. "Dorcas is right. You're tired. See if you can get ready for bed before the pain meds wear off."

Gracie nodded, and he got to his feet.

"I'll let myself out, Dorcas." He gave his aunt a hug. "Just be sure you lock the door behind me."

"I will," she said. "We'll see you tomorrow."

The cab arrived five minutes after he'd called for it. Quinn hated to leave Dorcas and Gracie, but his short wait in the lobby reassured him that James was monitoring the flow of traffic into the building carefully, and now that Gracie was out of the hospital, Quinn knew it was time for him to return to his apartment and work.

His unease over Calista's presence in the city continued to plague him, however, and as soon as he'd given the cabbie his address, he pulled out his phone and called Steve. "Any news?"

"The black Mustang Calista rented was booted not far from Brooklyn Bridge," Steve said. "The police found it this morning. They waited awhile to see if she'd come back to reclaim it, but it looks like she abandoned it there."

"Where is she?" Quinn did nothing to hide his frustration.

"She hasn't used her credit cards since she picked up the second car, so she's either using cash or she's sponging off someone."

Quinn's phone bleeped, and he glanced at the screen. It was Gracie.

"Hey, Steve, stay on the line. Gracie's calling through." He accepted Gracie's call. "Gracie?"

"Yes," she said. "Sorry to bother you again."

"You're not bothering me."

"Well, you may change your mind about that. Dorcas asked me to call and see if you could pick up more gauze bandages when you go for the crutches. She wanted me to contact you right now so we wouldn't forget."

"The fussing is spilling over," he said. She laughed, and he smiled, glad that she was in better spirits now than she'd been when he'd left. "Tell her I'll get them."

In the background, he heard a faint knock.

"There's someone at Dorcas's door," Gracie said. "Should that be happening?"

Alarm seized him. "No. Tell her not to answer it."

"Dorcas!" Gracie had obviously lowered the phone to call out, but he heard the hint of panic in her voice. "She can't hear me," she said. "I'm so slow in this wheelchair, I don't think I can—"

"Don't move, Gracie! Stay in the bedroom." He leaned forward and tapped the window between him and the cabbie. "Take me back."

The driver slid the window open. "You wanna go back?"

"Yes. As fast as you can."

The driver must have heard the urgency in his voice because he immediately moved into the middle of the road to do a U-turn.

"Quinn." Gracie was whispering now. "There are voices in the living room. It . . . it sounds like Mallory."

What was Mallory doing there? After what happened at the airport, he would have thought she'd have avoided all contact with Dorcas for a while.

"Calista, what are you doing?" Mallory's shriek was loud enough that Quinn heard it through the phone, and he instantly pushed the button connecting him to the other line.

"Steve! Are you there?"

"Yeah. What did—?"

"Call James. Calista's in Dorcas's condo."

Quinn didn't wait for Steve to respond. He flipped back to Gracie's line again. "Gracie, can you hear me?"

She was gone.

💎💎💎

It didn't matter that Quinn had told her to stay in the bedroom; Gracie wasn't going to let Dorcas face Calista alone. Pushing her wheelchair down the short hall, she turned into the kitchen. Hiding behind the large central island, she inched forward until she could see into the living room. Mallory was cowering behind one of the armchairs, her face pale, her wide eyes trained on Calista. Dorcas's back was to Gracie, but she was standing facing Calista, whose arm was extended, a small gun in her hand.

"Calista, why are you doing this?" Dorcas's voice was calm despite the fact that she had a gun pointed at her.

"You ruined everything!"

"I don't understand," Dorcas said.

"My father. He loved my mother. He loved Theo and me. We were his family. Then you came, and suddenly, he was not in

Greece anymore but in New York." She spat the words as though *New York* were a swear word. "His family—his real family—was not so important anymore. The friends he had known for a lifetime—not so important anymore. Why? Because of you. You stole him from us."

"I loved your father very much."

"Lies!" There was a wildness to Calista's eyes reflected in the erratic movement of the gun in her hand. "You used him. Used him for his money."

Gracie's heart ached for Dorcas. Calista's accusations were so unfair, so unfounded.

"I did not need your father's money to be happy, Calista," Dorcas said. "I simply needed to be with him."

"You cannot say such things." Her voice was rising. "Even now you spend thousands of dollars on trinkets—jewelry that shows your love for his money." She took a step forward. "Do you know what my mother wore? Do you?" She didn't wait for a reply. "A single gold crucifix on a thin gold chain. Nothing more. She remembered her humble beginnings always. She did not care for riches, only for her family."

"Your father spoke to me often about your mother. She was a remarkable woman, and he loved her very much."

"He loved *her*. Not you. He loved her and Theo and me." She repeated the words like an incantation. "That is how it was supposed to be." Her voice cracked. "That is how it was supposed to stay."

Dorcas took a small step toward her. "I'm sorry you lost your mother, Calista."

"You? Sorry?" Calista's laugh was hollow and harsh. "Even now, the lies continue." She used the gun in her hand to point around the room. "If my mother were alive, none of this would be yours. None of it!" Her eyes narrowed. "Would she have liked to wear the sapphire pendant Papa gave you? Of course. What woman would not? He gave it to you, but it should have been hers!"

"And so you took it," Dorcas said.

"Yes. *I* took it. I, Calista Katsaros." She stood a little taller, as though proud of her accomplishment. "But now you ruin my family again. My brother is arrested; my boyfriend is arrested. They did not take your jewelry, but their names are now black because of you."

Calista cocked the gun, and Dorcas froze.

"Calista. You can't . . . You mustn't . . ." Mallory was backing into the far corner of the room, as though a few more feet would distance her from the crime.

Gracie grabbed the pot of African violets sitting on the edge of the island. With one hand she pushed the wheelchair into the living room, and with the other, she launched the potted plant at Calista.

Calista saw it coming. She flinched, and the gun fired.

Mallory screamed, Dorcas ducked, and with a solid thud, the bullet entered the canvas above the fireplace.

Calista took a ragged breath, stared at the painting of the Acropolis at sunset, and crumpled to the floor. "Papa," she moaned. "Papa."

Behind her, the door flew open, and James burst in, gun in hand. "Don't move," he yelled at Mallory, going straight for Calista and putting her in handcuffs.

Dorcas staggered to the sofa. Gracie crossed the distance between them. Pulling herself out of the wheelchair and onto her uninjured leg, she pivoted, dropped onto the seat beside Dorcas, and wrapped her arms around her. She wanted to tell her how courageous she'd been and that Calista's toxic words were just that—poisonous and delusional—but instead, she just held on tightly while Dorcas wept.

The front door crashed open again, and Gracie looked up to see Quinn standing in the doorway, his chest heaving. The moment his eyes met hers, he ran across the room and dropped to his knees in front of them, touching first Gracie and then Dorcas. "Please tell me you're both okay."

"We're okay," Gracie said. She was sure a reaction to the terror they'd just experienced would hit her soon, but for now, her only emotion was overwhelming gratitude that they were safe and that he was with them. "Your aunt is the bravest woman I know. She stood up to Calista and her gun, and she never wavered."

His shoulders sagged with relief. He glanced at Calista. She was sitting on the floor, her wrists cuffed behind her, her eyes glassy. James had his hand firmly clasped around Mallory's arm and was leading her across the room as he spoke into his Bluetooth. The chaos of a few moments ago was already dispelling, the adrenaline ebbing. Gracie looked down at her scraped hands. They were shaking slightly. As though he sensed it, Quinn wrapped his fingers gently around hers.

From outside, the wail of police sirens reached them, and Dorcas raised her tearstained face toward the windows. "I thought I told you," she said, frowning at Quinn. "I wanted no police."

Quinn stared at her disbelievingly. Then he looked at Gracie and shook his head. "I guess she really is all right."

CHAPTER 30

TWO WEEKS LATER, GRACIE SAT on one of the bar stools in Dorcas's kitchen and watched as the older woman took a golden-brown apple pie out of the oven.

Dorcas placed it on a cooling rack next to a large pan of lasagna and gave a contented sigh. "Perfect," she said, checking the four place settings, the large bowl of green salad, and basket of fresh bread already on the kitchen island. "I think we're ready."

"It looks wonderful," Gracie said. Now that she was working full-time again, it was a special treat to come home at the end of the day to a homemade meal like this. Dorcas had taken great delight in spoiling her, and already, Gracie knew that moving back into her apartment next month would be hard on both of them.

A knock sounded on the door, and Gracie slid off the barstool and reached for the crutches lying against the island. "I'll get it," she said. Her ability to get around on crutches was improving every day, and she now reserved using the wheelchair for the times that she was especially tired.

Moving briskly across the wooden floor, she peeked through the peephole in the door, smiled, and pulled the door open. Quinn had loosened his tie and undone the top button of his shirt, but he'd obviously come straight from the office. The moment he saw Gracie, the weariness in his eyes dissipated and was replaced by warmth.

"Hi there," he said, stepping forward and wrapping his arms around her. "I missed you."

"You saw me last night," she said with a smile.

"Yep. It's been a very long day." He lowered his head and kissed her slowly and deliberately.

"All right. Enough of that mushiness." Steve's voice reached them from the elevator doors. "I can smell Dorcas's pie from here, and you're not blocking the doorway one more minute."

Quinn pulled back, keeping one arm around Gracie. "I promised myself I'd talk to him about his timing," he said. "Tonight may be the night."

Gracie laughed and turned to face the sandy-haired man. "Hi, Steve. I'm glad you could make it."

"Me too," he said with a grin. "Good to see you out of the wheelchair."

Repositioning the crutches beneath her arms, Gracie backed up so the men could enter the condo. "They're here, Dorcas," she called.

Dorcas hurried in and greeted them both with kisses on the cheek. "Right on time," she said. "Come on in. The food's all ready."

Quinn waited until dessert was served before bringing up the subject that had been hanging over them since Steve arrived.

"We haven't seen or heard from you since you and James took Calista and Mallory into custody. What can you tell us?"

Steve finished his last spoonful of apple pie and ice cream and slid the bowl to one side. "I have good news," he said, looking at Dorcas. "Yesterday, the French police received permission to access a safety deposit box rented under Calista's name at the Banque Transatlantique." He smiled. "They found a dozen extremely valuable pieces of jewelry inside. Among them were a sapphire pendant and a pink diamond ring."

Dorcas gasped, hope shining in her eyes.

"I didn't want to say anything to you until they'd been checked by a professional, but an hour ago, I received word that a jeweler in Paris has passed them all off as the real thing. Every one of your missing pieces is accounted for."

Dorcas covered her mouth with her hand, tears pooling in her eyes. "Thank you! Thank you so much."

"That's incredible," Quinn said, reaching across the counter to squeeze his aunt's free hand.

Steve nodded. "Unfortunately, you'll have to wait until after the trial to get them back. They'll be used as evidence—along with the forgeries. But when the time comes, they're yours."

With a lump in her throat, Gracie watched the emotions play across Dorcas's face. She knew that for the sweet, generous woman, the financial consideration meant far less than the sentimental value attached to the missing jewelry. Even for Quinn, whose company had stood to lose so much money with the theft of the jewelry, his happiness over this news had nothing to do with his work.

"What about Calista?" Dorcas said. "Will she be okay?"

"She's facing counts of theft and attempted murder," Steve said, "but she's also undergoing psychiatric evaluation, and those results will probably play a big part in her trial.

"Theo is making sure she has the best possible legal team." He shrugged. "It's looking more and more like Theo was unaware of his sister's scheme and was as shocked as you were when it all unraveled.

"Damien is claiming that he made the copies to hone his skills and didn't know they were being traded for the real thing—but we'll see if the jury buys that. Nikos, of course, is devastated by his son's involvement, but the people I've talked to claim that Nikos's reputation for honesty and expertise will carry him and his business through the fallout.

"Vlasis has a more shady background and may suffer because he has a previous record. We think he was in it for the thrill, although the money Calista paid him for his safe-cracking skills and silence was definitely a bonus."

"What about Mallory?" Quinn asked, his tone grave.

"I think her lawyers are going to try to prove that she was a pawn," Steve said. "She probably had no idea what Calista was doing with the photos. And when Calista called to tell her she was in town and that her rental car had broken down by the Brooklyn Bridge, Mallory went to pick her up and offered to put her up at her condo. Calista was already in the building—hiding out with Mallory—when we brought in the extra security downstairs. That's how she was able to access the penthouse suite without anyone in the lobby knowing about it."

"Mallory did seem genuinely shocked when Calista pulled the gun out of her purse," Dorcas said.

Steve grunted. "Yeah, the lawyers will probably play up that angle, although it seems to me that she'd have a stronger case if, instead of sniveling in the corner, she'd done something to help the situation—like toss an African violet plant or something." He grinned at Gracie, but before she could defend herself, his phone buzzed. He glanced at the text and frowned. "Sorry," he said, getting to his feet. "It looks like I've got to go."

Quinn stood, walked around the island, and shook his friend's hand. "Thanks again, Steve."

"We've been a great team ever since our freshman year," Steve said. "It was good to work together again." He turned and gave Dorcas a hug. "Thanks for the pie, Dorcas."

"Come for more when the jewelry's returned," she said.

"It's a date," he said.

Gracie hobbled over and stood beside Quinn. He put his arm around her.

"Thanks again, Gracie," Steve said. "We couldn't have done this without you." He tilted his head toward Quinn. "Keep him in line for me."

Gracie smiled. "Take care of yourself, Steve."

"Always," he said. Then he started for the door with Dorcas right behind him.

Swiveling to face Quinn, Gracie put her arms around his neck.

"So, you're going to keep me in line now, huh?" he said, humor dancing in his eyes.

"I guess I have to," she said. "FBI orders."

"And how's that going to work?"

She smiled knowingly, stood on tiptoe, and raised her lips to his. When they eventually drew apart, Quinn cupped her face in his hand and ran his thumb across her cheek. "I should never have doubted," he murmured. "You've totally got this."

ABOUT THE AUTHOR

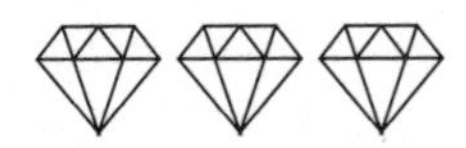

SIAN ANN BESSEY WAS BORN in Cambridge, England, and grew up on the island of Anglesey off the north coast of Wales. She left Wales to attend Brigham Young University and graduated with a bachelor's degree in communications.

The author of several novels and children's books, Sian has also written articles for the *New Era*, *Ensign*, and *Liahona* magazines.

Sian and her husband, Kent, are the parents of five children and the grandparents of three beautiful girls and two handsome boys. They currently live in Rexburg, Idaho, and although Sian has few opportunities to speak Welsh anymore, *Llanfairpwllgwyngyllgogerychwyrndrobwllllantysiliogogogoch* still rolls off her tongue.

Traveling, reading, cooking, and being with her grandchildren are some of her favorite activities. She also loves hearing from her readers. If you would like to contact her, she can be reached through her website at www.sianannbessey.com.